the downside to forever

JILLIAN LIOTA

Love Is A Verb Books

Book Cover Design and Layout by Blue Moon Creative Studio

Cover Photo by Regina Wamba

Editing by C. Marie

ISBN 978-1-952549-44-1 (paperback)
ISBN 978-1-952549-42-7 (eBook)
ISBN 978-1-952549-43-4 (kindle)

for mothers everywhere who make hard sacrifices
every damn day

and for some of the most incredible mothers I know:
Caitlin, Cheyenne, Marylou and Jaelynne

<3

prologue
busy

I stare at the two blue lines on the white strip resting on the counter in the bathroom, shock rippling through my body.

It never occurred to me that I might get pregnant. It feels naïve not to have even considered it...I mean, I'm a sexually active woman. Of *course* pregnancy is a possibility.

But I feel like I'm safe. I use protection. I always make the *guy* use protection, too, so I can't help the part of me that still wonders how this happened. Did the condom break? Did I miss a pill and not realize it? Or is the universe just so cruel that it felt the need to *once again* prove to everyone I know what a screwup I am?

Ever since I was a kid, my mom has called me her little troublemaker. Breaking rules and being mischievous was just part of my personality. When you're the youngest of five, sometimes you can get lost in the mix of things, and I often used that to my advantage.

As I got older, though, the teasing way she said it slowly fell away…less endearment and more concern. Like she was worried my rebellious nature might come around to bite me in the ass at some point.

Clearly she was right.

Licking my lips, I lean forward on the counter and stare at myself in the mirror then turn to the side, trying to examine my body to see if I can spot any small differences, any indication that there's a *life* growing inside me. If I'm doing the math correctly, it's possible I'm already two or three months along.

My mind flits back over the supposed stomach flus I've had, the missed period that didn't feel abnormal for my already irregular schedule, and it's easy to see how I didn't suspect anything earlier. I lift my shirt and examine my stomach more closely then tentatively run a hand over the soft skin just below my belly button. I'm surprised by the way my heart twists, a soft thump in my chest sending shivers through my body.

But underneath that unexpected jolt of joy…there's fear, too. I've never been the type to have particularly grand plans for my life. Becoming a mother at twenty, though…that was definitely *not* on my bingo card.

I roll the title around in my head.

I'm gonna be a mom.

The word feels foreign, as if I've never heard it before, never mulled it over. To be perfectly honest, I'm not sure I ever pictured myself being a mother at all, let alone before I finish college, before I even get to live a life. I've only been out of my parents' house for two years. I feel like I've barely lived at all. And now I'm going to be responsible for a whole other human being?

My stomach rolls at the thought and I dart to the toilet, dropping to my knees and emptying the contents of my sparse breakfast into the bowl. Once I've finished, I wipe my face, flush, and lean back against the wall, my arms on my knees, my head back as I stare at the ceiling.

I'm going to have to tell Jay, and the worst part is I have absolutely no idea how he's going to react because I don't actually know him that well. We've been hooking up for a few months, but it's nothing serious. Sure, there were some butterflies in the beginning, but that's just attraction, and I'm smart enough to know attraction doesn't equate to anything permanent.

Besides, Jay seems like the kind of guy who is just interested in a good time. I mean, that's what *I* was interested in, right? Just some carefree fun like the college kid I am? Who knows how he'll feel. Will he want to be a dad? How will he handle the news? Will he even believe me when I tell him it's his?

I push myself up off the floor and return to the sink, taking a few minutes to clean up. Then I look in the mirror again, my eyes focused on my belly, the uncertainty in my chest growing with each passing second.

Ultimately, it doesn't matter what Jay thinks, or even whether or not he wants to be involved. In the blink of an eye, my entire world has been flipped on its head. As terrified as I feel right now, though, I know without a doubt what my priorities are—what they need to be.

First and foremost, this little life slowly growing within me. Everything else comes second.

I'm going to be a mom.

This time, when I think the words, the joy outweighs the fear. And when my eyes find themselves in the reflection again, I smile.

chapter one
busy

The gravel pops underneath my tires, the unpaved road narrowing slightly as I drive toward the familiar green cabin at the end. It's too dark to see at this late hour, but I know the lake stretches out behind it, and I lament the fact that our drive took so much longer than I anticipated. It would have been nice to spend our first evening here sitting on the dock, watching the sunset. Junie loves sunset.

But I push that thought aside. There are going to be many, many sunsets for us to watch now that I'm back in Cedar Point, and I can't waste too much time worrying about a single missed one. Not when there are so many *other* things to worry about.

I slow to a stop and put my car in park on the parking pad just outside the cabin then turn it off, plunging myself into darkness, only the faintest hint of moonlight cutting a swath through the large cedar and pine trees scattered around the property. I've been here before, but it looks different somehow. Maybe it's the shadows of the trees, or because I'm just so damn tired. Truthfully, it's probably because the handful of visits I made when my sister used to live here were just that…visits.

Now, this cabin is my new home.

Our new home. Just the two of us…Junie and me.

My eyes briefly flick to the rearview mirror, to where my daughter sits in her car seat, her sleeping face reflected back at me through another small mirror positioned at her feet. Maybe I can take advantage of the fact that she's sleeping and try to do some unloading before she wakes up. It's been a long day for my baby girl, and driving all day with a toddler is not for the weak, that's for sure.

The fatigue of the long journey finally hits me, and I close my eyes for just a second, wanting to give them a brief rest—though the reality of knowing I still need to get Junie inside and settled as well as do some serious unloading from my car doesn't make those few seconds all that restful. Not for the first time, I wish I'd taken my mother up on her offer to let us crash at her place tonight. Her words from a few days ago taunt me.

"Why do you have to make everything so difficult? You're going to be exhausted. Come here and get a good night of sleep. You can unpack everything the day after you get to town."

Why do I have to make everything so difficult?

My original thought process did make sense. I assumed I'd be arriving in the late afternoon and would have plenty of time to get our stuff unloaded and manage dinner. Then we'd get to spend our first night in town in our new place, just the two of us. I didn't want any help; I just wanted the evening to ourselves.

Of course, the reality of driving such a long distance was completely different than I pictured. At almost two, my energetic Junie Bee struggled with being in her car seat for so long, which meant significantly more stops than I'd planned so she could get out her wiggles, get food, go to the bathroom. Now, it's nearing ten o'clock, and any hopes of an early evening of settling into the little green cabin are long dashed.

Snuggling into a made bed—even the twin mattress in my childhood bedroom—sounds infinitely better than lugging in the heavy air mattress that's shoved somewhere in the back of the car, probably in the least convenient spot because I was rushing this morning and not paying attention to how I was loading up our few possessions. Even so, I promised myself when I decided to move back to Cedar Point, I was coming back to make my own home, not to just return to the roost. Part of that is defining new spaces for myself, new routines, new relationships. It would be too easy to tuck myself into my parents' house and just let them take care of us. I might be *the* baby of the family, but I'm not *a* baby anymore.

Not to mention I have my *own* baby to take care of now, and part of that is doing as many things on my own as I can. Especially considering all the help that has already been extended my way. My job at Briar's store. Mom taking care of Junie. Dad getting this rental set up. It all came together because people who love me offered to step in and help, and even though it killed me, I took it. I knew being here would be a better life for my daughter, and no amount of pride is going to get in the way of giving Junie the best that I can.

I need to prove to them—to my parents and my siblings, but also to myself—that I am capable of handling things. That I'm not the same Busy, always getting herself into jams and needing to be rescued from her own choices. It's why it took me so long to finally come back in the first place, because I had things I needed to prove to myself.

That I could finish my degree, for one. That I could handle

being a mother on my own was definitely another.

So, even though it would be *easier* to go to my parents' house tonight and sleep in beds there—instead of living on an air mattress for the foreseeable future—I know sticking to my original plan is the better move. Even if it's the more exhausting one.

I sigh, the fatigue weighing even heavier on me now than it was a few minutes ago. Then I shove open my door and step out of the car, the sticky air of the early-summer night clinging to my skin. I shut it gently, glancing briefly in the back to make sure Junie is still sleeping soundly, then head to the front door, tugging out my phone to reread the instructions Lois sent me about the keys.

Key is taped under the pot out front

Sounds about right.

Chuckling to myself, I take the two steps up onto the wraparound porch, spotting the beautiful hydrangea plant in the orange pot next to the front door. Tilting it slightly, I reach under...

But no key.

I glance around, wondering if maybe I'm just looking under the wrong pot. The light on my phone illuminates the area, and I scan for another one before following the porch to the back of the house, facing the lake.

Still nothing.

I pull up Lois' number and give her a call, but it goes straight to voicemail.

Growling under my breath, I stalk back to my red RAV4 and pull open my door, digging around in the center console until I find two bobby pins. I don't care if I need to break a window. I'm getting into that house tonight. But I can start with something less dramatic, like picking the lock.

I take a quick look at Junie again, finding her sleeping peacefully, then quietly shut the door and head back to the porch. Dropping down onto my knees, I bend my bobby pins and get to work.

Picking a lock is one of those weird things I learned as a teenager that I've actually used a few times in real life. Once my freshman year of college, when I got locked out of my room and didn't want to pay a fee to have the RA come open the door, then again last year when I accidentally locked myself out of my apartment with Junie on the inside. I was a bit hysterical on that last one, sobbing and imagining my daughter—who couldn't even crawl yet—somehow getting her hands on a knife or catching the place on fire. It really is wild what horrifying visions the mind of a mother can conjure up.

I hear a click and grin to myself, knowing I've moved one of the pins inside the lock into place. I adjust my bobby pin, searching for the next one.

"Can I help you?"

I shriek, the sound of a male voice coming out of nowhere and scaring the absolute shit out of me. Scrambling to my feet, I extend my hand with the bent bobby pin in front of me like I'm brandishing some kind of weapon, my eyes locking on the silhouette of a man standing at the base of the porch's few steps.

"I'm not gonna hurt you," he says, putting both hands up as if to calm me. "Just trying to figure out why you're breaking into my place."

I blink a few times, my bobby pin still stretched out before me, and I glance around, wondering what the hell he's talking about.

"Breaking into *your* place? This isn't your place."

The guy takes a step up onto the porch but freezes when he

sees me take a step back.

"Hey now," he says, his voice calm and soothing, like he's trying to reassure a feral cat. "My name's Reid. I live here. Have for the past three years."

My brows furrow. "Reid?" I say, my hand falling to my side as I take a step forward. "Reid Cohen?

The cloudy haze of fear finally clears, my eyes straining to see him in the darkness.

"Yeah. Do we…know each other?" Reid asks, chuckling under his breath.

I put my hand to my chest and take a deep breath. "Jesus, you scared the shit out of me," I say, giving myself a moment to breathe. "I'm Busy. Patty and Mark's daughter."

My mom and Reid's aunt Lois have been friends for decades. If he doesn't remember me, he'll at least know my parents' names. Everyone knows the Mitchells. It's a reality of, one, living in a small town, and two, being a descendent of Cedar Point's founding family. It's a cool legacy thing, knowing the people who came before me planted the seeds of what this community has become. But it's also a little draining, knowing people are almost hyperaware of what you're doing.

As a kid who enjoyed sneaking around a bit, the last thing I wanted was a ton of eyeballs watching me and reporting back to my parents. Part of me thinks my mom wouldn't consider me such a troublemaker if people in this town weren't always narcing on me, but I guess that's all in the past. Hopefully.

"Busy Mitchell?" Reid takes a step forward, tugging on a small metal hoop on his belt loop, unhooking a set of keys. "Let me just…hold on."

He steps past me and opens the front door, then reaches in and flips a switch, illuminating a living room that is very much furnished, and a beautiful, shaggy dog stretching and yawning on the couch, tail wagging. With another flip of a switch, Reid turns on the porch light and shuts his front door.

I wince, the muted light still too bright for my eyes, which had grown accustomed to the darkness. Then he turns around to look at me, and I realize I might need another minute to catch my breath.

Reid Cohen is *everything* I remember him to be.

Tall, muscular, handsome. All-consuming, with his strong jawline covered in stubble and broad shoulders. He has a mustache now and his hair is just slightly longer and messier than I remember, but absolutely works for him.

I feel like I've been yanked into the past, to that summer when I was eleven years old. My friends and me giggling as we watched him sit atop the lifeguard tower at Cedar Point Summer Camp, slinking past his dad's shop on Main Street hoping to spot him inside. My crush on Reid slammed into me like a freight train that summer, and even though I forced myself to eventually move on, I can still feel the echoing pangs of those teenage emotions.

"Wow. I feel like I haven't seen you in…" He pauses. "How long has it been?"

"Five years," I say, remembering the last time I saw him with surprising clarity.

He was driving around in that truck that was older than dirt but was somehow cool because *he* was driving it. He rolled to a stop at the intersection in front of Ugly Mug, and I stood there like a lovesick fool, just admiring him with a kind of glazed expression you can only manage when you're a teenager.

His wife was in the passenger seat.

"No, it has to have been longer than that."

He furrows his brow, and I'm almost positive he's trying to conjure up any kind of real memory of me. The truth is, my adolescent daydreams aside, I'm pretty sure our only interactions were a few hellos stretched over many, many years.

Shaking my head, I swat a hand at the air between us. "It doesn't matter."

Then I take a second to look around again, my confusion surging back to the forefront. Only then do I spot a few things I missed before: a pair of worn steel-toe boots in the corner, the mat in front of the door that has clearly seen better days, and the multiple potted plants scattered around.

"Do you...live here? Really?"

How tired am I?

"I do. Have for a few years."

My shoulders droop, wondering how that's possible.

"But...I could have sworn..." I start, my brain scrambling as I try to make sense of it. "Lois said the place would be empty by yesterday."

Reid's head tilts to the side. "She did?"

I nod.

"I'm supposed to be renting this cabin from her."

He tucks his hands into his jeans, shrugging lightly like the world isn't about to fall apart. "Well, I'm sure there's just some kind of misunderstanding that can be sorted out with a phone call."

"She didn't answer." I tug my phone out of my back pocket and open up the text she sent yesterday. "Current tenants have moved out, blah blah blah, getting it cleaned and I'll have the cleaners leave the key under the pot."

"Wait, are you renting the *green* cabin?"

"This *is* the green cabin."

Reid gives me a gentle smile then hitches a thumb over his shoulder. "This is the *blue* cabin."

"What?"

I look again at the walls, certain he's wrong and…sure enough, they're blue.

At the realization that I really *was* breaking into his home, I laugh. Probably a little too long and a little more loudly than is warranted, but I blame the exhaustion of the long day and the reality that I was apparently on the verge of a B&E.

"I'm so sorry, I…" I rub my face with my hands, my laugh fading away. "It's just been a really long day."

I let out a lengthy sigh, wishing for the umpteenth time I'd just swallowed my ego and stayed at my mom's.

"Hey, you're alright. No harm, no foul. It's an easy mistake to make in the dark." Reid takes another step forward, pointing past where I'm parked. "The green cabin is just on the other side of that tree line. My aunt and uncle planted those a few years ago to give the cabins a bit more privacy. That's probably why you didn't see it."

Or at least I *think* that's what he said. His sudden proximity has me very aware of him, and I breathe in deeply, taking in the scent of him. It's something clean and masculine I wish I could bottle up and spray on my pillow.

Clearing my throat and trying to push that *very* embarrassing thought aside, I take a step away and nod.

"Thanks. Sorry again."

Reid gives me a soft smile. "Don't worry about it. It happens."

I roll my eyes. "People say 'it happens' a lot, but I really wish things would stop happening to me." I wave my hands out wide. "If the universe could spread *it* around a little more, that would be great."

He leans against the door jamb and crosses his arms, assessing me but not saying anything else.

Okay. Time to go.

"Alright well, I guess I'll be seeing you around, neighbor." I step down off of his porch. "Do me a favor will you? Maybe don't share the fact that you caught me trying to pick your lock?"

His lips tilt up on the side. "I won't tell a soul."

"Thanks. Not sure my already stellar reputation would survive it." I take a step back, knowing I need to head over to the correct cabin and get settled in. "Night, Reid."

He nods his head. "Night, Busy."

Giving him a small wave, I make quick work of hopping off his porch and heading over to my car. When I get settled back in the front seat and look in my rearview mirror, I see him still standing there, leaning against the door, his hands tucked into his front pockets.

I rest my forehead on the steering wheel, trying to let go of...all of that. He was far kinder than I deserved, far kinder than *I* would have been if I'd found someone picking the lock on *my* cabin door, whether I knew them or not.

God, Reid Cohen. Of all the people to be living next door to, it has to be him? The man who consumed my thoughts when I was a preteen noticing boys for the first time?

I shift my car into drive and roll down the gravel road until I spot the parking pad in front of the *green* cabin and come to a stop. I guess it won't be so bad to have Reid as a neighbor. Maybe we can be the types to exchange sugar and all that. My weary brain attempts to crack a joke about us maybe sharing more than one type of sugar, but I do my best to banish the thought. That is definitely not what I need right now.

This time, when I step up onto the porch, I find the key immediately and make quick work of getting inside and inspecting the place. It looks and feels almost exactly like I remember it from when Briar and Abby lived here a few years back. Same old hardwood floors and dated kitchen. Same slightly woody smell that surely comes from the cedar beams that cut across the length of the living room ceiling.

It's a tiny spot—probably only 1,000 square feet in total—but it's perfect for me and my rugrat. There's a primary bedroom with a private bath and a second much smaller bedroom and another separate bathroom in the hallway. I glance into each of the bedrooms, finding them clean and empty with the same wooden floors. Thankfully, the ceiling fans are already on and the screened windows are open wide.

Most of the spots around town don't have air conditioning, save for some of the newer builds or people who put in window units. I know the temps are just going to keep going up over the next few months until the summer heat finally breaks in September—Briar warned me about the heat in this cabin before I signed the lease—but I can't afford anything more than what this place currently offers. So…ceiling fans and cool evening showers and sleeping mostly naked will surely be the remedy. Tonight, we should be just fine.

Junie stirs as I hoist her out of her car seat a while later, but it's clear she's still mostly asleep.

"Shhhh, it's okay, baby," I whisper.

She glances around, but her eyes are still heavy, and she rests her head on my shoulder. I carry her inside then get her settled on the air mattress I've gotten all set up for us in my room. She rolls right over, her mouth open, completely dead to the world.

I let out a sigh of relief then slip out of the room and close the door behind me. I don't doubt she'll be up at some point in the night, but for now, I'm grateful she's as exhausted as I am.

I glance in the direction of the front door, knowing I should try to get the rest of the car unloaded. Instead, I head to the kitchen, eager to return to the bottle of wine I saw sitting on the counter when I first walked in. It's a twist-off, thank god, and I tilt it back, taking a long, *long* drink. Then I tug open the card that was sitting next to the bottle with a bouquet of tiny sunflowers.

Welcome home, Busy and Junie! Excited to see you.
Let us know how we can help get you settled in.
Love, Briar and Andy.

My lips turn up. Out of everyone, my oldest sister has been the most supportive about my decisions over the past few years. About school. About Jay. About motherhood. She sent money even though I told her not to and flew down to LA to take care of Junie during finals at the end of each semester so I could focus on my schoolwork. She's been a godsend, and I honestly don't know where I'd be without her.

I take another swig from the bottle and tuck the note back in next to the bouquet, then I step outside onto the back deck that overlooks the lake. The glowing moon shines bright, reflecting off the water and casting shadows on the ground. I can't wait to see this view again in the morning.

I leave the light off and take a seat on the steps that lead down to the shore, tilting my head back to look at the night sky, feeling small and tired and wondering not for the first time what the hell I'm doing. I have no idea what's to come from this new beginning, no clue if I'm really making the right choices—for myself, but more importantly, for Junie. All I know for sure is raising her near her grandparents and aunts and uncles, in the town that always felt so safe and welcoming, didn't feel like the *wrong* choice.

And maybe that's all you can do when it comes to being a mom: make as many not-wrong choices as you can and hope everything turns out okay.

chapter two
reid

The shrill sound of my alarm drags me out of a fitful sleep, and I swat at my nightstand, my hand finally finding my phone and shutting it off.

Fuck. I was up way too late last night to have such an early day. My head throbs, and I turn to my side, finding Sydney snuggled up on the pillow next to mine.

"Excuse me," I grumble, giving her a shove. "You know better."

My six-year-old Australian Shepherd looks back at me and lets out a whine, but she can tell by my facial expression that I'm not budging, so she slowly...oh so slowly...slides off the edge of the mattress and slinks over to where her cot sits in the corner, dropping into it with a huff.

I can't help but chuckle at her attitude, but it cuts off quickly as my head pulses angrily again. My entire body protests as I shove up and out of my bed, stumbling my way through the house into the bathroom then the shower.

I shouldn't have gone out for beers last night. The past few days at the shop have been more than enough to send me home completely beat, and the plan was a beer, some baseball, and collapsing into bed before I got back to it this morning. Instead, I convinced myself going out with Nick might be a good idea. Take the edge off the stressful week.

Oh, how wrong I was.

Once I've showered and dressed, I grab a cup of coffee and step out onto the back deck. Sydney rushes past me, bounding over to her favorite pee spot, and I take a few minutes to stretch my weary body before I drop down into my chair, looking out at the lake.

This is the way I like to start my mornings, exhaustion aside. A little caffeine, a good stretch, and a quiet, relaxing moment with nature. The temps are getting warmer much faster this summer than years past, but right now? The tiny bit of dampness in the air as I sit in the shade of a giant pine, the sun still low in the sky and barely beginning to crest the eastern ridge…it's perfect.

Quiet.

Serene.

Beautiful.

It took about twenty minutes to walk to the water from where I grew up, tucked into the southwest part of town, and I always dreamed of living on the lake. So when my life kind of fell apart three years ago, I decided to take my aunt's offer to live in one of her rental cabins.

Lakefront life suits me just fine.

Sydney finishes her inspections and joins me, curling up on the deck at my feet and falling back to sleep, both of us just enjoying the way the water quietly laps at the shore.

This spot is perfect. All the way at the northern end of Cedar Point, tucked away from all the other homes in a cove, sur-rounded by trees. Like I said: quiet, serene, beautiful.

Of course, it's as I'm musing about how quiet it is that I hear music turn on next door. I lean forward, resting my elbows on my knees and holding my coffee mug carefully in both hands, glancing over at the green cabin. At least it's music I don't have a problem with—an alternative rock band that was popular in the '90s and '00s. It could be much worse.

When the couple who used to live in the green cabin moved out last year, my aunt did a bunch of short-term rentals back to back. I've had to deal with the full range of annoying tempo-rary neighbors, though the partiers who gave zero fucks about town curfew and the families who fought their entire trip were definitely my least favorite. I didn't realize Lois had decided to go back to longer rentals, hence my surprise at finding my new neighbor picking my lock last night.

Busy Mitchell.

If she wasn't a surprise and a half…

I'm not much for listening to town gossip, so I don't know much about her except she's the youngest of the Mitchell kids. I remember she used to wear these funky mismatched florals and dye her hair constantly, but that's really the extent of it. Things from my early 20s are a little hazy because my grandfather was rapidly declining, and we were spending a lot of time over at my grandparents' house in Belleview.

Now, though…I doubt I'll ever be able to forget Busy Mitchell again. She's probably the most stunning woman I've ever seen, and she nearly knocked me over when she turned around last night, wielding her tiny hair pin like a sword.

I smile internally at the memory. That wild blonde hair. Those beautiful blue eyes. I felt a thrill run through me that I haven't allowed myself to feel since…well, in a while. And that was just what I was able to see by moonlight. Once I switched on the porch lamp?

Damn.

She's certainly not the gangly pre-teen I've managed to conjure up in my memory. Not by a long shot.

A beep on my phone drags me away from those thoughts.

Unknown: One hour out

Sighing, I take another sip of my coffee and push out of my chair, knowing I need to start the drive into town soon if I'm going to get to the shop before my delivery is set to arrive.

After making quick work of washing my mug and tugging on my work boots, I give Sydney a few good pets then hop into the old Chevy Cheyenne I bought when I graduated from high school, pulling down the gravel lane then out to the main road.

I don't normally work on Saturdays, but I'm getting a special delivery from a wood supplier who's doing me a big favor by hauling it all the way up here instead of forcing me to make the drive down to Oakland. So, as tired and weary as I feel, I know I don't have the option to relegate the responsibility to one of my employees. It's not easy being the boss.

The quiet, twenty-minute drive to and from town is one of my favorite parts of the day. I like the solitude of it. The music on the radio, the window down, the cool breeze blowing through my hair. Or warm breeze, depending on the time of year.

Whenever I can, Sydney hops up into the seat next to me and rides around town at my side, her head out the window, enjoying the views and the smells, probably just as much as I do if not more. Sometimes I bring her with me to work, depending on what I have going on. I hate leaving her at home. She's such a good dog and she loves curling up on the bed I have set up for her in the corner at the warehouse where I build pieces. When she was younger, she was a bit more squirrely, always snooping around and nosing her way into things. Now that she's older, she enjoys lazing around more than she used to. She's the perfect shop companion.

The music on the radio rolls into another '90s rock song as I pull into a spot on the street outside the coffee shop on Main. One cup in the morning is never enough, and I hop out of my truck and jog across the street, eager to get an extra boost of caffeine from Ugly Mug before I get to work.

"There's my favorite nephew!"

My head turns at the familiar sound of my aunt's voice, and I grin when I spot her sitting at a table on the patio with a few other women.

"Hey, Aunt Lois," I say, crossing toward her and leaning down to give her a hug. Then I turn, taking in the others. "Ladies."

My eyes scan as I silently greet each of the women my aunt gets together with on a regular basis, including Patty Mitchell, Busy's mother. Then my gaze falls to the identical books sitting in front of each of them.

"You working on a Saturday?"

I nod, returning my attention to Lois. "I am. Got a delivery coming in. What are you ladies up to?"

"Oh, just squeezing in a book club meeting."

Glancing at my watch, I chuckle quietly. "It feels early for book club. I'm not sure I could get into a conversation about *anything* this early, let alone…" I glance down at the novel sitting in front of my aunt. "What are you reading?"

"It's a historical romance," she says, a wide grin on her face. "It was made into a TV show, so we're all going to read the first book then have a watch party."

I shake my head, a smile still on my face. "Sounds like fun."

"Oh, it is," she proclaims proudly, and then she and the other ladies at the table titter with laughter I'm not quite sure I understand.

"Well, I'll let you all get back to it," I tell them, knowing I need to grab my coffee and head in. "Nice to see you."

"Before you go," my aunt says, stopping me before I can turn and head inside. "I should have told you this earlier, but things have been so hectic recently. I finally found a long-term renter for the green cabin. Do you know Patty's daughter, Busy? She just moved in yesterday."

I shake my head. "No worries about not telling me. I saw Busy when she showed up last night, actually."

A vision of her pointing her hair pin at me, her eyebrows tight and her lips turned down flits through my mind *again*, and I have a hard time hiding my smile.

"Oh, really?" My aunt beams. "That's wonderful. It would be great if you could kind of go out of your way to be friendly. Being a single mom can be so lonely sometimes, and I think she's had a bit of a rough time recently."

She says the last part as a whisper, and I blink, her words registering in my mind.

Single mom?

"Well, I won't keep you," she says, patting my hand. "Have a good day, and don't work too hard!"

I nod. "See you around," I tell everyone, giving them a wave before I push through the front door and head inside.

What my aunt said echoes on repeat. Busy is a single mom?

I didn't see any kids with her last night, though that doesn't mean anything. I highly doubt this is the type of thing my aunt would get wrong, especially with Busy's mother sitting right there listening to the conversation. I scan back over our very brief interaction last night, trying to dig for any kind of indicator that she had a kid with her. But, try as I might, there's nothing.

As I hop back into my truck a few minutes later, my black coffee in hand, I can't help but wonder what her kid looks like.

Though why that even occurs to me, I have no idea.

By the time I'm heading home around four, I'm sweaty and dirty and feel a little bit worn into the ground. My intention was only to assist with the delivery, but then I saw this one slab of wood that spoke to me unlike anything I've seen in quite some time. One thing led to another, and now I'm working on a new table I'm pretty sure is going to sell almost immediately once I'm done with it.

I love creating furniture. Carpentry is all I've ever wanted to do with my life, and I'm beyond lucky to get to do the exact thing I love every day. My father was a carpenter, as was my grandfather. It's in my blood, working with wood to create pieces that fill people's homes.

But I'm beginning to feel the stress on my body differently than I did when I was in my 20s and working in my dad's shop. Before it became mine, back when things were just…simpler.

Now, at 32, the aches linger, the recovery time needed after long days on my feet or hoisting lumber or dealing with the vibrations from any one of my large tools is a lot longer than it used to be, and I know it will only continue to get more difficult from here on out.

I've always been a bit of a homebody, so I've never been one to put myself through the wringer like some of my friends, partying until the wee hours then making it into work early the next day. Now, I'm feeling too old for that kind of shit anyway.

Still…it would be nice to get home and *not* feel like I want to collapse every once in a while. The reality is, on top of work, it's getting harder and harder to find the energy to do the other things I love doing: hiking, camping, exploring the nature that is my very large back yard filled with mountains and lakes and creeks and waterfalls. Over the past few years, I've started to realize I'm lucky if I get in a hike or two a month, and I can't even remember the last time I went on a camping trip. Though that's less about my weary body and more about the fact that my old man isn't around to go with me.

My heart pinches as I come to a stop in front of my house, a fresh wave of grief coming over me.

These emotions seem to come out of nowhere even though it's been over two years. Just the other day I was driving back into town from a trip down the mountain and my brain told me to call my dad to see if he wanted to grab lunch. The way that hit me in the chest…

I shake my head and shove my door open, my dirty boots kicking up some dust as I step out onto the gravel. Before I can even lock my truck, a blur races toward me and then Sydney is jumping up, her paws on my jeans, her tail wagging.

All I can think is, *How the hell did she get outside?*

"What are you doing outside, girl?" I ask, petting her head and rubbing at that spot above her tail that she loves. "Huh? How did you get out?"

I glance around, trying to wrap my head around why she's out here…and I spot Busy emerging from behind the tree line with a little girl resting on her hip, her blonde hair just as wild as her mother's.

"Hey," she says, giving me a smile that makes me think she's as tired as I am. "This is your dog, right? I found her sitting on my back deck a few hours ago, so I just let her hang with us while we were unpacking. I hope that's okay?"

I shake my head. "Yeah, she's mine. I'm so sorry about that." I glance toward my house then back at Busy. "You sure you didn't break in and let her out yourself?"

She laughs, and it is…wow. It's second only to the gorgeous smile that stretches wide on her face, her eyes closing as she giggles.

"Maybe that's the real story," she teases. "But I guess you'll just have to take a look around to see if I took anything while I was in there."

As I chuckle, my eyes fall to the young girl in her arms. She's watching me shyly, her head dipping to the side but her eyes still focused on where I stand.

"Well, you two have both met *my* baby. This is Sydney, by the way. But I haven't met *your* baby. Hi there, sweet pea," I say, dipping slightly and giving her daughter a smile. "I'm Reid. What's your name?"

Busy shifts slightly, trying to angle her daughter toward me. "This is Junie. Junie, can you say hi to Mr. Reid? He lives next door." When Junie tucks her face against her mom's chest, hiding away, Busy snorts. "Of course you choose *now* to get stranger danger." She looks at me again. "She's normally *very* friendly, almost to the point that I get worried she'll just hop into someone's candy van someday."

Busy jiggles Junie in her arms, and even though she's mostly looking toward the trees, I can see the smile growing on her face.

"Are we *sure* we don't want to say hello to Mr. Reid?"

"Mr. Reid," I echo, shaking my head. I grip the back of my neck and wince. "You're making me feel much older than I am."

"Sorry." Her nose wrinkles, but the small smile on her lips gives me the feeling she thinks that's funnier than I do.

"So…getting settled in okay?"

"Ooof. Yeah." Busy lets out a long sigh, switching Junie to her other hip. "It's just been a really long day of trying to put things away with *this* one running around and getting into everything that's sharp and small and not meant for her." She gives me that tired smile from before. "But yeah, getting settled."

"Do you need help with anything? Putting together furniture, or…"

My voice trails off, the thought out of my mouth before I can think better of it. Wasn't I just complaining to myself about how tired I am? What I need is to go inside and shower and stretch and sort through my bills for the month—so why am I offering to play construction worker for my new neighbor?

She gives me a soft look of appreciation, and I groan internally. *That's* why. That look would be enough to bring any man to his knees.

"Thanks, but I can do it on my own." She looks at her daughter and rests their foreheads together, her voice dropping to a whisper. "We got this, don't we, Junie Bee?"

My lips tilt up at the adorable interaction, though I can't ignore the sliver of disappointment I feel at her declining.

"Alright, well...Sydney and I will be just next door if you need anything. And apologies again about her escape artistry today. I appreciate you taking care of her."

"No problem. See you around, neighbor." She gives me a quick wave then turns and heads back in the direction she came from.

My eyes drop to the sway of her hips as she goes, to the jean shorts that fit snugly on her peach of an ass and her cute little cowboy boots and...

I turn and head into my own house, Sydney at my heels, ready to be fed. I'm not sure how old Busy is, but I *do* know she is far too young for me to be eyeing like that. Though really, I shouldn't be giving eyes to *any* woman, regardless. I might not be married anymore, but that doesn't mean I'm suddenly free to do whatever the hell I want.

Intent on distraction, I focus my attention on first setting out food for my girl, then hunting down the reason she was able to escape. Though, try as I might, I can't find anything.

Sydney's a great dog, so I've never needed to crate her. Instead, she gets to enjoy the place to herself on the days I leave her at home while I'm at work. Not once have I returned to a bag of food ripped open or stuffing from a pillow on the floor. She doesn't chew on anything I don't explicitly give to her. Normally when I get back, she's lying comatose on the couch or sprawled on her back in the strip of sun that comes through the back door. The idea that she escaped somehow just feels...mind-boggling. Especially since I can't figure out how she got out of the house.

After a while, I give up the search and head to the shower, rinsing away the sweat and dust from the day before tugging on a pair of shorts, grabbing a beer, and plopping onto the couch in front of the TV.

But before I can even reach for the remote, my phone rings. I groan when I see who it is, though I still hit accept and put it on speaker.

"Hey, mom."

"How's my baby?" Her voice comes through the line and fills the room, and I wince slightly at the sound of it. Maybe that makes me a jerk, but right now, with how exhausted I feel, I can't muster the energy to care.

"Tired," I tell her honestly. "How are you doing?"

I glance around, realizing I didn't grab a bottle opener. Shoving up from my seat, I return to the kitchen as my mom replies.

"Amazing. Vance took me to the Caribbean last week, remember?"

I *do* remember. She called me from the car on the way to the airport to brag and then hung up on me when I didn't get as excited as she wanted me to.

"It was incredible," she continues, not waiting for me to respond. "We went to this all-inclusive resort and danced and drank and sunned by the water. Ugh, it was perfect. Exactly what I needed."

Finally, I find the bottle opener and snag it, turning to head back to the living room, but my eyes catch on movement outside the window over my kitchen sink.

Busy and Junie are walking out onto the shared dock that sits between our two cabins. My mother's voice fades into the background as I watch them, the setting sun sparkling brightly on the water behind their silhouettes as they take a seat on the wooden jetty and share bites from what looks like a sandwich.

They paint a cute picture.

"Reid! Are you even listening?"

My mother's voice cuts through and I turn away, heading

back to the living room to the beer that's waiting for me.

"Sorry. Say that again?"

The reality is I don't want to hear anything about Vance or my mom or this stupid vacation. Why she is nearly relentless about sharing this stuff with me when I've tried to make it clear I don't want to hear it is beyond me.

But I'm all she has now, no matter what has happened in the past. She might have let me down in ways I'm not sure I'll ever be able to forgive, but she's still my mom. So I listen as she recounts their trip, trying to be the dutiful son, trying to give her the attention I know she wants, even if I'd rather be doing literally anything else.

chapter three
busy

"Good morning!" I call out, a bell ringing as I shove the front door open, my eyes scanning the nearly empty shop.

There are cans of paint stacked in the corner along with a few folded-up tarps lying in a heap and other supplies sitting on a pop-up table, but not much else. It's the first time I'm seeing what will eventually be Happily Ever After, the bookstore that will open next month on Main Street. There used to be a boutique clothing store here, but it closed years ago and the space has sat empty for that entire time, so it's great that a new business is going to open downtown. Especially because this bookstore is the life's dream of one of my favorite people.

Briar emerges from the back, a small smile on her face.

"Hi, Little Bee," she says, using the childhood nickname that always makes me roll my eyes even though I love it.

Someone who doesn't know my sister might assume she's not actually that happy to see me based on how reserved she's being. But Briar and I have grown very close recently, and I can see in the slight upturn of her mouth and the way she's wringing her hands together just how excited she is.

Almost as excited as I am to see her.

I bounce across the room and fling myself at her, laughing at the way her eyes widen in shock and an awkward chuckle tumbles out of her mouth as I throw my arms around her shoulders. Briar embraces me as well, her rigid frame softening as she lets herself sink into my hug.

"I've missed you so much!" I tell her, pulling back, my hands on her biceps. "Junie will be so excited to see you."

At the mention of her niece, a genuine smile stretches across Briar's face. "I can't wait to see her, though I'm sure she's already forgotten who I am."

I scoff. "Her Auntie Briar!? She could never."

My sister shakes her head as if to dismiss what I've said. It's not just lip service, though. Junie *loves* Briar. My kid has been a bit on the slower side when it comes to speaking, but she definitely knows the word 'auntie' and shrieks excitedly whenever my phone rings because she thinks it's my sister.

We're doing a family dinner at mom and dad's this weekend, and I know everyone is excited to see both of us—but *nobody* is as excited to see anyone as Junie is to see Briar.

"So, what do you think?" she asks, turning to look at the empty room, possibly trying to see it the way I do. "It feels a lot bigger than I remember it when I did the first tour a few months ago."

The nerves are rolling off of her in waves, and I step up to her side and loop my arm in hers.

She looks at me, and I give her an encouraging smile. "It looks fantastic. I can't wait to see what you're envisioning."

Briar takes a deep breath, almost like she's bolstering herself, then nods.

"Alright, boss. Put me to work!" I clap my hands and rub them together. "What will you have me start with? Cleaning? Painting? I have my coveralls in the car just in case."

"Andy and I did the cleaning over the past few days," she replies, referring to her husband. "Today is absolutely going to be a painting day."

"Yes!" I bounce on my feet and clap my hands together. "I know I ended up going the photography route, but you *know* I love any chance to pick up a paint brush. Just tell me what to do!"

My sister chuckles and shakes her head then goes into detail about what she wants done with the paint cannisters in the corner: dark green on the ceiling and the top half of the east and west walls, sage green on the entire back wall. Eventually, the plan is to hang lots of plants and flowers and greenery to make it feel like a magical realm, but that will come after we've installed the bookshelves and hung some specialty plant holders around the room. I'm hoping she'll let me get creative with the painting on the ceiling, but I'll hold off and ask that on a day that isn't my very first.

"I'm in the process of negotiating buying up the stock from a used bookstore that's closing in Elk Grove, so I'll just be in the office," she says, hitching her thumb in the direction of the doorway she emerged through just a few minutes ago. "Let me know if you need anything, okay?"

I beam at her. "Got it. Good luck!"

Once Briar has disappeared into her office, I head back out to my car parked on the street and snag my coveralls. I don't normally wear these when I paint, opting to just allow my clothing to get speckled and sprayed as a sign of my dedication to the arts.

But during my victory lap—the extra year I spent finishing up my degree after I had Junie—I did some large-scale installation work as part of my senior thesis. I printed out these massive photographs then spent weeks adding paint and oil, and the process was really messy, so I opted for some more coverage. Plus, by that point, I was also doing *tons* of laundry because apparently babies spit up and poop on everything, and I just didn't have the time or money to do an extra load just because.

After I've set up the tarps across the base of the western wall and taped off a line about halfway up, I pop in some headphones and get started. As the sounds of one of my favorite rock bands echo through my ears, I open the cannisters, pour the paint into the trays, clean the rollers, and dip in.

I'll give my sister this: she picked two gorgeous colors of green. I feel like they perfectly encapsulate her personality. One is muted, the other is very deep, and both are eye-catching. It doesn't surprise me that she wants her bookstore to be filled with plants and flowers. Briar spent years working as a florist, and it's so like her to figure out how to bring two things she loves together in a way I never would have pictured.

Like I do any time I'm working, I zone out as I roll the forest green color onto the walls, and before I know it, three hours have passed.

"Wow!"

I glance at Briar as she walks out from her office, her eyes scanning the work I've done so far.

"I considered going with a lighter color for the ceiling because I worried it would make the space too dark, but I really like how it looks."

I nod. "Too many people just lean into millennial gray," I tell her, tilting my head back and staring at the ceiling. "This has personality."

Briar snorts. "Millennial gray?"

"Ah, you know. It's supposed to be calming, but really it's just bland."

"I happen to *like* gray."

I smirk, somehow completely unsurprised.

"Well, regardless of your judgments about *other* colors, I'm glad you like this one," she adds, continuing to examine my work.

I roll my shoulders, trying to ease the way my muscles have tightened over the past few hours. Painting a ceiling is no joke.

"You ready for lunch? I was thinking about swinging by One Stop to grab sandwiches from the deli."

"And I'm sure the fact that Andy is there has no impact on that choice?" I tease.

Briar rolls her eyes but doesn't dispute my observation. She and my brother-in-law got married last year, but the honeymoon period certainly hasn't faded in the slightest. Any time she talks about the guy, her cheeks turn all rosy and she gets this…look on her face. Briar isn't the bashful type, so it always makes me want to laugh. I don't though, because I don't want to mock the fact that she's so in love with him. It's something I am so glad she's found, especially because he looks at her with the same twinkle in his eyes.

"I actually brought my lunch," I answer, crossing to where I chucked my bag in the corner. Tugging out my water bottle, I take a long sip. "But you don't have to worry about me. Go. I know you want to eat lunch with Andy."

Briar rolls her eyes. "I want to eat lunch with *you*, weirdo. You just got to town and I want to hear how the move has been. Grab your lunch and let's walk over there together. I can get a quick sandwich and then we can sit outside and chat."

Smiling, I acquiesce, reveling in the idea that she wants to spend time with me. "Sounds good."

There was a time when the concept of sitting down to 'chat' with my oldest sister would have felt daunting, like I was in trouble. I mean...what would we even have had to talk about?

Growing up, Briar was closest with our older brother Boyd, while I was closer with our other two siblings, Bellamy and Bishop, who are only two years older than me. But ever since I got pregnant with Junie, my relationship with Briar has changed in ways I never even imagined were possible. And honestly, probably in ways I wouldn't have been interested in when I was younger.

Back then, I was a lot more complicated.

"Feeling settled at all?" Briar asks, dropping down onto a bench and plopping her purse next to her hip. We've grabbed her lunch from the deli at the grocery store and settled in at the beach park that overlooks the lake and the marina, and Briar stretches out her long, lean frame before she tilts her face back, her eyes closed as she soaks in the sun.

"Not really." My reply is maybe too honest, because my sister brings her hand up to shade her eyes from the sun, looking at me with concern. "I mean, I've unpacked what I can. But I still need to buy a few pieces of furniture, so I'll be digging things out of suitcases for the foreseeable future."

Even with the sun, I can feel Briar's eyes burning into me as I take a bite of my PB&J, and I know what she's going to say before she even begins speaking.

"I wish you would just let us *help* you a bit, you know?"

Giving her a tight smile, I shake my head. "You *are*. Mom's watching Junie...*full time*. You've given me a job, and don't pretend you're not paying me way more than what you'd pay a normal assistant. And I *know* dad talked with Lois about me renting from her."

"But that's not help, that's just family," she says, shrugging her shoulder and bumping it against mine. "You were away at college when I moved home, but I had to accept a lot of help I didn't want." She makes a face. "I mean, I moved back in with mom and dad."

"That was different."

"Why? Because I was escaping an emotionally abusive relationship?"

I don't answer, surprised by how candid she's being. I remember Boyd talking about Briar's ex like he was scum who treated her badly, but I've never heard *her* talk about it that way.

"Here's the thing to remember, Busy. I wanted a new start. The same can be said for you. You've been through *plenty*, and it's only normal for the people who love you to want to rally around you to help in whatever way makes sense for them. For mom, it's offering childcare, because she has free time and wants to hang with Junie. For dad, it's helping get your housing sorted, because he has connections in town. Let me help, too."

I scoff. "You gave me a *job*."

At that, Briar grins. "Honey, you took a job I needed to have filled. Trust me when I say you're going to be *earning* that paycheck."

Chuckling, I bite into my sandwich, thinking over what she's said. Each of my siblings have their own thing. Boyd is Mr. Independent and Bellamy is the people pleaser and Bishop is the charmer. I guess if I had to label myself, I'd be…I don't know. The problem child, maybe.

But Briar? She's the best listener. It's probably because she's never been super talkative, always kind of keeping to herself and doing her own thing. She's a quiet observer. So when she shares her opinion about me moving back to town and accepting help from the family, I can't just write her off. She's saying it because it's something she really believes *and* because it's something she wants me to hear.

Maybe that's why I have loved her checking in on me so often. She's careful with her words, so I know the ones she shares with me are important.

"I'll think about it," I finally tell her, though I roll my eyes when I see the hint of satisfaction that comes across her face.

We chat a bit more about the cabin and Junie before moving on to things that have changed around town over the past few years since I've been gone. Eventually we chuck our trash and head back to the bookstore. It's a casual lunch with my sister, and I can't help the ember of happiness that settles in my chest at the knowledge that we'll get to do this kind of thing on a regular basis. Maybe with Bellamy, too.

There's something about spending time with your siblings as adults that's just...different than what it was like when you were a kid. It's like you get to know them in an entirely new way, and I'm looking forward to seeing how my relationships with my sisters will change now that I'm home.

"There she is!"

Junie is plucked from my arms the second I cross the threshold into my childhood home, my mother barely even looking at me, too absorbed with seeing her granddaughter as if they didn't just see each other yesterday.

I share a look with my dad, who opens his arms and pulls me into a big hug. "Hey, Little Bee."

"Think she noticed I'm here?"

He gives me a squeeze then pulls back, holding each of my biceps. "Probably not."

I roll my eyes as he closes the door behind me, but I can't help the tiny bit of sting at his comment. Sure, *he* wasn't serious. But *I* was.

I've seen my mom only a handful of times since Junie was born, and she's always so focused on my daughter she seems to forget she has her *own* daughter who wants some attention, too. Then again, I've always dealt with feeling a bit forgotten, so I guess it isn't anything new.

"How's the cabin working out?"

My movements are slow as we make our way through the entry toward the living room. I can hear everyone in there, commenting on how much Junie has grown, and I can't help wanting just another minute or two before I join them.

"It's great," I tell him, not wanting to give him the same honesty I gave Briar earlier this week over lunch.

If I tell *him* I'm living out of suitcases, he'll show up with a trailer full of furniture tomorrow and I'll be forced to accept it all. I might be able to rebuff my mom when she makes demands, but I've always been a daddy's girl.

What I *can* do is tell him how wonderful the cabin is, especially because I know he took the time to find somewhere great for Junie and me to live.

"The spot is so perfect and it's quiet, which is a nice change from the apartment we used to have near campus." I shrug a shoulder. "My neighbor seems really nice."

"Good."

I nod, unsure why I brought Reid up at all. I've seen him a few times this week, usually hanging out on his patio with his dog. He always gives me a friendly wave and chats with Junie for a few minutes. It's really sweet, actually. And Junie *loves* Sydney.

"It's Reid Cohen," I continue. "My neighbor."

Dad smiles. "Oh, that's great. He's a nice kid."

We stop at the threshold to the living room, watching as everyone coos over Junie.

"Shame about him and Sarah."

I nod at that too, though about a million questions sprout up. I heard about Reid and Sarah's divorce through the grapevine when it happened a few years ago. There was a time when I knew *everything* that was going on in this town even though I lived over 400 miles away. Then I found out I was pregnant and promptly checked out of Cedar Point gossip.

Before I can ask my dad anything about it, he speaks again.

"Have you gone over to say hi to Don and Margie yet?" he asks, bringing up their best friends, Sherriff Perry and his wife. "I know they're excited to have you back in town."

"Not yet. Still just trying to get settled, you know?"

He nods, and then I follow my dad into the living room, my eyes tracking over where everyone is scattered on the couch, chatting animatedly and fawning over Junie. It's been over a week since I moved home, but it's the first night everyone has been free for a family dinner. Briar is here with her husband, Andy, and Bellamy with her boyfriend, Rusty. Plus mom and dad, and now me and Junie Bee.

Having a big family feels chaotic more than it doesn't, but

it's also familiar, and my nerves and slightly standoffish attitude fall by the wayside as I'm enveloped in hug after hug and answer questions about the move and being back in town. Being back here feels like putting on a comfortable pair of shoes that had been forgotten in the closet, and I sink right in, chatting away with Bellamy and laughing at dad's stupid jokes.

But there's something in the back of my mind that lingers, a feeling I've long tried to get rid of but continue to struggle with, no matter how much I try to ignore it. I glance around the table, at my siblings and their partners, at my parents, and I'm reminded of the fact that I've always, *always* felt on the outside of my family. Sure, I know they love me. That has never been in question. But I've never really felt...connected the way I think the rest of them do.

I was a bit closer with Bellamy and Bishop, but they're twins. They had a special relationship no one else could touch. It always felt like everyone in my family had a partner in crime, and I was left to fend for myself. Mom had dad. Boyd had Briar. Bishop had Bellamy.

And then there was me.

Living at college and filling my life with people who had nothing to do with my family usually allowed me to hide that in the back of my mind, like something I didn't want to remember. But now, being back home, I know there's no way I'll be able to avoid feeling that way again.

It's a reminder that sometimes, those comfortable shoes were chucked in the back of the closet for a reason.

chapter four
reid

"No cigars tonight," Nick says as he walks through my front door, carrying a case of beer from Cedar Cider in one hand and the poker chip container in the other. "Claire says if I come home smelling like an ashtray again, I have to sleep in the guest room."

I smirk at him, taking the beers and setting them on the counter. "There are worse things than wanting to sleep next to your wife."

"I knew you wouldn't call me a little bitch."

Nick pats me on the back then cracks open one of the cans as I begin unloading them into the fridge.

"Not me. But tell that story to Teddy or Carlos and that's *exactly* what they'll call you."

He chuckles and takes a long sip. "I guess we just won't bring up the cigars, then."

I laugh. "Sounds perfect."

Once I've finished with the beer, we lug a folding table and a few chairs to the back deck and begin setting up. I've been part of this monthly poker night since Nick started it up five or six years ago, and I'm pretty sure I've only ever missed it two times. Once when a buddy from high school got married, and once when my dad died. That's it, and I wouldn't *dare* to miss on a month when it was my turn to host.

As a confirmed introvert, a night like this *should* make me break out in a cold sweat. The truth is if I thought about it too hard, I probably *would* break out in a cold sweat. But Nick is my best friend, and the rest of the guys who come—*his* friends, because I tend to keep to myself—are pretty easy to hang out with. Being around them doesn't usually feel like work, so for whatever reason, this is one of the very few group things I enjoy doing. Especially because when I host and it's a night like tonight, we get to play poker out on the deck with the lake in the background.

Brilliant.

Over the next twenty minutes, the group of guys who show up month after month for poker night begin arriving. Carlos and Brad, two guys who work for Nick's construction company, arrive together carrying a stack of pizzas they picked up in town. Jeremiah has his phone to his ear and an irritable expression on his face. He's only lived here for a few years and I can't say I'm a big fan, so I'm thankful when he immediately steps out onto the deck and closes the door behind him to finish his conversation. My cousin Marie's husband, Craig, shows up with two more boxes of beer—good man—and as we're all standing around, eating pizza and drinking beer, Nick's younger brother Teddy walks in looking stoned as hell.

Sunday poker nights are always kind of messy, but I wouldn't have them any other way.

"Read 'em and weep, boys," Teddy says an hour later, laying

his cards down on the table to a chorus of groans. "Royal flush."

"You know, one of these days, we're going to figure out how you manage to get one of those almost every month."

Brad says a variation of this at every poker night. Nobody has ever figured it out.

"Look, the poker gods have bestowed luck upon me in a way that defies reason. I'm not a cheat, *especially* not at poker."

Nick snorts as he reaches out and collects everyone's cards then begins shuffling. "That makes it sound like you cheat at other things."

Teddy shrugs, giving us a devious look. "You can take what I said however you like."

I roll my eyes and accept the hand Nick deals out, leaning back in my chair and chewing on my toothpick as I eye the new cards. It's a dud, and I decide to stick with my ace of spades and chuck out the other four. Nick gives me new ones, and when I look at them, I chuckle. No better than the last ones I had. The odds are not in my favor tonight.

"Holy damn."

I glance up at Jeremiah's words, muttered under his breath, wondering what kind of hand he has. Which is when I realize he's not looking at his cards. I follow his gaze, looking over to my left, and my stomach dips when I spot Busy stepping out onto her deck with Junie, wearing a bathing suit that cuts high on her hips and shows off that gorgeous peach of an ass.

I swallow thickly. Holy damn is right.

I've allowed myself a few moments to admire her figure over the past week or so since she moved in, but she was always fully clothed. Jean shorts, tank tops, and bare feet are her normal attire, but this is…like a daydream.

Busy drops her towel on the ground and tugs her thick

blonde hair up into a messy bun at the top of her head, then bends over to help Junie with something, though I couldn't say what if I was offered a million dollars.

My throat goes dry and I groan internally. When I glance around the table, I'm not surprised to find every man watching her.

"Jesus. That's your new neighbor?" Jeremiah asks, sitting up straighter in his chair, not even trying to hide the blatant way he's staring at her.

Nobody's hiding it.

"Busy Mitchell," Teddy says, drawing out her name like he knows her, and when I glance his way, I'm relieved to see he's staring at his cards. "She's *always* been a bombshell."

"You two are friends?" I ask, putting out a few chips without really paying attention. I might have a shit hand, but I can't fold every time.

"We went to high school together."

It doesn't surprise me. Teddy's in his early 20s—about ten years younger than me—which tracks with what I know about Busy and the few memories I have of her, as vague as they are.

I look back over to where she's now hoisting her daughter up on her hip. Junie sees us then and waves her hand wildly in our direction, making me smile. Busy turns, finally spotting us out on my deck.

"Hey," she calls out, nodding her head at our group.

A chorus of hellos are sent back her way, then she turns and steps down off her deck and follows the short path to the dock, where we all have the perfect view of her putting Junie down then bending over again.

"Man, she is…" Jeremiah starts, then shakes his head and makes a humming noise like he wants to eat her up.

I don't like it.

The thought surprises me, but I try to set it aside and refocus on the game. I'd *really* like it if *everyone* would return their focus to the cards, but it doesn't look like I'm going to have that kind of luck.

"So what was she like in high school?" Jeremiah asks Teddy.

I try not to roll my eyes. Does it matter? Does it really matter what she was like in high school? Most of the men at this table are far too old to be staring at her the way they are, myself included.

Of course I can't help but lean in slightly, more than happy to take in the information if Teddy's going to be sharing it anyway.

"She was a partier, that's for sure. We weren't friends, but we ran in the same crowd." He takes a swig of his beer and looks back out toward where she's sitting on the edge of the dock. "She was kind of a loner, though. Kept to herself a lot."

Now *that* surprises me.

"I wouldn't mind getting to know her better, if you know what I mean."

In most situations, I'd keep my opinion to myself. I'm not friends with Jeremiah. It's no skin off my nose if the guy wants to run his mouth about a woman I know is way out of his league.

But for whatever reason, tonight, I can't keep my mouth shut. I don't like the way he's eyeing her.

"She's a single mom, man."

He nods, his eyes oscillating between his cards and where Busy and Junie are now down at the end of the dock. "Single and ready to mingle, or what?"

His response makes it clear he didn't hear me the way I intended.

"Single and maybe *not* in need of someone sniffing around who just wants to get in her pants."

I don't know where this protectiveness is coming from. All I know is watching him look at her like a piece of meat he wants to sink his teeth into has me all kinds of riled up.

Jeremiah turns to look at me, one eyebrow raised. "You heard Teddy. She likes to party." He looks her way again, biting his lip in a way that makes me want to bust it open. "If she wants to party, I'll give her a party."

Disgust roils through me, and I take a deep breath then let it out long and slow.

"Folding this one." I drop my cards on the table, face down. "I'm gonna grab another beer. Anyone?"

Teddy nods, but everyone else declines. I head inside and into the kitchen, retrieving two cans from the fridge.

I don't know Busy any better than I know the dozens of other neighbors who have come and gone over the past year or so. She's been in town a week, we've talked a few times, she's kind to my dog. I have a few memories of her when she was a kid, but that's really it. The kind of protectiveness I felt when Jeremiah said what he did—it came out of nowhere.

I crack my can open and take a long sip, giving myself a beat to move past whatever this bristly irritation is before returning to the deck and retaking my seat. Thankfully, they're no longer ogling my neighbor and are now talking about the A's game from a few nights ago.

I'm normally pretty good at poker. It requires a kind of shrewd attention to detail that comes naturally to me. But tonight, all my mojo seems off. I feel distracted and a bit restless, my mind scattered when normally I keep it carefully focused.

I can't seem to shake off Jeremiah's comments. They might

have been slightly uncouth, but it wasn't anything wildly inappropriate. And yet I wanted to leap out of my fucking chair and launch myself at his throat. As someone who considers himself to be a fairly calm, easygoing guy, I can't say I particularly liked that feeling. I have no idea where it came from or why it bloomed so quickly in my chest, but it did. Even as Nick deals us a new hand and everyone has clearly moved on, something prickly is humming through my veins.

"Reid. You in?"

Nick's question drags me out from under the current of emotion I'm feeling, and I find everyone staring at me, waiting for my bet.

"Yeah," I say, sitting up in my chair and returning my attention to the cards in my hand.

I guess the reason doesn't matter. The reality is that I feel… protective of Busy, warranted or not. I didn't like what Jeremiah said, not one bit. But I also didn't like everyone watching her in her bathing suit. I didn't want them to sit around talking about her, eyeing her the way they were.

So while, yes, it was protective, it was also…possessive. Something I definitely shouldn't be feeling.

Not about Busy Mitchell.

Not about anyone.

It's dark when the guys finally take off, and for the first time, I'm glad to see them all go. I remained distracted for the rest of the game, and when nine o'clock finally rolled around, I brought up the workday tomorrow. Everyone seemed to be as glad to wrap up the evening as I was to see them out the door.

Which is a shame.

I slump down into my chair on the porch, having finally finished putting everything away, and I just stare out at the lake, my feet resting on the small coffee table and my hands folded in my lap. Just like how I feel about mornings, I love watching the lake at night. The gentle glow of lights in the distance and the moon in the sky, the way it all dances in the reflection of the water. It's beautiful.

After while, I hear the familiar squeak of the screen door opening at the green cabin. Busy emerges, a bottle of wine in one hand and her phone in the other. I'm sitting in the dark, but the light of the moon is enough to illuminate us both, so when she turns, glancing in my direction, she waves.

"I thought all you guys went back inside."

I nod. "We did, but everyone's gone now, so…" I shrug. "Just enjoying the night."

She bobs her head then looks out at the water for a beat or two. "Mind if I join you?" she asks. "I'll gladly share my wine in exchange for a chair so I don't have to sit on the ground."

Part of me thinks I should say no, thinks my little outburst earlier means I'm stepping into murky waters by spending any time with Busy. The flare of interest I felt and my resulting attitude at the other guys is enough for me to know better.

But I ignore that small voice, and instead, I nod and gesture to the chair next to mine. Busy smiles and hops off her deck, crossing over to the edge of mine, her bare feet padding softly on the grass between our cabins. When she plops down next to me, I get a waft of something sweet and fruity—jasmine, maybe.

"It's on the cheaper side," she says, twisting off the top of her wine bottle, "but I promise it won't give you a hangover." She takes a long sip before she shrugs, licking her lips. "Most likely."

Then she extends the bottle my way. I look at it for a beat then back at Busy before reaching out and accepting it. Apparently we're drinking straight from the source tonight, and *sharing* the bottle—two things I haven't done in at *least* a decade. I've never been a big drinker, but you have lower standards in your early 20s.

Groaning internally at the reminder that Busy *is* in her early 20s, I take my own sip, careful to hide my wince at the bitter taste, then pass it back to her.

"Were you guys playing poker?" she asks, her feet joining mine on the coffee table, her head tilting back to look up at the stars.

"Yeah. It's a monthly thing Nick started. You know Nick Waltham, right?"

"I do. He's friends with my brother. He did all the construction work on Cedar Cider, too."

I nod. Boyd was a year ahead of me in school. I didn't know him that well, but I was friends with a few of his friends, and we were both athletes, so we were friend*ly* even if we weren't friends.

"A regular poker night with friends sounds like fun."

I shrug a shoulder. "It can be."

Busy's head lolls to the side, her eyes connecting with mine. "Ooof. Was it *not* tonight?"

Licking my lips, I chuckle slightly, surprised she was able to read me so easily.

"Let's just say...if it were up to me, there might be one less seat at the table."

I know that's harsh. Clearly, I'm not at my best tonight.

"Ouch," she says, returning her eyes skyward as she takes another long drink from the bottle.

"How about you?" I ask. "How was your day?"

Busy's lips tilt up at the sides. "Pretty good. Got a few pieces of furniture set up in Junie's room and mostly took it easy. I went over to Briar's for a bit, which was nice."

"That's your sister, right? She's the one married to the guy who owns the grocery store?"

Busy snorts. "What kind of small-town boy are you?" she asks, though her question is teasing. "Don't you know anyone's names? Or is everyone classified by their job?"

Smirking, I roll my eyes, feeling sort of embarrassed because *yes*, that is how I keep track of people. "Not everyone in this town is a Mitchell. I probably couldn't name more than a hundred people, if that."

She gasps and slaps a hand against her chest. "Sacrilege."

I just laugh and shake my head. "Apologies." I narrow my eyes. "I'll work harder at learning everyone's names."

"You better. I might quiz you on it."

I watch her for a long minute as she takes another sip of her wine, my eyes roving along the elegant length of her neck and up to the apples of her cheeks before they drop down and focus on the plump pout of her lips, which I can only imagine now bear the tinge of stain from her drink of choice.

When she hands the bottle my way again, I take a much longer sip than I should, this time barely even noticing the taste.

"My dad was always a lot better at knowing people's names," I eventually tell her, remembering the easy way he talked with customers, and also the importance he placed on knowing people around town. "I never really picked up that skill."

She hums and smiles. "How is your dad doing? Still owns

the furniture store in town, right?

I lick my lips and stare at the bottle in my hands for a long minute.

"Dad passed away. 'Bout two years ago." I want to take another long drink, but I refrain, reminding myself that drinking through my grief has only ever brought me even more sorrow.

"Oh, Reid. I'm so sorry," she says, her voice soft. "I usually stay up to date on stuff that happens in town and I...didn't know."

I shake my head and give her a sad smile. "It hasn't been that long, so..." But I trail off, not sure what else to say.

"Can I ask how he died?"

"Heart attack while he was alone in the shop." I reach out and set the bottle on the coffee table.

It's probably one of my greatest regrets. I was supposed to meet him for lunch, but I went on a hike instead, needing the time to myself and wanting to clear my head. Nature usually provides that for me. I'll never know what might have been different if I'd gone in, if he might still be here today.

"I'm so sorry, Reid."

I nod like I do any time someone expresses their condolences, but when I look at Busy, I see my own grief reflected back on her face. It's pained, as if she cared for him as much as I did. Something about that makes me feel grateful.

"How was the lake earlier?" I ask, knowing it's an abrupt change of topic but not wanting to linger any longer on my regrets from the past.

Busy watches me for another beat before she follows my lead.

"It was really nice," she finally says, looking back out to the water. "I forgot how wonderful it is to just float around in the water. In LA, I was over an hour from the beach, and even when I *did* go, there were waves, you know?" She shakes her head. "Lakes beat the ocean so hard."

I nod. "I completely agree. I like the calm of it. It's always steady." Consistent. No surprises. "I'm almost embarrassed to tell you how long it's been since I've gone for a swim."

"Really? It's right there." She waves her hand in the direction of the lake, only about ten yards away from us, then reaches out and snags the wine again. "Weren't you like, a swimmer? Wasn't that your thing?"

"I was," I say, surprised she knows that. "I *am*. But sometimes you just...get out of the habit of doing something you love. Or you fall out of love with it."

It's hard to admit that about swimming. It *was* something I loved, but it's been a few years since I've felt that way.

"Anyway, it's probably been...a year. Maybe more."

Busy's jaw drops. "What? Reid. First, the names. Now, the lake?" She lets out a long sigh. "You are so lucky I moved in right next door."

I shake my head, trying to hide the way I want to constantly smile when she's talking to me. The shit she says just makes my soul feel lighter, even with the subject matter of our earlier conversation still lingering slightly. It's been a while since I've smiled this easily, without the looming fears of the future hovering and sapping me of the joy most people experience in the day-to-day. And I don't know whether it's a good thing or a bad thing.

It's good because talking with Busy feels like my soul has taken a much-needed breath, and I can't help the voice in the back of my mind that says I want to get to know her better, want to understand the things that make *her* smile.

But it's a dangerous feeling, too.

A reminder of the decisions I've made for my future and what's to come
Of things I will never have.

chapter five
busy

The paint looks like shit.

I stare at the wall, at the light green layer I just finished, my eyes narrowed and my arms crossed.

Like literal shit.

The color looked more sage when I opened the jar, but now that it's on the wall and contrasting with the forest green of the other two walls and ceiling, it has taken on a hue that reminds me of one of Junie's diapers that made me want to hurl myself through a window.

What is that? A moss green? Olive, maybe?

Gross.

There's no way Briar's going to dig on this. Not a chance in hell. Or if she *does* like it, I need to strongly advise her that we need to go with a lighter color, something with a bit more brightness and poppy energy. Definitely not...*this*.

Sighing, I decide to break for an early lunch instead of continuing with a second coat. Until I know for sure what my sister wants to do, I don't want to move forward with any more painting.

Every day this week, Briar and I have eaten lunch together, heading down to the beach park and chucking a blanket down on the grass. It's been great, catching up on some of the goings-on around town and hearing about how she and Andy are doing.

But she's down the mountain today, picking up an actual truckload of books she purchased from a bookstore that's closing, so I'm on my own.

I roll my eyes. I'm *always* on my own. That's the reality, isn't it?

Shoving that thought aside, I grab the lunch bag I packed for myself this morning and wander out to Main Street, looking left toward the mountains and the direction of Cedar Cider before turning right and heading toward the lake. Just because Briar isn't here doesn't mean I can't still enjoy the view and some vitamin D.

"Oh, sorry," I say, bumping into someone coming out of one of the shops.

Reid.

I'm instantly overwhelmed by him—by his scent and his height and that soft grin that's had me going weak in the knees since before I knew how to explain what that meant.

I blink, trying to get my bearings. "Sorry," I say again, shaking my head and tucking my hands into my back pockets.

"You're fine."

I glance behind him, realizing I'm standing in front of Cohen Custom, his father's shop. Or I guess, maybe *his* shop? I haven't been inside in a long time. For about a year after that summer when Reid was a lifeguard at camp, I found any excuse

I could to wander inside, hoping to bump into him. In those preteen dreams, we'd strike up a conversation and he'd realize I was *so much more* than just the girl from summer camp.

It's hard not to laugh at my younger self and just how clueless she was.

"You been painting?"

Glancing down, I realize I'm still wearing my coveralls. "Oh, yeah." I laugh, slightly embarrassed. "We're trying to get the inside of the store painted before we get the bookshelves put up. Except it looks more like baby poop than sage so I'm going to have to completely repaint the back wall, which is…" I trail off, not wanting to ramble too much.

Reid's smile grows. "Well, that's unfortunate." He glances behind me briefly before returning his gaze to mine. "Can I help at all? I'm pretty good with a paint roller."

I'm tempted to take him up on it, though it's more from the selfish vantage point of wanting to get to know him better than because I actually need the help. I don't want to come across as the needy girl who can't do anything without assistance.

"That's alright." I bat a hand his way. "I appreciate it though. Briar's actually paying me to do it, and I can't afford to pay you myself."

"I wasn't assuming you'd pay me." He chuckles. "I was just offering because apparently it's important to get to know your neighbors, you know? Engage in small talk, ask about how things are going."

Something tiny blooms in my chest at his words, knowing he's taken the things I said and tucked them away to remember. I watch him for a long moment, seriously considering his offer. A montage of scenes plays through my head. The two of us painting together. Maybe a quick paint fight. Rolling around on the tarp, paint in my hair and maybe other places it shouldn't be.

And *that* is why I decline.

"I really do appreciate it, but I'll be fine."

Part of me thinks I see a bit of disappointment in his eyes, but I bet I'm just imagining it. Surely.

"Well, I'll let you get on to where you're going, then," he says, nodding at me. "Good to see you, Busy."

I smile. "You, too."

We both turn at the same time and walk in opposite directions. For whatever reason, I find it oddly difficult to walk away from him. Not only did I want to take him up on his offer of painting help, I also oh-so-briefly considered asking him what he's doing for lunch. Which would have been foolish.

Reid is…so gorgeous. So unbelievably handsome he's almost hard to look at.

I let out a sigh. I thought I'd moved on from this adolescent crush, really and truly. But in just two short weeks, the man has officially planted himself back into the same position he occupied before: the star of my daydreams.

Not that it matters.

Taking a seat on the familiar bench I've been sitting on with Briar, I pull my sandwich and water bottle out of my purse. The last thing I need right now is to be looking at any man the way my eyes seem to peruse Reid every time he's near.

The Busy I used to be wouldn't have been so cautious. She would have stared him right in the face then given him elevator eyes and a playful smirk. Flirted her heart out and hoped it would result in a fun night or two.

Now, though…I know better.

I mean, obviously I can't lump all men in with my ex. Jay was…well, he wasn't good for me. I doubt he'll be good for anyone, for that matter. But when things between us didn't work out—exactly as I expected—I resigned myself to a life of single mom-ing it. The idea of managing a child *and* navigating a new relationship just feels too daunting. Besides, I don't want anyone inserting themselves into my life and making things any more challenging than they already are.

Maybe that's harsh. Maybe that's me just looking at everything as a half-empty glass. Maybe that's me refusing to see something that could be so much better than being on my own.

But that's the thing…it *could* be better—finding a man and falling in love—but it also could be much, much worse. And that's the thing I'm not willing to take a risk on. I used to be that girl. The risk taker. The one who was willing to bet big and lose bigger if it meant I gave it a chance.

But I can't afford to be that person anymore, not now that I have Junie. Now, it's all about the safe choices, the things that will give her the best chance at a happy, healthy life. It's the main reason I came home.

It's also the reason I will need to continue to choose to do it all alone.

When I open the door to my parents' house on Friday afternoon and spot my mom holding a sobbing Junie, I'm instantly on high alert.

"She's okay, I promise," mom says as I fly across the entryway and over to where she's sitting on the floor of the living room. "She just took a small tumble *right* before you walked in the door. Bonked her head on the edge of the coffee table."

I pluck Junie from my mother's embrace and snuggle her close, my entire body radiating in pain as my daughter cries in my arms. There is nothing that hurts as badly as hearing your child cry. Nothing.

"You okay, sweet girl?" I ask, my voice gentle as I rock her slowly, trying to use my own calm as a way to help calm her down. I place a kiss on her forehead and try to examine her for a bump or red mark. "Where does it hurt?"

Junie takes a hiccupping breath, her tears beginning to subside. Then she points at a spot on the other side of her head, and when I turn her to look, I see some faint redness.

"Yeah, sweet girl. Looks like you got a little knock, huh?"

My daughter nods then tucks herself against me, her hands gripping me tightly. When I glance at my mom, I find her watching us with a concerned expression.

"I'm so sorry, honey," she says. "I feel horrible."

I shake my head. "Hey, she's a kid. She's going to fall and hurt herself sometimes, you know?"

"I know," she replies, planting her hands on the evil coffee table and pushing herself up to stand next to me. "Doesn't make it any easier to see this sweetie crying like that."

Mom lightly touches Junie's arm, her eyes gentle as she watches my daughter.

"I *hate* hearing her cry. I can't handle it."

At that, mom gives me a knowing glance. "Oh I remember that feeling."

"How long until it goes away?"

She holds up both hands, her fingers crossed. "Any day now."

I snort. "Great."

We move into the kitchen, starting the handover routine we've begun now that she's watching Junie full time.

"She took two naps today, so she might have some extra energy tonight," she offers, shoving various items into the diaper bag I drop off every morning. "And she refused to eat the broccoli at lunch."

I gasp. "Junie Bee!" I exclaim, wiggling her in my arms. "You didn't eat your *broccoli*? But it's your favorite!"

Junie giggles through a watery expression.

"No child loves broccoli," my mom teases, giving Junie's stomach a poke.

"It's really her favorite," I say, shaking my head. "I don't know why she loves it so much but…" I shrug. "I'll try to feed it to her for dinner. She might have just been in a mood."

"I mean…do you want to stay and eat dinner with *us* tonight?" Mom gives me a smile. "I'm making chicken piccata."

I let out a sigh, feeling guilty about my answer before I even speak.

"Thanks for the offer, but I'm wiped. I just want to get home, feed us, give this rugrat some time to run around, and then hit the hay."

She nods, but I don't miss the tiny hint of disappointment in her eyes before she turns away quickly and focuses on tucking the last few things into Junie's diaper bag. I don't know what caused this weird rift between me and my mom, but things have been stilted ever since I told her I was pregnant. Sure, there isn't any easy way to hear that your youngest daughter is going to be the first to make you a grandmother when she's only 20 and single and already six months along.

Not one of my finest moments.

It took me a while to muster up the courage to tell my family about the pregnancy, long enough that the reactions were understandably bigger than they would have been if I'd told them straight away. But mom just...checked out, almost completely, something she's *never* done before in my entire life. It hasn't ever felt like she's really checked back in, not with me at least. With Junie, absolutely. She's a wonderful grandmother. And the fact that she watches my daughter every day? Her willingness to make that sacrifice so Junie has someone she loves watching her every day instead of strangers?

It's amazing, and I'm so lucky. But that stiff awkwardness is still there between us, and I don't know how to fix it. So I just let it be. Someday, we'll figure it out, I'm sure.

Well, I hope we will.

Surely, things won't *always* be like this. When I was younger, I was the troublemaker, but I still always felt like I could go to my mom when things went sideways.

Maybe *that's* what the issue really is. It felt like, with the pregnancy, I'd finally pushed her too far. I'd finally gotten in *too* much trouble, caused *too* much of a problem. While part of me understands that my mother is entitled to her emotions and opinions, I guess there was something inside me that broke when I realized the truth: there *was* a limit to how much she was willing to put up with.

It makes me sound selfish, I know, but as the baby of the family, the one who always felt a little bit forgotten and a little bit on the outside, the one thing that comforted me whenever I felt the most forgotten and alone was believing I was loved, even if I wasn't always understood.

Now, I'm not so sure.

Mom and I exchange our goodbyes and talk vaguely about another family dinner in the next week or two, and then I head out, wishing I knew what to do or say to make things...better. Unfortunately, finding the right thing to say hasn't ever been my strong suit.

When I get home, I shove open the front door and set Junie down.

"Run wild, baby girl."

She shrieks and barrels through the house, the bump on her head long forgotten. I step into the kitchen and tug open the pantry, pulling out a blue box of mac and cheese. Movement on the deck outside has me leaning over the sink to look out the window, then I laugh to myself when I spot the familiar dog lying on the porch, looking out at the lake, her tail wagging.

"Sydney," I say, shoving the window to the side and speaking to her through the screen.

Her head perks up and she looks at me.

"What are you doing, girlfriend?"

The dog's mouth opens, her tongue flopping out, and I swear she's smiling at me. Probably reveling in however it is she's sneaking out of Reid's.

Shaking my head, I walk to the back door and swing it open, Sydney immediately barreling through and heading right into Junie's room.

My daughter shrieks again. "Sinny!"

I chuckle to myself and return to the kitchen, putting a pot on the stove to boil water as Junie and Sydney chase each other around the house for the next fifteen minutes, my daughter giggling like a maniac and Sydney bounding around like Junie is the coolest toy she's ever played with. It really is one of the cutest things I've ever seen, and I'm feeling eternally grateful for Sydney's ability to run my daughter ragged. Hopefully, this helps get out that extra energy my mom was talking about and Junie sleeps hard tonight.

I'm mixing in the highly nutritious powdered cheese when I hear Reid's voice outside.

"Sydney!"

I lean over the sink again and look out the window, spotting him on his deck, looking around.

"Sydney!" he calls out.

"She's in here with us," I shout to him.

His head whips to the side, and I spot the way his shoulders droop. A few beats later, he's standing on the porch, looking in through the screen door.

"Is she seriously here again?"

The sound of the door opening precedes him as he steps into the living room, his large body making the already small space feel even tinier. That's when Sydney sees him and bolts across the room toward him, her tail wagging. She twists around his legs then drops onto the ground, belly side up. Reid drops down into a squat and begins stroking along the soft fur of her tummy.

Junie crosses the room slowly, inching toward where Reid is petting Sydney, then lies down on the ground next to her four-legged friend, her own belly in the air.

"Oh, are you a dog, too?" he asks her, poking her stomach, an easy smile on his face.

Junie squeals then turns and wraps her arms around Sydney, snuggling in close. I watch him as he talks to Junie, my eyes scanning the lean muscles of his biceps, the firm roundness of his shoulders, the way his ass looks in those dusty old work jeans.

When his eyes connect with mine, catching me watching him all googly-eyed as he pets his dog and talks sweetly to my daughter, I spin away, clearing my throat and returning my attention to the boxed pasta that could use another few stirs before it's ready.

"Thanks for always letting her hang out when you find her out there."

I nod but don't turn around. Instead, I reach up and grab one of the plastic bowls out of the cabinet that Junie picked out over the weekend at the thrift store. It's white with a red rim and has a Care Bear in the middle. I had one just like it as a kid, so I was thrilled when she pointed at it and clapped when I added it to our cart of kitchen items.

"I promise I'm trying to figure out how she's getting out. I'm not a...neglectful owner."

"I don't think you are," I offer, scooping a small portion of the neon orange noodles into the bowl. "Honestly, I think you're missing out, though."

When I glance his way, I find his head tilted to the side as he watches me with confusion.

"Clearly, your dog is a magician. You could take her to Vegas. Make some of the big bucks."

He chuckles and rolls his eyes then pushes up to standing.

"Well, we'll get out of your hair and let you two eat dinner."

Licking my lips, I glance at the pot on the stove then back at Reid. "You're welcome to join us, if you want," I say, the words flying out of my mouth faster than I can manage to stop them.

Reid pauses his movements toward the door.

"It's just blue box pasta, but..." I shrug, suddenly feeling a bit foolish.

He probably has a *real* Friday night planned out back at his house that doesn't include a wily toddler and neon food.

"Actually, that would be awesome," Reid says, surprising me. "Thanks for the invite."

"Okay, well..." I pause, feeling somewhat flustered by his

acceptance. "I'll just get Junie served up and then I'll make another box."

Reid smiles. "Sounds perfect."

chapter six
reid

I can't remember the last time I ate mac and cheese from a box.

Maybe that makes me a snob, I don't know. I try to be really careful about what I eat, making sure I'm giving my body the best that I can. But as I scoop up another spoonful of the most horrifically orange pasta from my Ninja Turtle bowl, I can't help but admit…it's pretty delicious.

"How was your day?" I ask Busy as I lean back against the kitchen counter, bowl in one hand and spoon in the other.

She bobs her head, finishing off her own bite before speaking.

"Good. Had lunch down at the beach park near the marina and got a little too much sun, but otherwise it was a pretty good day. How about you?"

"Same, basically," I reply, scooping up another spoonful of mac and cheese. "Work, lunch, work."

My eyes scan her exposed skin, taking in the hint of pink on her shoulders and nose, highlighting the freckles that are already there and surely adding more.

"Up until last year, there were umbrellas at the picnic tables at the beach park, but some kids lit them on fire over the summer."

At that, Busy's head rises, her eyes wide. "Seriously?"

I nod. "I didn't see them lit up, just the aftermath. But Teddy can see the beach park from his girlfriend's apartment, and he said it was wild."

Busy shakes her head, still looking shocked. "It *sounds* wild. I feel like this town has had enough of things being lit on fire."

I nod, knowing she's referring to the fire that nearly burned down One Stop a few years back. Losing our town's only grocery store was quite the ordeal and had a huge impact on everyone. Nick had to collaborate with a construction crew from Belleview to get the work done, with everyone working long days and late nights to make sure things were repaired as fast as possible. Those of us who had experience with tools and construction stepped in as often as we could to help. Even still, it took months before it was back up and running.

"You're friends with Teddy Waltham?" Busy asks, bringing me back to our conversation.

I shrug. "Kind of. Nick's my best friend and Teddy kind of just...comes with the territory," I joke. "We get beers every so often. He's a good kid."

Busy nods. "Teddy and I were in the same year in high school."

I remember him saying as much during poker night, but I think I still assumed she was a few years older than him.

"How old are you?" I ask her, the question out before I can help myself.

"I'll be 23 in October."

I snort at the way she says it, the way kids talk about their next birthday, certain it will make them sound older than they really are. But really, hearing Busy tell me she's 22 years old makes me feel…

I don't even know. Far older than I actually am, that's for sure, and fucking guilty as hell for how my eyes have wandered over her body since she moved in three weeks ago. I knew she was young, but it's one thing to tell yourself someone is too young for you, quite another to hear that they're a full decade younger. If I think Teddy's a kid, Busy's not much different.

"Why? How old are you?"

She asks it like it's a challenge, and I chuckle as I respond.

"I'll be 33 on Christmas."

There was no reason for me to say it like that other than to imitate her, and she rolls her eyes, her lips turning up in a smile.

"You're not *that* old."

God, I feel even more ancient when she says it like that.

"Trust me. My body disagrees," I tell her, taking the opportunity to roll out my shoulders, which are still feeling particularly tight from my long day at work.

I forgot to stretch and do my exercises this morning, having woken up a bit late and rushing out the door with only a few minutes to spare. As I stretch one arm and then the next, I don't miss the way Busy's eyes scan my arms and chest. I certainly feel younger when she looks at me like that.

Licking my lips, I shake my head, knowing that being here is trouble. That I should grab my dog and head back home, leaving Busy and her daughter to their evening.

"Wait…did you say you'll be 33 *on* Christmas?"

I chuckle, nodding. "Yeah."

"Oh, I'm so sorry." Then she freezes. "I mean…not that I'm *sorry*, but I've always wondered what that's like."

I shrug. "It's about what you'd expect. People lump your birthday in with Christmas, so it never really gets celebrated."

"That is…so sad."

"It sucked as a kid, but now, I can't complain. I take two weeks off of work every year to make up for it, so…"

"Well, at least you're staying positive," she says. Then she hitches a thumb at Junie. "This one's also a holiday baby."

My eyebrows rise. "Really?"

She nods. "She was born on the Fourth of July." She looks at Junie. "Huh, Junie Bee? And mom struggled to get you to latch all night because fireworks kept going off and you'd just cry and cry."

I wince. "That sounds tough. Lucky girl, though. She'll get fireworks every year on her birthday."

Busy nods. "This year will be the first time she'll get to truly experience fireworks. Last year I put headphones on her to protect her from the sound. She hated them, but at least she didn't lose her hearing." She giggles again. "Though I'm not looking forward to the day she's old enough to realize the fireworks are not actually *for* her."

"All done!"

I turn, grinning when my eyes land on Junie, both her hands in the air, completely covered in orange "cheese." She's beaming, clearly proud of herself.

"Let me wipe you off and then you can give the puppy a kiss goodbye, okay? Sydney and Mr. Reid probably have better things to do with their evening."

I'd *like* to tell her I'm doing exactly what I want to, but I keep that thought to myself.

Busy grabs some wipes and cleans up Junie's hands and face, the sweet kid squirming and giggling, before letting her down out of the chair. She immediately grabs onto Sydney, who has been waiting dutifully at her feet hoping for a scrap or two of food, which I don't doubt she got judging by all the lick marks on the floor.

"Thanks again for dinner."

I take my empty bowl to the sink and give it a rinse. I'll need more food once I head back to my place, but she doesn't need to know that. She made an extra box of pasta to share with me, and I don't doubt that was a sacrifice for a single mom, even if a relatively small one.

"And for loving on Sydney," I continue. "She and Junie are clearly turning into best buds."

Busy crosses her arms, a smile on her face. "Oh trust me, I have *loved* watching Junie chase Sydney around. My kid is going to sleep *so* good tonight."

I grin, too. "Well, any time my dog can be of service, let me know."

A funny expression crosses Busy's face, but it's gone in a flash, her eyes following Junie around the room until they veer into a bedroom and disappear.

"So you and Teddy were friends in high school?" I ask, returning to our earlier conversation.

I lean back against the counter and cross my arms, stalling, not exactly ready to go.

Busy nods. "Kind of. We were in the same friend group, had a lot of overlapping friends."

I try to reconcile what I know about Teddy with the image I've been creating of who Busy is, and something about it feels... off.

"What's that look for?"

I grin sheepishly. "I just…can't picture the two of you being friends."

Busy shrugs and lets out a humorless chuckle. "Well, I've changed just a bit from my high school days."

"How so?"

She leans against the counter, her arms braced wide. "I don't get high anymore, for one."

Clearly, she knew where my mind was more so than I was expecting.

"Unless the occasion really calls for it," she adds on.

At that, I can't help but laugh, and Busy's resulting smile nearly bowls me over. I barely know the girl, but somehow that natural, easy, effortless expression of hers has become something I look forward to.

My laugh tapers off, but my own smile remains, my eyes fixed on her.

"I can't picture *you* being friends with Teddy," Busy says, drawing my attention back to her. "I mean, what do you even talk about? You know, since you're *so much older than him.*"

She says the last part dramatically, and I shake my head.

I shrug. "I don't know. Sports. Hiking. Camping."

"You like to go camping?"

Her entire face brightens when she asks that question, and I nod. "I do."

"Ugh, I love camping. My family and I used to do the Kilroy hike every year together and camp at the top so we could see the sunrise in the morning. It was one of my favorite things, every summer." She shakes her head, her smile still wide as she remembers. Then her face twists slightly. "Then I got pregnant, and let me tell you…these buns weren't hiking *anything.*"

My lips tip up.

"I've skipped the past two years."

"You gonna try to do it this year?"

Busy lets out a long, slow breath then shrugs. "I don't know actually. Maybe. If they want me to."

There's something odd about the way she says that, as if her family might *not* want her to join them. I open my mouth to comment on it, but before I can, Busy puts her hand up, a single finger in the air, her head turned to the side.

"Do you hear that?"

I turn my head in the same direction, listening.

"No."

"Exactly," she whispers.

She wanders off, coming to a stop at the threshold of the bedroom just off the living space. She chuckles then looks back to me, tilting her head toward the room and waving me over.

"Forget what I said about becoming best buds," she says quietly as I step up to the doorway. "These girls are sisters."

Lying on a blanket in the middle of the room, Junie and Sydney are snuggled together, both with their eyes closed, completely tuckered out. It really is adorable, and part of me wishes I could let Sydney stay the night, like a little sleepover.

"They're pretty cute," I say. "I almost hate to wake them up."

Busy hums, and that's when I realize how close we are. Inches apart, my body hovering just behind hers. God, I can smell her, something floral and bright. Maybe it's perfume or her shampoo or some kind of lotion. I can't tell. All I know is it smells delicious.

When Busy turns, looking up at me, a smile still on her face, I can't help the way my eyes dip, taking in that scattering of freckles across the bridge of her nose, the tiny dimple on the right side of her mouth, the slight crease at the center of her plump lip.

What is this…possession that comes over me when she's near? This inability to think straight when we're within feet of each other? All I can imagine is what it would be like to reach out and bring her in against my chest. Move her petite body flush with mine, feel her softness pressed against me.

I swallow thickly, my brain conjuring images of what it would be like if I could just…bend down and press my lips to hers. I dip just slightly, my eyes glued to her mouth, and I know I don't imagine it when her chin tilts up just a bit.

But you can't, a quiet voice whispers. *You promised.*

Gritting my teeth, I step back, putting space between us, repeating the same words over and over in my head like a chant.

You promised.

You promised.

You promised.

Busy clears her throat then steps further into Junie's room, and I watch as she slowly maneuvers her daughter, releasing her little hands from Sydney's fur one at a time before carrying her carefully to her bed. Sydney hops up then and walks out of the room, coming to my side.

"Well, we'll get out of your hair," I say quietly, patting Sydney on the head.

Busy tucks a strand of loose hair behind her ear as she steps out of Junie's room, shutting the door softly behind her. Then she spins around and smiles, though some of the lightness that was in it just a few minutes ago is missing.

"Have a good night, Reid."

I don't linger any longer, even though I wish there were something I could say to eliminate the weird tension that's suddenly hovering in the air. Unfortunately, I don't think there's anything you can say to someone after you almost kiss them but don't to make the situation easier. You just kind of have to let it…be.

Like I told Jeremiah, Busy's a single mom. She doesn't need someone trying to get into her pants, and the truth of my life is that I wouldn't be able to give her more than just a good time. And even *that* isn't something I should be doing.

I know I made the right choice by pulling away, keeping myself from making such a huge mistake. But at the same time, as I crawl into bed later that night, my belly full of neon pasta and the space next to me cold and empty, I can't help but wish things were different.

"Sydney." I pat the space next to me, knowing I'm breaking my own rules by calling her over to snuggle. She's there in a flash, plopping down at my side, resting her head on my stomach.

Eventually, I fall asleep, but not until I've played and re-played my moment with Busy over and over again, wishing I didn't always feel the need to do *the right thing*.

Because making a mistake with Busy Mitchell sounds like a hell of a lot of fun.

I bring the circular saw down and slip the wood along the rotating blade, slicing off the live edge. It clatters to the ground, though the sound doesn't register over the whine of the blade and the protective earwear I have on. Flipping the wood around,

I measure then do the same with the other edge.

As much as I enjoy any kind of woodworking, there's a certain kind of sadness I feel when I take a slab as beautiful as this one and cut off a live edge. Mostly because I think it adds a bit of character and personality that a 90-degree angle doesn't provide, but also because it isn't the way *I* would do it if it were up to me.

But that's the thing about taking on clients who want custom projects. The final result has to be *their* vision, not mine. That's why they pay me the big bucks.

Movement at my side pulls my attention, and I glance toward the open rolling door that faces the parking lot, grinning when I spot Nick stepping inside. I hold up one finger then make quick work of cutting the other two edges before shutting down my saw and tugging off my headphones.

"Hey, man. How's it going?"

Nick nods. "Good. Here about the leather chairs we talked about."

"Yeah, gimme a sec to move these and wash my hands, then we can chat?"

I hoist the two slabs of wood over my shoulder and take them over to the large shelves I have set up against the wall, sliding them in place in the area I have labeled for this particular project. Then I head to the work sink and wash up.

"Okay," I say, leading Nick into my office. I pat Sydney on the head where her bed is set up next to my desk, take a seat, then wake my computer. "Remind me again what this is for?"

"Ellis wants new chairs for the lounge area buildout at Dock 7."

I nod. "That's right."

"Said she has always loved the ones you made for Cedar Cider and wants something with a different look but a similar feel."

With a bit of pride, I pull up the details for the chairs I made for the local brewery—one of the only custom projects I handled completely on my own before my dad passed away—and open the specs on my computer screen.

"I did love those chairs."

Nick chuckles. "They're works of art."

Leaning back in my seat, I cross my arms. "So what's the deal? I know you're doing the buildout to add the lounge area, but are you doing design now, too?"

"Nah." He bats a hand my direction. "Ellis is just old school, you know? She hasn't worked with you before and I've done a few projects for her over the years." He shrugs. "I think she just wants to make sure someone she trusts is handling it."

I bob my head, though I can't completely ignore the pinch at the unspoken truth. Ellis used to go to my dad for furniture for Dock 7, but he's gone. Even though she's known me practically since I was born, she's putting on her business hat and adding a middleman because she doesn't entirely trust *me*.

I look back at my screen and the detailed notes I have for the project I did for the brewery, knowing I can't allow myself to spend too much time dwelling on that. As much as I know Ellis likes me as a person, business is business.

"Well, if she wants a dozen of them, I'll need about three months once I've sourced the wood and leather. So, maybe four months to delivery?"

"That's perfect. We're aiming to be done with the project by mid fall, so that'll be a good time for install."

"Makes sense to finish up before it gets cool. I'm looking forward to that fireplace."

I love Dock 7. It's a restaurant on the west side of the lake with a really cozy vibe and beautiful deck area that books out weeks in advance during the summer because everyone wants to eat with a view of the lake.

Locals call the place Lucky's, because during high tourist season, the bar is a veritable hot spot for finding casual hookups with people just stopping through town. I might have taken advantage of that truth during my 20s, before Sarah, but eventually I moved on from that kind of life, and I haven't really been back to Lucky's for more than a dinner or two since.

With the renovations happening, I might need to reconsider, if not for the hookups, certainly for the new whiskey tasting lounge Nick's building off the bar. It's going to have a fireplace and dark walls and sconces and, apparently, wood and leather chairs made by me. Sounds like a dream, and I can't wait to see the finished work.

"Getting the guys together to grab a beer tonight," Nick says as we step out of my office a while later, once we've finalized the details for the chairs. "You wanna join in?"

A beer sounds nice, but I've been feeling overworked this week.

"Nah, I think I'll pass," I say, massaging the joints in my right hand with my left. "But thanks."

We come to a stop at the doorway that leads out to the parking lot. "Well if you change your mind, you know where we'll be."

I nod. "I do."

We shake hands.

"I'll catch you later," he says, then heads off in the direction of where his truck is parked a ways away.

I turn, flexing my hands and doing a few stretches before I tug a different project off the shelf, a table top with a stain that has finally finished drying. Then I get back to work. As much as I enjoy spending time with Nick and the guys, I enjoy time on my own just a bit more, and a quiet night with my dog and a book sitting on my deck sounds like a perfect evening.

If Busy and Junie happen to be there?

Well, I wouldn't hate it.

chapter seven
busy

"You're going to hurt your back if you keep lifting it that way."

I turn and pin Andy with my eyes. "You're going to hurt your mouth if you don't keep your thoughts to yourself."

Andy laughs and rubs his hands together. "Oooh, someone's testy today."

"Not testy," I correct him. "Focused."

"Hey, if that's how you see it..." he replies, smiling.

Rolling my eyes, I return my attention to the bookshelf we just finished maneuvering into place. These things *are* really heavy, but the last thing I want today is my brother-in-law, who I love on most occasions, giving me advice on how to lift something. I'll do it how I want, thank you very much.

Okay, so maybe I'm a bit testy.

It's been a long few days of unloading box after box after box of books, plus finishing up the last bit of paint on the back wall once Briar picked a new shade of green. Now, we're setting up the shelves, and they are *far* heavier than I was expecting. Not to mention the temps in Cedar Point have been rising steadily, which wouldn't be such a problem if there wasn't also a record high in humidity. Junie hasn't been sleeping well, and neither have I.

So, yeah, not quite at my best today.

I move over to where the last bookshelf is waiting in the corner. I squat, bracing my core, and once Andy has counted it off, we lift and walk it over to the opposite wall.

"You're right," I tell him, once we've gotten it in the right spot. "It was easier your way. Sorry for being a brat. It's just been a long week."

He shrugs, an easy smile on his face. "Don't worry about it, Busy. We all have off days. You need any more help before I head out?"

I shake my head. "No, I've got it from here. Thanks."

Andy gives me a wave then heads into the office where Briar is working to say goodbye to her, leaving me to the rest of my work.

Things in the store are picking up pace, Briar's vision beginning to truly come together the closer and closer we get to opening day. The plan is to open Happily Ever After on Fourth of July weekend to capitalize on the crowds, so the pressure of that looming date, less than ten days away, makes every moment feel important. Thankfully, it feels like the last true task is to get the books on the shelves. Though it would feel a lot easier to do if we had more hands than just mine and Briar's.

I make quick work of wiping down all the shelves now that they're all in place, and then I take a break, wandering out onto Main Street and over to Ugly Mug. With how poorly I've been sleeping, splurging on some caffeine to boost me up for the rest of the day doesn't feel like a waste.

Once I have my coffee in hand, I take a seat outside in the shade, enjoying the light breeze that's funneling off the lake and wafting through downtown. Now, if only that breeze would blow the *other* way and whip through my house. *That* would be something special.

My phone rings, and when I look at the screen, my heart falls.

Incoming Call: Jay

I know why he's calling. I can feel it in my bones. And to be honest, right now, I don't have the strength to deal with it, another instance of him letting Junie down—letting *me* down. I send it to voicemail, slip my sunglasses on, and take another sip of my iced coffee.

Jay is the kind of guy who likes to believe he's a stand-up man, but in reality, he does whatever it is that makes *him* the most happy, regardless of anyone else. What that looks like is an inability to be faithful in a relationship, a lack of interest in showing up when he says he will, and absolutely no clue why someone he has let down is upset with him.

It's pretty infuriating.

Thankfully, I clocked the kind of man he was beneath all that smooth charm, which allowed me to make decisions with logic instead of emotion—not an easy feat when your body is overwhelmed by hormones. If I *had* gone by pure emotion, Jay and I would be married right now, he'd be cheating on me left and right, and I'd *still* be at home by myself with a toddler.

Cheers to choosing a better life for my kid over a man.

Once I've finished most of my coffee, I head back across the street, intent on returning to the bookstore. But as I do, my eyes flick across the businesses on Main Street, snagging on Cohen Custom just a few doors down.

Before I can think too much about why I want to pop in, I walk the short distance and tug open one of the two glass doors, heading inside. It's been years since I've been in this place, but it still smells exactly the same: like freshly cut pine and that earthy scent that comes from old leather. It takes me back to the days when I would slip in here and wander around, sitting in all the different chairs, as if there was any chance I would be buying a piece of furniture. In reality, I was taking my sweet time, hoping to run into Reid. Just over a decade later, clearly, not a lot has changed.

I step up next to a beautiful wooden chair with a dark green leather cushion and take a seat, loving the way my body sinks into it, like it's already been broken in. I could use a chair like this back at the house. I mean, I could use *any* living room furniture, but this is just so…

I flip up the price tag and wince.

Shit. More than a month of my rent. No wonder it's so damn comfortable.

"That chair is one of a kind."

I glance up, smiling at the employee. Heather, I think. The daughter of one of my mom's friends. "I don't doubt it."

"Each of our pieces are crafted from some of the best wood in the country, cut right here in Northern California. And the leather you're sitting on was made using natural tanning methods. So, no toxic chemicals."

I nod then rub my hand along the soft grain of the armrest. "It's beautiful."

"Are you interested in purchasing a piece for your home today?"

Twisting my lips, I shake my head. "Unfortunately no. I don't think it's in my budget."

"We do offer layaway. The owner usually handles that. I can call him, if you'd like."

I glance behind her. "Oh, is Reid not here?"

Her smile widens. "He is. But he spends most of his time making furniture at the warehouse. I can let him know you're here, Miss…"

I shake my head, feeling thankful that she doesn't seem to recognize me. Having been away for a while has its perks.

"I don't want to bother him while he's working." A lie *and* a truth. "But thanks for your help."

"Well, we'll be here if you change your mind."

Nodding, I take another minute to admire things before I push up out of the chair. It's better that Reid's not here. Perfect actually. I got a bit of my nostalgia out, gave in to my impulse, and didn't get myself into any trouble in the process.

Because that's all that can come from me wandering over to his shop in the middle of a work day—trouble.

Sure, it might be completely normal for a neighbor to pop in to say hello at work, but I'm not here to be neighborly. I'm here to flirt, to assuage that thing inside of me that likes the way his eyes rove over my body when I walk toward him.

But after our almost-not-a-kiss a few nights ago, I know that mentality is foolish. It's one thing to flirt, to feel that pitter-patter in your chest because you've garnered some attention. It's quite another to let things become physical. And I'll be honest, I was a hair's breadth away from pushing up onto my toes and planting my lips against his as he hovered behind me in the doorway.

It would be far too easy to fall for a man like Reid Cohen.

Kind. Considerate. Handsome.

God, is he handsome.

But like I've said to myself over and over…there's just too much risk in getting involved with someone, with anyone. Not only for me, but for my daughter.

And with that final thought, I give Heather a pinched smile and head back out to Main Street and over to the bookstore. Back to reality, leaving the daydream behind with my teenage self.

Junie giggles, her head of blonde curls whipping around her face as she swings away from me. Then momentum brings her back and I grab the toddler-style seat.

"Ready?" I ask, stretching out the word as I hold her up, bringing her a bit higher, holding her in place to heighten the suspense.

"Swing!" she says, her tiny fingers holding tight to the black rubber seat as she waits in anticipation.

She lets out a joyful shriek as I let go, swinging away from me in a long arc again. We've done this same thing about twenty times, and her enthusiasm hasn't waned. It's one of those things about kids that blows my mind, how they like doing the same thing over and over and over again, never getting tired of it.

My arms are certainly tired of it, though, and after a few more minutes, I tug her out of the swing and set her on the ground. She totters happily over to a boy sitting in the sand pit, playing with yellow Tonka trucks and scooping sand into a bucket. She plops right down next to him and picks up one of his toys, and the two begin playing together.

If only friendship stayed that easy as we get older.

The playground at Cedar Point Elementary is much more conducive to toddler play than the modest park I used to take Junie to near campus when she first started to walk. It was rare for other kids to be there, so she often just wandered around with me hovering close as she plucked grass out of the earth and picked up leaves. I know she had fun exploring, but I always wished there were more kids around so she had someone to play with. It's nice to see other kids and parents here on a midweek evening, letting their kids get out their wiggles and socialize as the sun sets on the weekend.

When my mom suggested I check out the playground for a place Junie could run around like a nut, I nodded and promptly set the thought aside. Kids thrive on routine, and getting my daughter home for dinner felt more important. But once I got in my car, I realized the real reason I wanted to head back to the cabin wasn't because I wanted to get Junie home for anything. It was because I was hoping to have a run-in with Reid when he inevitably stops by the house looking for Sydney, who continues to jailbreak the blue cabin to make her way over to hang out with us.

Instead of heading home, I turned and drove directly to the elementary school. A smarter decision, and one Junie is enjoying immensely, even if I'm left to wonder what Reid's reaction was when he got home and we weren't there.

I shake my head. He probably doesn't care at all, and thinking otherwise is a recipe for disaster.

"She's so cute."

I turn toward a very put-together-looking woman sitting on a nearby bench and smile, thankful for the brief reprieve from my own thoughts.

"Thank you," I reply, stepping in her direction, trying not to be self-conscious of my stained pants and plain gray tank that I'm pretty sure has a hole somewhere near my belly button. It didn't seem to matter when I was heading out the door to work because I knew I'd be a sweaty mess today, but for some reason, it feels like it matters now.

"Is that your son?" I ask, dipping my head in the direction of where Junie and the boy are playing together.

She nods as I drop down on the other end of the bench. "Yes, that's Leo. I'm Marie."

"Oh, Marie." I laugh, shaking my head. "Lois' daughter, right?"

Her head tilts to the side, then recognition hits her. "Oh my goodness, Busy!" She stands and walks toward me, surprising me when she wraps me in a hug. "How have you been? You've grown up so much!"

Chuckling, we both take a seat. "Good, I've been good."

"And you have a daughter. I thought I heard about that from my mom."

A gracious way to say she heard about my unplanned pregnancy through *my* mom gossiping with hers. The reality of small-town life.

"I do. Her name is Junie."

Marie looks over to where Junie and Leo are playing. "What a cute name."

We both watch our kids for a moment in easy silence. If I remember correctly, Marie is around the same age as Boyd and Briar, though I can't recall whether any of them were friends.

She's also Reid's cousin, the two of them growing up super close, almost more like siblings.

Licking my lips, I look back toward where our kids are playing, trying my best to shove all thoughts of Reid to the side.

"How are you liking being back in town?"

I cross my legs and rest my hands in my lap, nodding. "It's going good, I guess?" Then I shrug. "It's an adjustment, for sure. But I know we're better off here than we were before. Being near family, especially."

Marie's eyes turn soft. "Change is always hard, but it's so much easier when you have a great support system. My mom mentioned that Patty's watching Junie?"

"Yeah. It's been amazing, having that kind of help."

"I know what you mean. Mom used to watch my daughter Nina, until she started pre-K this year, and she does the same with Leo."

My shoulders droop, relief coursing through me at the fact that Marie is in a similar situation as me, relying on her parents for help with her kids. There's a kind of guilt I feel, leaning on my mom, needing her help.

It might be because things between us are strained right now, but I know it's mostly because I feel like if I had been married or had my life more together when I finally had a kid, I wouldn't *have* to rely on her like this.

"Do you ever feel guilty?" I ask her, feeling suddenly desperate to get someone else's thoughts. "I mean, my mom used to garden all the time and do farmer's markets and play bunco with her friends. Now she's a nanny, and I keep waiting for her to get sick of it."

Marie smiles. "She's not a *nanny*. She's a *grandmother*," she says, her eyes twinkling. "My guess, knowing Patty, is she wouldn't have offered if she didn't want to have that time with your daughter—if she didn't want to help *you*." She shrugs. "My mom quit working at One Stop to watch Nina when she was born, and my husband and I didn't even need her to. She just wanted the responsibility. She said it gave her a 'renewed purpose' when she was starting to feel like her usefulness on earth was waning, though she tends to be kind of dramatic."

I laugh at that, even as I consider what she's just said. I feel surprisingly buoyed by her response. It hadn't ever occurred to me that, yes, my mom is doing something amazing for me, but there's also probably something she gets out of it, too.

"That's actually…really helpful," I tell her, grinning sheepishly. "Thanks for sharing."

"No problem."

We sit in silence for a few minutes, just enjoying the sun and watching our kids giggle as they dump out all the sand they just finished putting into the bucket.

"Hey, I don't know what you're up to on Friday morning," Marie says a few minutes later, bringing my attention back to her, "but I have a group of women who come over to my house every week. The kids run around in the yard and we sit around complaining and drinking mimosas. It makes me feel a lot more sane to chat with other moms who get what I'm going through. Do you want to come?"

Warmth blooms in my chest at the unexpected invitation. I literally can't imagine something I want more.

"I would love to. Let me just check with my sister? I'm working for her at the bookstore, so I want to make sure it's okay for me to shuffle around my hours."

Marie smiles, and I smile back. It's been a long time since I've made a new friend, and being a single mom during my last year of college meant the few friends I *did* have scattered faster than I ever could have imagined. It never even occurred to me to hang out with other moms because there just *weren't* any.

But it makes sense, the idea that spending time with women who also have kids would be cathartic somehow. A chance to find people who understand how incredibly hard it is.

Marie and I chat for a bit longer, until she leaves with Leo, letting me know she's looking forward to seeing me in a few days.

The entire interaction leaves me with a kind of uplifted feeling I haven't experienced in quite some time. Pregnancy and motherhood have been—for the most part—incredibly lonely. This…makes me feel like there are good things around the corner, like this is a sign of what's to come.

I guess I can only hope.

chapter eight
reid

I'm late getting back to the house on Wednesday, my doctor's appointment running long. I hate getting bloodwork done, not because I'm squeamish about needles or blood, but because every time something gets checked, there's the possibility of getting bad news. It's a little pessimistic, considering my otherwise positive views on most things, but I figure it's okay to have a few areas in life that are less than perfect.

Shoving out of my truck, I drop down onto the dusty drive, slam the door, and walk through the clearing between our two cabins, straight up onto Busy's deck. There's no use going into my house, looking for Sydney, stepping out on *my* deck, and calling her name when I know exactly where she is—where she has been on the handful of days I've left her at home over the past few weeks that Busy and Junie have lived in the cabin next door.

Junie's sweet giggles escape from the open windows, and I stand at the edge of the deck, just listening to the sound.

"You're a princess," I hear her say.

"Oh, *am* I?" Busy replies, her tone teasing. "I thought I was the queen."

"Granna's the queen."

At that, Busy bursts into laughter. "She certainly is, isn't she?"

I lean back against the wooden siding, knowing I should just head in and get my dog and call it a night, but for whatever reason, I just want to stay here for a minute. Maybe two.

It's been a few days since our near-kiss, and my hope is that enough time has passed that we can move past it without causing any kind of rift. I truly enjoy my time with Busy and Junie, and I don't want the fact that I'm attracted to her to fuck up this burgeoning friendship we have developing.

I listen to them playing whatever princess game they're enjoying for five minutes. Something in my soul feels soothed by it, then just as I tell myself it's time to head in, I hear a phone chime.

"Hey."

I'm instantly on alert at the sound of Busy's voice getting sharp, the muscles in my body going taut as I shift my head, listening for her next words.

"No, Jay. That's not what we…"

She trails off, but only a few beats pass before she's talking again.

"What do you mean you're not going to come?" Her voice drops slightly, becoming hushed. "It's her *birthday*. You said you would be here."

I grit my teeth. I can only assume this is Junie's dad. The only thing I know about the guy is that he obviously let Busy get away, which was very clearly his first mistake. Now, I'm starting to feel like I might have some inkling of the type of man he is.

"Of *course* she'll care," she continues. "Someday, she's going to look back on these moments and she's going to see that her dad wasn't there." A pause. "It *does* matter, and you saying it doesn't is just your way of trying to make yourself feel less guilty for wanting to drink yourself into a coma on a holiday weekend instead of spending time with your daughter."

My fists clench.

Yeah. I know *exactly* who this guy is.

"Okay, so what if I move her birthday party? It doesn't have to be *on* the Fourth."

More silence, and something inside me knows whatever it is the guy is saying, it isn't what a father *should* be saying.

"Fine, Jay. Fine. You want to make up excuses? That's your choice. But your daughter misses you, and that's a truth you're going to have to live with."

A few more beats pass and I don't hear Busy speak again, so she's either hung up on the guy or moved into a different room. Quietly, I step down off her deck, giving myself a minute to collect myself before I noisily step back up and cross over to the door, hoping she thinks I'm just arriving.

When I look through the screen, though, I don't see anyone.

"Knock, knock," I call out.

Junie comes barreling around the corner wearing a purple gown that's about three sizes too big, a crown on her head and a wand in her hand, Sydney following dutifully behind her. "Misery!" she shouts, giving me a big smile as I open the door and step inside.

I tilt my head to the side, amused but also wondering where she learned that word.

"Hi, Junie Bee."

"Mommy's a princess," she tells me.

I nod, agreeing wholeheartedly. "She is." I crouch down and pet Syd's head, then give a tug to the dress Junie's wearing on top of her clothes. "Are you a princess, too?"

She twists from side to side then sits on the ground, her hands caressing Sydney's tummy. "Uh-huh."

Glancing around, I take in the stack of particle board and box of screws in the corner that I'm assuming is going to become a bookshelf or small table. I'm not completely surprised that Busy doesn't have a lot of furniture. She did just graduate from college and had to pick up her entire life to move home, after all.

Still, though…I'm sure it would be nice to come home and be able to sit on a couch or turn on a TV. My brain scrambles over the pieces I have in the shop, wondering if I might be able to help out in some way.

"Where's your mom?" I finally ask Junie when it seems like Busy isn't going to appear any time soon.

Junie shrugs.

"Will you take care of Sydney for me while I go talk to her?"

She nods her head dramatically then reaches out and wraps her arms around Sydney. "Yeah."

I grin. "Thanks, kiddo."

I walk through the house and over to where I assume Busy's room is, knocking twice on the door jamb as I come to a stop outside.

She looks up at me from where she's sitting on the floor, her eyes red. It's like a punch in the gut, seeing that, but I don't want to bring attention to something if she doesn't want to talk about it. Busy seems like the type to keep things close to the vest, something I understand.

I glance around, taking in the pieces of metal scattered

around her, the mattress and base leaning up against the wall, and the white folded paper she's reading that looks like directions.

"I was just going to say I'm grabbing Sydney, but...do you want some help?"

She looks back down at her instructions, and for a minute, I assume she's going to tell me no. I've offered to help her several times since she arrived, and she's always turned me down with a very clear, "I can do it by myself."

But then she surprises me when she nods. "I bought this thing online and the instructions seem easy enough but, I don't know, maybe I'm just tired. It's been a long day."

"Hey, not a problem. Just gimme a second to grab my tools."

I make quick work of heading outside, grabbing the smaller of my kits from the toolbox that sits in the bed of my truck, and going back in.

Busy snorts when she sees it in my hand. "I don't think you need that. It's supposed to all be able to fit together with just this thing." She holds up an Allen wrench.

"We'll see."

Twenty minutes later, we're still both sitting cross-legged on her bedroom floor as I re-read the directions again.

"This doesn't make any sense," I finally say out loud, not wanting to look like I have no clue what I'm doing, but also not wanting to just sit in silence anymore staring at the worst instructions I've ever seen.

Busy sighs and leans back against the wall. "Thank god. I thought it was just me."

"It's like they sent only half the parts *and* the wrong instructions. I would recommend sending this back and just getting something completely different," I offer, scratching at the back of my head. "There are probably tons of similar bed frames that will be way easier to put together than this."

She groans and then begins crawling around on her hands and knees, collecting the pieces and shoving them back into the long cardboard box they came in.

"At least I'm off the air mattress," she says, though part of me thinks she's actually saying it out loud to herself more than she's saying anything to me. "Even if it *is* on the floor for a little longer."

I studiously look away from where she's bent over, instead reaching out and grabbing a few pieces myself. Once I pass them over, I push up off the floor, wincing at the way my right knee pinches. That's new.

"Thanks for trying," Busy says, standing as well. "I appreciate it."

"Seriously, any time. I'm *normally* a lot more competent than this."

She smirks. "I'll believe that when I see it. So far you can't put furniture together *or* figure out how your dog is sneaking out."

I chuckle, especially at the furniture jab, and we both walk out to the kitchen, finding Junie using a brush on Sydney, combing her hair gently.

"Here, Sinny," she says, her voice quiet, almost like she's telling Sydney a secret. "You're a princess, too."

Then she puts her own crown on Sydney's head, and my heart melts just a bit.

"Sorry I couldn't be more help," I say, tugging my attention away from Junie and back to Busy at my side. I slip my hands into my pockets. "But once you get the new bed frame, let me know. I'll help you get it set up."

Busy nods. "Thanks. I appreciate it."

We stand there for a few minutes, just watching Junie as she continues swiping a brush through Sydney's fur, talking quietly to the dog about who knows what. She really is a sweet kid, and I can't help the frustration that bubbles up at the reminder that she has a dad out there somewhere who doesn't care enough to visit his daughter for her birthday.

"Hey, listen," I say, turning to Busy, my mind mulling over the conversation I overheard.

But when she looks my way and I spot the faint hint of redness from her earlier tears, I realize I can't say anything about what I heard. Who knows if it might make her cry even more, and the last thing I ever want to do is make Busy cry.

I lick my lips, suddenly scrambling for something to say, something to ask.

"I'm heading out on a hike on Saturday morning. You and Junie wanna join me?" I don't know exactly why I asked, especially when I keep telling myself I need to spend *less* time with Busy, and this is the exact opposite of that. But I can't seem to help it.

She gives me a tired smile. "Can I think about it? I might need to work some this weekend because the bookstore is opening *next* weekend, so I'm not sure how it will all shake out."

I nod. "Yeah. Just let me know."

Something occurs to me then.

"And actually, I should probably give you my number. That way you can just text me one way or the other."

Busy blinks but then pulls her phone out of her back pocket. She unlocks the screen and hands it to me, and I punch in my number. When I pass it back, I see her give me a call and feel my own phone buzz in my pocket.

"And now you have my number, too."

It's the simplest thing in the world, but still, I can't help the spark of excitement I feel at knowing her number is in my phone.

We stand there for another beat or two before I realize I need to head out or else I'm at risk of asking her something stupid, like if she wants to meet me out on the deck for a beer after she puts Junie to sleep for the night.

I clear my throat. "Alright, Sydney. Let's go."

Sydney looks up at me with the saddest eyes I've ever seen, and I laugh at how ridiculously pathetic she looks.

"Let's go," I say again, and she finally gets up, walks over to the screen door, and waits patiently.

"I'll see you later Miss Junie."

Busy snatches Junie up as she tries to race past us, and she squeals, the sweet sound piercing something inside my chest.

"Say good night to Sydney," Busy says.

"Night Sinny!" Junie calls out.

"And good night to Mr. Reid."

"Night Misery!"

We both laugh, and Busy shrugs. "She's still learning her 'st' sound."

I grin and shake my head. "What a nickname."

"Have a good night, Misery," Busy says teasingly.

I shove open the door and motion for Sydney to head out. Once she's past me, I turn back to Busy and Junie. "See you two later." Then I head home.

When I pull up in front of Ugly Mug, I spot Sarah immediately, sitting at a table outside, talking on her phone. I can tell just by the way she's moving her hands, the stern focus on her face, that it's something related to work. She was always that way about her business. Extremely focused, nose constantly to the grind, something I always admired about her.

Sarah waves as I step out of the cab of my truck, but when Syd jumps down to the asphalt, even behind the fancy sunglasses, I can tell she's displeased. She holds up a finger, letting me know she's almost done with her call, and by the time I've approached the table, she pulls it away from her ear and presses a button.

"I didn't realize you were bringing her," she says, standing to give me a hug. "Now we can't sit inside."

I shrug. "The weather's not too bad this morning. We can sit out here, right? It's shaded."

Sarah is easy to read, and I know finding a solution *other* than taking my dog back to hang out in my office isn't what she wanted.

"I'll grab our drinks and be right back," I say, before I look at Sydney. "Be good for Sarah."

I turn and head inside, walking right up to the counter to put in our orders—a black coffee and a croissant for me, an iced americano for Sarah.

Almost the first thing I did after we got divorced was get a dog. I had dogs growing up and always wanted one of my own, but Sarah's allergic, and no amount of discussing allergy meds or air filters or grooming schedules could convince her to get one. I even tried offering to get one of those frou-frou hypoallergenic dogs, but she didn't budge.

I guess you could say Sydney was my divorce present to myself.

Once I return outside with our drinks, I rip off a piece of my croissant and feed it to Sydney, then take a piece for myself.

"So, how have you been?" I ask, settling into my chair, resting my ankle on my knee and holding my coffee with both hands. "It's been a few weeks. You went out of town right?"

"I've been good. I went with Alton on that work trip to Texas."

I nod.

Alton. Her new boyfriend.

I have a few feelings about the guy, mostly because I think he's self-absorbed. But that's Sarah's problem, not mine, and I have no plans to turn our friendship—which is already complicated enough—into one where I offer critique about her new choice of partner.

"Have a good time?"

There's a beat that passes where I wonder if she's going to say something other than yes. It's a particular way her mouth opens, like she's considering her words before she says them.

"We did," she finally says. "But I'm glad to be back in town and back to work. You know I love my work."

"That I do."

Soon before we got married, Sarah got her real estate license. Over the years, she has created quite a reputation for herself as the go-to person if you're trying to buy in several of the small mountain communities around here, including Cedar Point.

After the divorce, I think she got sort of lost in her work, trying to distract herself from the end of what we had. As much as I might not be a huge fan of the guy she's dating now, I'm glad she has someone. The last thing I would want is for her to be alone. We might not be together anymore, but I still care about her, still want the best for her.

"So, what's new with you?" Sarah reaches her hand out and very lightly taps my knee with two fingers. "How *are* things?"

I know what she's really asking, but I don't want to talk about it. I *never* want to talk about it. So I play dumb.

"I started working on a new custom project for Ellis Darrow, for the new buildout at Dock 7," I offer. "A dozen leather chairs like the ones I made for Cedar Cider."

Sarah nods. "I love those chairs."

Everyone does. They're gorgeous chairs. I had planned to make two additional ones for us to have in the living room of our apartment, but we ended up getting divorced instead. So I used the remaining wood to create the frame of a dog bed for Sydney.

It wasn't supposed to sound as vindictive as it does.

"How's Marie and the kids?"

At that I smile wide. "They're doing really good. Leo's picking up all kinds of things right now, so I have to be careful what I say around him."

She laughs. "I've heard that's a fun time. I've been meaning to connect with her recently. I feel like we used to be so close, and now..." She trails off. *Now, with the divorce, it feels awkward* is probably what the rest of her sentence would have been.

It makes sense. Marie and Sarah became close friends while we were dating and then even more so after we got married. I know the divorce came as a shock to everyone, but particularly my cousin, probably because neither of us ever truly explained it. The two of them have tried to maintain their friendship to some degree, especially because I have explained to Marie over and over again that our decision to break up was mutual and I wasn't angry about it.

There might be a tiny lie in there somewhere, but Marie doesn't need to know that.

"Well, I'm sure she'd love to hear from you," I reply, taking another sip from my coffee.

"And how's the cabin?"

I snort. "Still perfect."

Sarah grins at me and shakes her head. "You and your lake-front dreams."

Shrugging, I set my coffee on the table between us, leaning forward slightly. "Don't deny it. You're a little jealous."

"Not of that little cabin, I'm not," she says, laughing. "You know I always preferred the shiny new over the old and rustic."

I nod, still smiling. "Ain't that the truth."

When we moved in together after we'd been dating for a year, the *only* option for Sarah was the apartment complex just off Main Street. She wanted walkable access to town and sparkly new finishes. Having only ever lived in a much older home with wood paneling and a wood-burning stove and super old appliances, the apartments on Main felt like a hospital to me.

I made do. We tried to 'warm it up' a bit, as Sarah referred to it, by adding décor to the stark white walls and bringing in a handful of pieces of furniture that previously belonged to my parents. But it always felt plain and bare and boring to me.

The cabin is a *much* better fit. In many ways.

"Although, if Lois ever decides to sell, make sure you point her my way." She tilts her head from side to side. "If she doesn't hate me."

"She doesn't hate you," I insist. "But there's no way she's selling. Especially not now that the green cabin is back to being a full-time rental."

Sarah's eyebrows rise. "Oh you must be so relieved." She

chuckles, having heard a number of my stories about the antics of my variety of neighbors over the past year.

"Definitely."

"New neighbors are better?"

I nod. "Much. Busy Mitchell moved in with her daughter about a month ago."

"Huh."

I blink, my brow furrowing. "Huh, what?"

Sarah's smile stretches slyly across her face. "Oh, just…she had a huge crush on you when she was a kid," she says, laughing quietly to herself.

My head jerks back. "What? No she didn't."

Sarah nods, leaning back in her chair. "She did. She used to go into Cohen Custom and hang out because she wanted to bump into you."

I scoff, feeling like she's making it up, even if it *is* flattering. "That can't be real. How do you even know that?"

"Kelsey's younger sister was friends with Busy in junior high," she says, referring to one of her old friends from high school.

Knowing someone you're attracted to *now* had a crush on you a decade ago is…an odd feeling, a convolution of emotions. And I'm not too ashamed to admit to myself I'm pleased to hear the rumor, even though I would *never* admit it to someone else.

"But don't tell her I said anything about it," Sarah says, reaching out and placing her hand on mine briefly. "Keep it to yourself, okay?"

I laugh. Like I would *ever* bring it up to Busy.

"Don't worry. I plan to repeat this to nobody, ever."

Except maybe Nick, but I'm even on the fence about that one. Because…what would be the point?

We move on to other topics, touching briefly on my mother's trip to the Caribbean with Vance and how Sarah's parents are adjusting to their new life in Oregon, before saying goodbye and promising to catch up again soon. We do this every other month or so, both of us leaning into a friendship instead of cutting off all communication like most people do.

I mean, we care about each other. If life had turned out differently, we would have stayed together. So, maintaining our friendship, especially when we were friends first, before we started dating, felt like a natural choice. An easy choice. A simple one. A way to maintain a slice of normalcy even as we grieved the end of what we were.

chapter nine
busy

It takes exactly two seconds for Junie to wobble off in the direction of where Marie's son Leo is playing in the yard with a few other children of varying ages, and my heart swells and pinches at the same time. I love that my daughter seems comfortable running off to play with other kids, but it hurts a bit, too, knowing she can let go of my hand so easily, not even looking back.

"I wish Nina had been that easy to set up with other kids," Marie says as we step back over to where her group of friends are sitting on cushioned outdoor furniture in a large circle. "Any time I tried to do a playdate, she wanted to drag me around, too. It was exhausting."

The woman to my right—a redhead with a large smile— leans forward. "My Tessa couldn't be left with anyone other than my parents until she was almost four. She'd literally scream so hard and for so long she'd pass out."

I wince. "That sounds hard."

"It was a *nightmare*. Be thankful your girl can run off early."

"It's nice to see Junie like this," I share, "but it wouldn't hurt to see a little more 'stranger danger' in her, you know?" Shaking my head, I glance over to where she and Leo are tottering around after a soccer ball. "I'm just always terrified she's going to go missing one day because she's so dang friendly."

It's a thought that plagues me more often than I'd like to admit. Sometimes I'll find myself lying in bed, staring at the ceiling, listening for the soft sounds of her sleeping, as if she might have somehow gotten up and wandered out to the road, like she could hitchhike away from me.

She can't even open a door yet.

Even so, I've heard from quite a few people that the fears infiltrating the minds of a mother are rarely rational.

"I'm Busy, by the way," I say to the redhead.

Her eyes flash. "Oh, so *you're* Patty's daughter who just moved home."

I'm not sure I like the way she says it, as if she's heard so much about me. I nod anyway.

"That's me."

"I'm Tilly. My daughter Tessa is the one who looks just like me," she says with a laugh. When I glance over to where the kids are and spot the girl with wild red hair flying around her head, it's easy to see what she means.

"Let's do a round of introductions, actually," Marie interjects, and the chatter around the circle slowly fades. "I'm Marie, I'm thirty-three, and I have two kids. Nina is four and Leo is two."

With that first spiel out of the way, the rest of the women launch in behind her. Sophia and Marlow and Becka and…it's honestly hard to keep them all straight and after a few people, they all begin to blend together. Some of them look familiar and

I try to place how I know them, though don't really have much success. I honestly feel slightly bad for how intense I was with Reid about how important it is to remember people's names because if *I* were the one getting quizzed after today, I *know* I'd fail.

When the intros finally get to me, I give my friendliest smile and try to greet everyone with my eyes. "I'm Busy. I'm twenty-two and my daughter, Junie, is almost two. We just moved back to Cedar Point at the beginning of June."

The faces all appear friendly, and I get a lot of smiles and 'welcome home' comments. Maybe this doesn't need to be as intimidating as it feels.

"So, Busy, you're helping Briar open that bookstore, right?" Tilly asks, crossing her long, elegant legs and taking a sip from her champagne flute.

I nod. "Yeah. I'm her assistant. Painting, cleaning, lugging things around." I shrug. "If she needs it, I'll do it."

"Bless you for being able to work with your sibling," she says on a laugh. "I don't think I'd ever be able to work for my sister. It would feel too much like I'm getting bossed around."

"I'm sure working with family isn't a good setup for everyone," I reply, knowing plenty of people who fit that bill. "But Briar's amazing, and it's really fun getting to spend so much time with her."

"Ignore Tilly. She just knows *she* would want to be the one to do the bossing," says a beautiful brunette sitting next to Tilly who gives me a friendly smile. "I know all those introductions can run together, so I'm Sarah, by the way."

I nod my head with a smile…that promptly freezes on my face, realization dawning.

Reid's Sarah.

Sitting there looking…like a fucking model and perfection

embodied. Long and lean and elegant, with her hair perfect and her makeup spotless and her nails done. She's tall, like Reid, and her body is lithe in that willowy way I would never be able to manage at my petite 5'3".

"She doesn't have kids," Tilly offers, smiling at me. "She's just here for the mimosas."

The two of them laugh as I sit frozen, my eyes glued to the woman who used to be married to the man I can't get out of my head.

"Nice to meet you," I finally manage, thankful when Sarah turns back to Tilly and says something I don't hear.

I don't know Reid *that* well, even though I might have memories of him from since I was basically a kid, but what I *do* know about him I really, really like. Obviously he's handsome—that's a no-brainer—but he's also all those other things that make me want to kiss him whenever I see him. Warm and kind and funny and good with my kid.

It's hard to imagine anyone ever being married to him and then getting divorced.

"Where on Main is it?" Tilly asks, leaning back against the cushioned seat.

"Where on Main is what?" Marie asks, plopping down across from me.

"My sister's bookstore. It's a great spot. We're right between Ruthie's and that art gallery I'll never be able to afford anything from," I reply on a laugh.

Tilly turns to Marie. "Oh, that's right by Reid's shop."

Marie's eyes flick to Sarah before she looks back at Tilly. "It is."

Sarah sighs. "I've told you plenty of times, you don't have to tiptoe around me. He and I are just fine." Then she turns to me, rolling her eyes. "Just because people get divorced doesn't mean they can't stay friends, right?"

I manage a smile and a nod.

"So, Busy...how are you getting settled?" Sarah continues. "Reid said you moved into the green cabin, right?"

I can't help the new wave of surprise that rolls over me. I don't like *that* feeling. Not at all. Even though I have no right to the jealousy that courses through me, something about knowing Reid and his ex are not only still friendly but on speaking terms—that they've spoken about *me*—ruffles something in my chest that I don't like. At. All.

"It's going great," I finally spit out. "I like being on the water."

Sarah laughs. "You sound like Reid."

"It'll be great on the Fourth," Marie interjects. "Sitting on the dock to watch the fireworks. Although if you don't have plans, you're always welcome to come here."

I nod. "I'll probably go to my parents' house."

After a few beats, Tilly, Marie, and Sarah begin talking about Fourth of July plans as I sit there...in stunned silence. I only speak to Jay out of strict necessity. If he wasn't Junie's dad, I would *never* speak to the man again. And we weren't even married—thank god. We didn't have to go through all the emotional upheaval of separating our lives the way I can only assume Sarah and Reid have had to do.

But I guess that's only an assumption, after all. Who knows what their relationship was really like?

I listen as intently as I can and try to laugh in the right places, but I feel a little distracted and a whole lot tired. I forgot how exhausting it is to be around people like this, in a place where I feel like I have to be so social and friendly and smiley all the time. I know that's something I've imposed upon myself, but I can't help it.

Licking my lips, I glance toward Junie, wishing she'd call out for me or something, because I am suddenly desperately ready to go. Unfortunately, I find her plucking flowers from a weedy bush, completely oblivious to me. I want to grab Junie and leave, flee to our cabin in the woods. But I don't.

Instead, I stay and continue my conversation until Junie runs over to hand me her flowers and weeds, and I take my chance. I excuse myself from the women I'm sitting with and walk with Junie a few steps away, and then when I feel like nobody is watching, we slip out through the side gate unnoticed. I kind of feel like an asshole, not even saying bye to Marie or thanking her for inviting me over, but sometimes it's just easier to disappear and say nothing.

That said, as I pull down the drive and away from Marie's, I can't help feeling incredibly guilty. Maybe I shouldn't have darted so quickly. The last thing I want to do is seem ungrateful. I'll have to make sure I talk to her and say thank you soon.

"How did it go?"

I glance at my mother as I unclip Junie from her car seat and tug her out. The question isn't unexpected or even unwarranted, but it is unwanted. I'm not really sure what to say.

So I shrug. "It was alright."

Mom's head jerks back. "Just alright? I feel like all the moms love going over to Marie's for mom-osas."

I snort. "They do not call it that."

"Yes, they do."

Giggling, I smooch Junie on the cheek then set her on the ground, my heart pinching again when she lets go of my hand quickly and races over to my mom.

"Well it's a cute name. I'm just not sure it's for me."

My mom picks Junie up and settles her easily on one hip. "Maybe give it another shot. Those are some wonderful ladies, and you could learn a lot from them."

My spine straightens, the underhanded comment hitting me square in the chest. "Excuse me?"

Mom sighs, her face falling. "Busy, that's not what I meant."

"Well, it's what you said."

We're silent for a long moment, the tension between us thick and uncomfortable and making me want to cry because I miss my mom.

"I'll be back at 4:30," I say, taking a step closer and pressing another kiss to Junie's cheek. "Bye, baby. Love you."

"Bye!" she says, smiling wide and waving her hand dramatically.

My eyes connect with my mother's briefly, and then I spin around and hop into my car without saying another word.

When I get home from work, I'm nearly ready to collapse. Briar and I spent most of the afternoon shelving books, an action that requires bending down and standing up over and over and over again. And we're only halfway done, if that.

I'm in my early 20s. Shouldn't I be more spry than this?

When we get back to the house and I hear Junie call out "Sinny!" as I tug her from her car seat, I nearly cry with relief.

Please, Sydney. Run around with my daughter.

Reid's dog comes barreling over, her tongue lolling out of the side of her mouth. Sydney promptly licks Junie's face, and my girl lets out the most precious giggle. I glance around, assuming she got out again, but then my eyes lock on Reid where he's walking toward us from his cabin.

"Hey." I look around again. "Did you take the day off?"

He smiles. "Kind of. Had a doctor's appointment today, so I took a half day."

I shut the car door and give him a smirk.

"Prostate exam?"

Reid looks like he's about to choke before he bursts into laughter.

"Yep. How'd you know?" he jokes back, coming to a stop a few feet away.

I shrug. "You have a special glow about you."

Reid just shakes his head. "God, you really *are* a menace, aren't you?" he asks, but the smile on his face says he's teasing.

He crouches down to pet Sydney, though she ignores him as she continues snuggling into Junie, who is giving her soft pets on her ears and back.

"Hey, I don't know what you have planned for the rest of the day, but…I think Junie and I are gonna jump in the lake." I glance at Reid. "You and Sydney are welcome to join us."

I don't know why I ask.

Maybe it's because I want to keep Junie preoccupied with the dog. Maybe it's because I'm hoping for a distraction from the way my mind continues to return to my shitty interaction with my mother. Or maybe it's just because I like when Reid is around.

I'm not entirely certain, but what I *do* know is how thrilled I feel when he nods his head and says, "We'd love to."

The thud of Junie's footsteps are too precious as she toddles quickly toward the end of the dock, her floatie swimsuit bouncing with each step. She hurls herself off the edge with a squeal before landing with a splash in the water, where Reid is waiting for her.

Seconds later, Sydney dives in behind her. The two of them have been doing this same routine over and over again for the past twenty minutes or so, without tiring in the slightest.

"Again!" Junie cries out, laughing wildly as Reid swims her over to the dock and hoists her back up.

I glance over to where Sydney is paddling toward the shoreline, trying desperately to catch up. Junie's energy and speed just can't be matched, and as soon as she's back on her feet, dripping with water, she totters away. Then she turns around and races right back, barely giving Reid enough time to prepare for her before she launches into the water again.

"I think you're raising a fish," Reid jokes as Junie giggles in his arms.

I nod from where I'm sitting at the edge of the dock, my feet dangling ankle deep in the water. "I think you're right. It's probably time to start with some swimming lessons."

I've been thinking about it ever since we moved back. With such easy access to the lake, the best thing I can do for her is make sure she knows how to swim as quickly as possible.

Reid lifts Junie up above his head, and she squeals again as he chucks her into the air then drops back down with a splash.

"Though I'm not sure *I'm* ready for it even if *she* is."

"Well...I taught both Nina and Leo how to swim," he says, floating slowly on his back over to the dock again. "If you want, I can teach Junie."

I'm floored by his offer, and I swish my feet in the water, the mental image of Reid teaching Junie to swim fluttering through my mind.

"But no pressure," he adds just as he lifts Junie back up onto the dock.

I shake my head. "Sorry, I was just... That's so generous of you. Thank you for offering. Can I think about it?"

"Absolutely. And if you'd be more comfortable having someone else teach her, I completely understand."

Licking my lips, I let out a sigh. "It's not about comfort, I just...have a hard time accepting help from people," I say, far more honestly than I intend. Something about talking with Reid brings that honesty out in me. "I came home, intending to do all these things on my own, and it feels like I've done nothing but step back and let other people do things for me."

Reid flicks some water at me, the droplets hitting my legs where they hang over the edge.

"I wouldn't offer if I didn't mean it," he says, his lips tilted up at the sides.

The pitter-patter of Sydney's feet sounds as she comes barreling down the dock then launches past me, and a few seconds later Junie's footsteps follow suit. I tuck my hands underneath my thighs, feeling a pinch in my chest at the way Reid smiles at my daughter, at how bright he is, how present. Like she's deserving of his attention.

If only Jay felt that way. If only he felt even a fraction of what seems to come so naturally for Reid.

After a few more jumps into the water, I can tell my girl's energy is fading. "I think it might be time to head in and get some dinner and go to bed," I say, taking a slightly sluggish Junie from Reid and bringing her little body in snuggled against mine. "Are we getting sleepy?" I ask her.

Junie shakes her head even as her eyes begin to droop, and I chuckle under my breath.

Then I about swallow my tongue as Reid hoists himself out of the lake and up onto the dock, his muscles bunching and flexing with the movement, and I can't help the way my eyes scan over his near-perfect physique. I can't remember the last time I watched a body like this, with such rapt attention to detail. It's as if I'm magnetized to him and can't look away.

Which is, of course, when I realize Reid is watching me watch him, and I look back at Junie in my arms, feeling completely mortified. The man was literally just being a sweetheart and playing with my daughter, and I'm over here just...basically drooling.

Grow up, Busy.

"Well, thanks for hanging out with us," I say, turning slightly and trying to figure out how I'm going to stand up with Junie in my arms.

"Here, let me help."

Before I can say or do anything, Reid's hands are under my arms and he lifts me so I'm standing. His hands brace me, making sure I'm balanced.

"You good?"

I swallow thickly then clear my throat. "Yeah. I'm good."

Even though I could feel your fingers barely grazing the edge of my breasts.

Shoving that thought aside, I turn around so I'm facing Reid, hoping any kind of pink in my cheeks can be explained by our time in the sun.

"I'm gonna try to get her to eat dinner then get her ready for bed," I tell him, glancing at where Junie is already beginning to doze in my arms.

"Well, if you're looking for something to do once she's down," he says, shrugging a shoulder, "maybe I can teach you to play poker."

I lick my lips, wanting to say yes, wanting to race inside and put my daughter in her bed then return to his side for more of this feeling I get when I'm around him, like I'm a dead battery getting plugged in.

But before I can get ahead of myself, I'm already shaking my head. "I think I'm pretty beat, too. I'm gonna take advantage of Junie's early night and call it for myself."

Reid nods, his hands on his hips. "Alright, well. I hope you enjoy your rest."

"But…we'd like to join you on the hike tomorrow," I add on. "If you're still up for some tagalongs?"

His smile grows and he crosses his arms. "I'd love that."

"We're not huge hikers, though, and I'm gonna assume hiking with a toddler is a very different game than hiking with friends."

He's already shaking his head. "Don't even worry about it. I've done hikes with Nina and Leo. I know it takes forever."

I chuckle. "Okay, well…just text me the details and I'll make sure we're ready to go."

"Sounds good. Have a good night, Busy."

I give Reid a small smile then turn, heading back up to the house and inside. I make a few sandwich bites for Junie, which she eats without complaint, even if she starts dozing as she does, her mouth chewing slowly and her head lolling forward before jerking back up as she tries to stay awake.

Once she's finished eating, we do a quick tub before I finally get her settled in bed. Then, I finally get to think about myself, and what *myself* needs is a nice long shower before I crawl into my own bed and collapse.

I do a quick pick-up, cleaning Junie's high chair and putting away all the sandwich supplies before I hop into the shower, turning my face into the water and bracing my hands against the tile wall. The exhaustion finally catches up with me as my sluggish brain attempts to reflect on the long day. Marie's, work, and swimming have sapped all the energy out of me.

Though I'm clearly not *so* exhausted that I feel like I can't do the hike tomorrow with Reid.

I roll my eyes. Didn't I *just* tell myself it would be far too easy to fall for him? What happened to all those mental pep talks with reminders of how important it is not to be too risky?

And then there's the fact that he still talks regularly with his ex-wife. Younger Busy wouldn't have seen any of this as a problem. The idea of hooking up with my neighbor who is still friends with his ex? No biggie.

Now, though, I can see that it's messy. So, so messy.

I growl at myself and rest my forehead against the wall. I've *got* to get over this stupid crush. It's a mistake. Reid is just a nice guy who is being nice and friendly and neighborly, and I'm over here in my head, hyperaware of his hands and irritated at his ex-wife for knowing I live next door. Tomorrow is a friendly hike in the woods. Just a friendly hike.

I turn and tilt my head back, enjoying the water as it beats down on me. Then I begin to wash away the lake water, first from my hair, then from my body.

But that proves to be a mistake as well. The feeling of my soapy hands roving over my skin sends a thrum of need racing through me that I haven't felt in…quite some time.

Before I can think better of it, my mind pictures Reid helping me put my bed together again, but it's just the two of us in the house, his strong muscles working as he hoists a thick bed frame into place and then sets my mattress into it.

"Want help breaking it in?"

I shake my head, knowing he wouldn't say anything so obvious. Reid is a softer animal, gentler. I can tell, just from the way he speaks to me, the way he moves his hands.

"This wood is sturdy and strong," he says instead, tracing the grain along the footboard. "Should last a good long while."

I crawl up onto the bed and flop onto my back then look at Reid before gently patting the spot next to me.

"Wanna help me test it out?" I ask him.

His eyes flash but he hoists himself up next to me, then lies back so we're side by side. Our heads turn to look at each other.

"God, you're beautiful," he whispers, his eyes roving over my face in my mind the way I've seen him look at me in real life.

Then, unlike the night he pulled back as we stood in Junie's doorway, this time, he leans in and presses his lips to mine.

My hands dip down, sliding through the slick crease between my legs, and I can't help but whimper, the sound echoing around me in the shower.

In my waking dream, Reid's hands reach out for me and draw me close, pull me in against his body. They rove and touch and caress as our tongues duel before he pushes me back and brings himself over me. He blocks out the light, blocks out anything but him, his hips coming between my legs and grinding against me.

My fingers circle my clit, my forehead pressed against the tile wall. Fuck, it feels so good. So good, so good to feel this spark between my legs again after so long without it. Desire pools in my belly and I rotate my hips, searching for the move or thought or *something* that will take me over the edge.

But the longer I hover there, the longer I imagine Reid and me in bed, the more frustrated I become, because I can't get there. I can't get there on my own. I've never been able to. No matter how…desperate or needy I feel.

When the water begins to cool, I let out a frustrated growl and finally give up, washing quickly then storming out of the shower. As I dry off and slip on a pair of panties and a tank top for bed, I become more and more infuriated with myself.

I didn't mean to re-cast Reid in the role of 'hot guy' in my fantasies, but he is quickly beginning to take on that position and I don't know what to do to stop it. Maybe swearing off men until Junie is in college was the wrong move. Maybe I just need to swear off relationships.

There can't be any harm in enjoying some sexy time with a faceless man, right? Someone who can take the edge off for me—get off himself—and then we exchange high fives instead of phone numbers?

When I return to the bathroom and begin brushing my hair, my eyes scan over my body with critical eyes. I haven't had sex with anyone since Jay. It was good sex, don't get me wrong, but it was with a man who treated me like shit. A man I *allowed* to treat me like shit for far too long before I cut him out of my life as much as was possible.

My body is desperate to be treated right, desperate to be craved, and worshipped, and brought over the brink.

But the idea of no-strings sexy times feels a lot more daunting than it did when I was in college and having the time of my life. I had quite a few one-night stands with absolutely no cares about whether or not the guy was using me to get off, because I was doing the same.

Now, it feels a whole lot more intimidating. My heart is shaped differently now than it used to be. When I was younger, it was kept safely behind a wall and in a cage surrounded by a moat that no man could penetrate.

Then I had a daughter, and after plenty of time in therapy, I realized if I kept my heart walled off like that, I wouldn't be able to be the mom she needs me to be. One who can be honest and open with her, who can love her with her whole heart. Doing that makes me feel so much more vulnerable, and you can't be vulnerable with a one-night stand. That's the whole point.

So just as quickly as my mind dabbles in the idea of taking a night for myself and going to Lucky's to find some fun, I flip right back to my original plan.

No men until Junie's 18.

I'll survive. Nobody ever died from lack of sex.

At least, I hope not.

I guess I'll just have to wait and see.

chapter ten
reid

I swing Junie up high, her giggles echoing around us as we walk along the mostly flat path I selected for our hike.

"Again!" she calls out, and I indulge her, ignoring the fatigue of my muscles.

"Junie, I'm sure Mr. Reid is tired of throwing you in the air," Busy says. "How about we try walking for a bit?"

"No! Again!"

I grin and look at Busy. "With Marie's kids, I'd just keep tossing them. But if you want her to walk, I can put her down."

Busy shrugs. "Up to you. I'm not the one who is going to have dead arms later." Her eyes scan briefly over my muscles, and I decide once more can't hurt.

I toss Junie up one more time then set her on the ground. "Alright, let's race," I tell her. "Fastest one to that rock up there wins a prize."

"Yay!" Junie says, charging ahead of us with Sydney tottering along at her side.

Then I look to Busy again. "Fair warning—I haven't thought of a prize yet."

She laughs. "Pluck a flower or something. She's easy."

I glance around, spotting some wild geraniums in a nearby bush and tugging a couple free. Busy gives me a thumbs-up, and when Junie reaches the rock that's maybe 50 feet in front of us and spins around, I hold the flowers up in the air. "Junie wins!"

She giggles and races back, her hands out, ready to accept her winnings. A few minutes later, we get to the end of Washburn Trail, a small lookout on the west side of the lake. From this vantage point, we can see South Bank Resort & Marina and all of downtown to the south, the beautiful lakefront properties along the eastern shoreline, and Drucker Landing near the middle of the lake. It really is a great view for such an easy hike, and we take a seat on a wooden bench for a minute to enjoy it. Sydney hops up next to me as Busy opens up her backpack and retrieves an applesauce pouch for Junie.

"Any fun plans for the Fourth?" she asks before she bites into an apple.

I shake my head, petting Sydney's head as she pants next to my ear. "I'll just be working, for the most part."

She looks surprised at that. "Really? Don't you get to like… make your own hours? Take some time off and enjoy the holiday?"

"Nah. Holiday weekends are usually super busy, and I like to be in the store to answer questions."

Busy nods. "I'll be working, too. The bookstore opens on Thursday."

I smile. "That's right. You must be so excited."

Her head dips from side to side as she chews. "Mostly. A little nervous."

"How come?"

"Well, I've been working in an empty space with no customers. Painting and shelving books is one thing. Answering questions and problem solving and managing the issues a new store undoubtedly presents is an entirely different animal."

"That's true. Anything I can do to help before the doors open?"

Busy laughs. "You can come by and help me shelve the million books still left to go up if you want."

"Just let me know when."

She blinks, her head jerking back. Then she laughs again. "I was joking, Reid. You...do *not* have to come in and help with that. I promise."

"I know I don't *have* to. I *want* to."

Because I want to spend more time with you, no matter how foolish it might be.

We sit in silence for a bit before she responds, and I get the feeling she's debating if she wants to accept my help. When she actually relents, I'm far too happy about it.

"Can you come around noon tomorrow? I told Briar I'd go in this weekend to work for a few hours."

I nod. "Happy to."

She takes a deep breath then lets it out, nodding. "Thanks."

For whatever reason, it feels like accepting my help is a big deal to Busy. Based on some of the things she's said over the past few weeks, it seems like doing things on her own is really important to her. It feels good to know she believes she can accept that help from me.

Sydney hops down from the bench and begins snooping around, marking the edges of the overlook a few times before she lies down in a shady spot, staring out at the water.

"So what's the plan for Junie's birthday? Having a big party or just something small?"

Busy's lips tilt up. "Just something small at my mom's on Thursday night. We'll barbeque and watch the fireworks from the back deck."

"Sounds like fun."

"It will be. I just want Junie to feel like she's loved, you know? Like she's worth celebrating."

I nod, my mind conjuring up the memory of Busy on the phone with Junie's dad. It makes sense, how much she tries to make her daughter a priority. She has to make up for a man who doesn't do it at all.

"Well, I'm sure a party surrounded by family will make her feel like a princess."

"I'n a princess," Junie says.

"That's right, sweetie. You *are*." Busy brings Junie in close and kisses her forehead. "You absolutely are."

The walk back to the car takes far less time than it took to get *to* the overlook, and before I know it, we're hopping into Busy's SUV and pulling out onto the main road, the windows down. I close my eyes, tilting my face up to the sun, enjoying the way it feels as it warms my face.

But that simple, easy calm I feel dissipates when my eyes lock on the black Mazda parked next to my truck as we pull down the gravel lane back to the cabins. Instead, dread fills my body.

I must sigh louder than I realize, because when Busy comes to a stop on her parking pad, she reaches out and touches my shoulder in a gentle caress.

"Everything okay?" she asks, her voice soft.

Nodding, I give her a pinched smile, trying to ignore how

nice it feels to have her hand on my arm. "Yeah. It's just…my mom is here."

Busy's eyes glance past me, through the window and over toward where my mom's car is parked.

"She's just…not who I want to see today. Which I know makes me sound like an ass and a horrible son, but…"

"No need to explain," she interjects, patting me gently. "I'm not judging, trust me. Mothers are hard."

I rub at my perpetual five o'clock shadow, trying to decide how I want to handle this. But before I can even begin to come up with a plan, I see my mother emerge from the backside of the house. She was probably sitting on my deck, something she's done in the past when she's just…shown up unannounced.

"You've got this."

I glance over at Busy, who is looking at me with eyes filled with encouragement and care. Chuckling at her sweetness and sincerity, I nod then push open my door.

"There's my sweet boy!" my mom says as she walks my way, a wide smile stretched across her face.

"Hi, mom." I rise out of the passenger seat, my long frame looming over hers. "Fair warning: I'm a little sweaty."

"Oh, that doesn't matter," she says, wrapping her arms around my middle and giving me a squeeze. "What matters is that I get to see my baby. It feels like it's been so long since I've seen you."

I don't tell her it *has* been a while, mostly because I don't want to imply that she should come around more often. But even as I think it, I feel a piercing sense of shame for how I'm thinking about the woman who raised me, who loved me, who showered me with attention and encouragement growing up.

With everything we've been through, it's just hard to see her sometimes.

"I gave you a call once I got here, but it went straight to voicemail," she says, stepping back, her eyes flicking over to where Busy is coming around the front of the car. "And who is this?"

I can feel my mom suddenly vibrating with excitement at the sight of me with a woman, and I know I'll have to be swift and clear with her that nothing has changed. I'm still single and still plan to stay that way.

"Hi, Mrs. Cohen. Good to see you. My name's Busy, I'm—"

"Patty's baby girl, oh my goodness!"

Mom throws her arms wide and envelopes Busy in a hug as well. Busy's eyes widen, and she looks at me with both surprise and amusement. When my mother pulls back, she holds Busy by her biceps, her eyes assessing.

"I can't believe it's you! You've grown so much, and into such a *beautiful* young woman, too."

Busy blushes, and I can't help the pang of jealousy at the freedom my mother has to tell Busy something I've been thinking since the moment I laid eyes on her.

I round the back of the SUV, raising the rear door to let Sydney hop out.

"Well…thank you, Mrs. Cohen, I…"

"Oh, call me Tabitha, please." She swats at the air between them.

"Okay. Thank you, Tabitha."

Mom looks back at me. "Honey, I'm in town for a few days staying at South Bank—just wanted to see you before things get crazy for the holiday—and I booked a table for us at Dock 7."

I'm not exactly surprised by the fact that my mom is staying at the resort, but it's still a stark reminder of how many things have changed over the past few years. Growing up, my mother would *never* have spent that kind of money. She was frugal to her core. So was my dad.

Now, though...well, things are different, I guess.

"And I'd love for you to join us."

That last bit was directed at Busy, and panic suddenly fills my chest. But before I can even open my mouth, Busy responds.

"Oh, thank you so much for the invite, but...I don't think we can make it." She tugs open the rear passenger side door and begins to unbuckle Junie from her car seat. "Dock 7 is probably too fancy for a toddler," she continues, "but I really appreciate it."

A few seconds later, Junie has been freed and set down on the ground, and she looks up at my mother with a big smile.

"Hi!"

My mom blinks, then looks at me, then back at Junie. "Well, hello there."

Junie tugs on Busy's finger, pulling her in the direction of where Sydney has shot off toward the water, probably chasing a squirrel or something.

"Sorry, I need to..." Busy hitches a thumb in the same direction. "Thanks again for the hike," she says to me, her eyes flicking back to my mom, "and I hope you both have a great time at dinner."

She turns and chases after Junie, who is laughing hysterically and shouting "Sinny!" as she heads toward the lake. I watch them for a beat or two, and when I look back to my mom, I find her staring at me with a pleased smile on her face.

"We're just friends."

"Says every man before he falls in love."

I scoff, shaking my head, barely containing my eye roll. She's been like this ever since Sarah and I got divorced, constantly making up fairy tales in her head about me finding my true love. I don't believe in that kind of stuff anymore.

"Sorry I didn't answer my phone," I tell her, leading us toward my cabin, hoping the change of subject will distract her. "We were on a hike and I turned off my ringer."

My mother hums as she follows me into the house. "Well, you're here now. That's all that matters." She clasps her hands together, glancing around my house while I cross to the fridge to get some water. "The reservation for tonight is at six. Does that work for you?"

I take a long moment to drink from my glass, trying to find a reason to decline. But in the end, I can't come up with anything that doesn't sound like complete bullshit.

"Yeah, that'll work."

She nods. "Wonderful. I'm gonna head back to the resort. I have a spa treatment in an hour, so..." She trails off, her eyes assessing me as I stand in my kitchen. "It's good to see you, baby. I've missed you."

I nod. "Missed you, too."

The words are true, but the reality is that I miss who my mother *used* to be, before my father died and she ran off to travel the world with *Vance*.

"Well...I'll see you at dinner."

"Sounds good."

She gives me a wave then heads out, closing the door softly as she goes. I let out a long, exhausted sigh, knowing I'm in for an even more exhausting evening. Dinner with my mother...I only hope it's short and sweet and we don't dive into anything too deep.

For both our sakes.

When I arrive at Dock 7 just before six, I spend a few minutes just sitting in my truck, staring at the entrance before I finally head inside.

When I greet Jennica at the host stand inside, she gives me a wide smile. "Your mom's already here. I'll take you out to your table," she tells me, grabbing a menu and leading me through the restaurant and out to the patio overlooking the water.

As we approach where my mother is seated against the edge of the deck, my entire body tenses when I see she's not alone.

Vance.

He stands, adjusting his sport coat and reaching out a hand to shake. I grit my teeth and sit, ignoring him completely and focusing my attention on where my mother sits, holding a glass of white wine, a shawl draped over her shoulders.

"You should have told me."

Mom just continues to smile at me. "I said I made a reservation for us for dinner."

"Us," I repeat, motioning to her and me. "Not…us," I draw a circle in the air, including Vance. "And you said it that way on purpose because if I'd known, I wouldn't have come."

Mom sighs and sets her wine down. "I know. I *know* you wouldn't have come. Excuse me for doing what I needed to in order to get the two most important men in my life at the same table."

I clench my fists. "What was dad then, huh?"

Her face pales, but a server approaches, rattling off something about their specialty summer drinks. At least I think that's what she's talking about, though I'm completely blanked out and have no memory of it.

I'm the only one who needs to order, my mother and Vance having already gotten their drinks before I arrived, and I know without even looking at the menu what I want, though I doubt I'll be here long enough to enjoy it.

I order a whiskey. The server nods and retreats with the promise of returning with my drink and a basket of bread, and when she goes, the silence at the table is thick. I look out to the water, the sun still high enough in the sky that it twinkles in the rippling pools below. The heat from last week has cooled a bit, and it really is a beautiful night to sit out here, enjoying dinner.

If only being here right now were something I could enjoy.

"How's the shop?" Mom asks, her manicured fingernails tapping lightly at the base of her wine glass. "Still prepping for the big Fourth of July sale?"

I don't even want to answer her. She wants to ask me about the shop—my father's legacy—in front of this man? The one she ran off to with barely a backward glance at my dad's gravestone?

"Come on, Reid. I'm trying. Can't you try, too?"

"Try what?" I ask. "What can you possibly imagine would come from a dinner like this?"

My eyes flick to Vance's briefly before returning to my mother's.

"Well, I guess...I hoped you would be able to sit and enjoy dinner, tell me about your life, that's all."

"And *he* has to be here for that?"

"Reid, I know you think—"

"Don't." My words come out on a bark, and I don't miss the

way silence expands around us, the neighboring tables quieting slightly.

There are few things on this earth that anger me to the point that I will speak exactly what's on my mind, and one of them is sitting across from me. My mother's new boyfriend.

I lower my voice and lean forward. "I don't care what you think. About anything."

"Reid." My mother's voice is hushed and admonishing, reprimanding. It's a tone she hasn't used on me in years.

The server returns with my drink, and it takes all my effort not to toss it back in one gulp. Instead, I sip it, trying to savor the way it burns my throat.

"Can't you just...try to be happy for me?"

I shake my head, not as an answer, but in plain disbelief that she would even say that to me in the first place.

"You want me to be happy for you? When you ran off with this joker literally *months* after dad died?" I lean forward again, glaring at my mother, suddenly unable to keep my thoughts to myself any longer. "You left me to handle everything alone while you went on fucking cruises and vacationed in Mexico. And you want me to be happy for you?"

I take another sip of my whiskey, my hands gripping the glass tightly for fear of dropping it.

"I want you to be as happy for me and my choices as you want me to be for you and yours."

At that, my jaw goes tight.

"Tabitha." Vance says my mother's name in a firm tone then takes one of her hands in his.

"No," she replies, tugging her hand free. "If you're going to say exactly what you think, I'm going to do the same."

Vance sighs and takes a sip from his own drink as my mom

crosses her arms, her eyes narrowing.

"You've made some of your own choices that I don't agree with. Divorcing your wife. Taking this ridiculous…vow of loneliness or whatever it is you're doing…"

I scoff, shaking my head at the way she's characterizing my choices.

"…and I might not have understood them, but I've supported you anyway. I've stood by you, regardless of how I actually felt about it."

"You didn't stand by me," I say. "As soon as dad died, you were gone. Like you didn't even care what *I* was going through. As if you couldn't wait to be rid of this place, of his memory."

"That's *exactly* why I left!"

Her voice rises, and my head jerks back at the pain I see in her face, pain I haven't seen in…years, if I'm honest. Since that night almost two years ago when she collapsed on the floor after finding out he was gone.

I've never known that kind of grief before. Not when my grandfather died, even though we'd spent years watching him deteriorate before our eyes. Not when Sarah said she wanted a divorce, even though I thought we'd be together forever.

Those both felt inevitable. Like I'd been preparing for them, somehow.

But the pain of that night, of the doctor saying he was gone, just like that, no warning, no preparation, no…hint that he'd be there one day and gone the next, no chance to say goodbye…

I don't know if I'll ever get over it.

Which is why it's been even more painful to watch my mother gallivant around the globe like she doesn't have a care in the world. Like she's completely fine, unhindered by grief, unwounded by the shrapnel of loss that has left me with many,

many scars.

My mother glances around, her eyes welling with tears, her face flushed.

"My memories of your father are...everywhere," she whispers, tears beginning to trickle down her face. "I see him in everything. In everyone. I don't go a single day without grieving the fact that he's gone." She shakes her head, using her napkin to dab at her face. "So don't you *dare* judge me for trying to grasp at the things that might make me happy again."

I swallow thickly, overcome with emotion at seeing my mother like this, seeing the true pain she keeps so carefully hidden behind that mask of hers.

She turns and looks at Vance. "I'm so sorry," she says, giving him a soft smile.

He shakes his head, lifts one of her hands, and gives the back a gentle kiss. "You have nothing to apologize for." Then he reaches up and lightly swipes away another tear as it falls.

"I'm gonna head to the restroom and clean up," she says, looking at me. "And when I get back, I'm going to order a damn steak and enjoy the rest of my evening. Got it?"

I grit my teeth and nod, that same shame from earlier today creeping up the back of my neck as my mother leaves the table.

Vance and I sit for long minutes in silence before he speaks. And for the first time, I don't cut him off.

"Next to you, your father is the most important man in your mother's life," he says, his voice quiet, his eyes focused on the table where his fingers play with the stem of his wine glass. "That will never change."

I look out to the water, a swell of emotion brewing in my chest.

"But I love her, and all I want to do is to make her smile," he continues. "Which is more difficult to do every time you make her feel guilty for…not living in the most painful part of her grief every second of every day."

Gritting my teeth, I glare at Vance. "That's not what I want."

"Well, it seems like it," he replies, his curtness surprising me. "Let her be happy. Let me try to make her happy. She deserves that, don't you think?"

I sit in silence for a few more minutes, my mind at war with itself. About all of it.

Eventually, though, I look at Vance in the eyes and I nod. "I'll figure it out," I tell him, knowing if my mother and I are ever going to sort things, I'll need to let my grievances with Vance fall by the wayside.

When she returns to the table, her makeup refreshed, a smile on her face, I promise myself I'll really give it my best effort. This isn't what I pictured for our evening, obviously, but maybe it was for the best. Maybe finally being honest with each other about things is what my mother and I need to do to get past this emotional chapter and on to the next.

As painful as it might be.

As awkward and uncomfortable as it might feel.

Peeling back the layers of a wound never feels good, but it's the only thing you can do if you want to clean away the bad and let it heal.

chapter eleven
busy

The tinkling of the bell has me spinning where I stand, and I can't help the smile that stretches across my face at the sight of Reid, dressed in a pair of joggers and a tight cotton tee, walking through the door.

"Wow, this place looks great!" he enthuses, his eyes tracking over all the work that has gone into getting the shop in shape over the past few weeks. He points at the leaves on the ceiling. "You seriously painted all of this?"

I nod, my eyes following his around the room, trying to see everything from his vantage point. He stands smack in the middle, staring up at the ceiling, taking in the large leaves Briar agreed to—and that took me many, many hours and created a little pinch in the back of my neck that I can still feel when I think about it—his mouth slightly open.

"You're incredibly talented."

I roll my eyes, trying not to let his words carve too deeply into my chest.

"They're just leaves."

He shakes his head. "I couldn't do something like that. Don't downplay your talent when you've clearly worked very hard at it."

Okay, so maybe I let *those* words trickle through the heart of me.

"I really like the vibe. It feels like…a fairytale forest."

I beam at him. "That's what I said! Briar was talking about making it feel like you're hunting for books, and I said those exact words, fairytale forest."

He continues strolling around, examining the special plant holders we finally got installed on Friday, a variety of live hanging plants peppering the room. Boston ferns and English ivy, philodendrons and string of hearts. It has really brought this place to life.

Now, all that's left are the books.

Once Reid has finished snooping around, we get to work on the final boxes that need to be shelved. It's primarily thriller and fantasy/sci-fi that remain, and I take a few minutes to explain to Reid how we're organizing things before we get started. Then, I turn on some music and we get moving.

We're mostly silent over the next two hours, though I do regular check-ins to see how things are going. It's not every day someone gives up his Sunday afternoon to help you shelve books, and I can't help but feel pleased at the fact that he's doing it for me.

Or for Briar. Or the community. I shouldn't assume it's about me. Right?

After three hours, we finally finish, and we head to Ugly Mug for a caffeine boost and a pastry to celebrate.

"Thanks again for all your help," I say as we take a seat at a table in the corner. "It would have taken me all day to do it on my own."

Reid shrugs. "Not a problem. Glad I could help."

"And thanks for inviting Junie and me on the hike yesterday, too. She's been talking about it almost non-stop. I think you've officially converted her into a hiking girly."

He grins. "Good. Glad to know I'm having a good influence."

"Absolutely. And on me, too. I was on the fence at first, but it was actually really great to wander around in the woods for a bit."

Reid chuckles. "You say that like you weren't sure you were going to enjoy it."

I shrug. "Sometimes you get out of the habit of doing something you love, remember?" I tell him, calling back to our conversation a few weeks ago. "It's just been a long time."

"Well, for what it's worth, I understand how you feel. It's exactly how I felt when I jumped into the lake on Friday."

I can't help the pleased smile that stretches across my face. "Really?"

He nods. "Yeah. I think I've been avoiding swimming because I'm afraid of accepting that I'm not the same swimmer I used to be. That as I get older, my body will struggle to achieve the things it used to excel at."

"But I think that's some of what makes a hobby so special, right?" I reply. "It isn't about being *excellent*, it's just about the joy."

I know it sounds cheesy, and if I had to guess, he's trying not to roll his eyes at me right now. But it really is the truth.

"So I guess what I'm trying to say is…don't be so hard on yourself. You know? Just get in the water."

He studies his coffee for a minute, his large hands engulfing his cup, before he looks at me again. "And what's your water?"

My head tilts to the side in confusion. "What do you mean?"

"Well, based on this conversation, it originally sounded like hiking was your love, the thing you've been avoiding. But somehow I don't feel like that's true."

"Oh," I say, shaking my head firmly. "No, definitely not hiking. It's art."

"Really?"

I nod. "Yeah. I got my degree in photography with a focus in mixed media, so…taking photos and paint and oil and pretty much anything and combining them all together to create something completely unique."

"Wow, that sounds amazing."

"It's really fun, and there is just…so much you can do with it. For a long time, my goal was to create pieces that sell in galleries, have a dedicated studio space to create things that inspire me."

I wanted to be a household name, maybe even be the kind of photographer that would be showcased in the gallery next door to the bookstore. That's where I originally got my inspiration from. I used to stare at the pieces hanging in the window for long minutes any time I was downtown, envisioning mine in their place, trying to manifest for myself the kind of success that gets you into a position where galleries carry your work.

But…life doesn't always go to plan.

"Then I had Junie," I continue. "And I don't regret it for a second, I just want to make sure I'm super clear about that. She is…the best thing to ever happen to me. She absolutely changed my life in the best ways, has made me a better person."

"But?"

I want to laugh at how easily he saw that there was something else, something I didn't say.

"But…" I add, "choosing my daughter meant I had to let go of a part of myself. The part of me that was willing to take the big risks to become that creator, to make a name for myself. So maybe…maybe *that's* my water. Taking risks. It's not about the photography, necessarily, it's about throwing myself into it with all my passion and energy. Now, I give those things to my daughter instead. I can't afford to take big risks, because who knows how that will impact her life in the long run."

We're silent for a few minutes, and I wonder if I might have been *too* honest, *too* vulnerable about the realities of what it's like to be a single mom, the sacrifices you have to make.

But when Reid speaks again, he surprises me.

"So…get in the water."

I laugh. "What?"

He leans forward, a brightness in his eyes that draws me in.

"There has to be *something* you can do. Something small, something simple. You don't have to risk *everything* in order to risk *something*, right?"

I want to shake my head, almost by default, want to shut down his words before they take hold, take root.

"I mean, I don't get into the water to swim in competitions anymore. I haven't in years. But I jumped back in and it felt magical, made me feel more like me than I've felt in quite a while. Maybe it's the same for you. Maybe you need to take a tiny risk with art in some way—painting, photography, whatever—something just slightly out of your comfort zone, to feel like yourself again."

I mull over his words, trying to sort them into the space in my head where I categorize things based on priority. Junie is in the top box, because she's the most important. Everything else is kind of scattered beneath that, taking precedence only in the moment when it feels urgent.

But maybe that's the problem. Maybe I need to be more intentional about how I prioritize the things in my life that aren't about Junie, the things that are just…me.

"I actually think…you might be right," I finally say as we're getting up a while later and stepping out onto Main Street. "Maybe I do just need to try something small. I have literally no idea what that might look like. But…thanks, Reid. Seriously."

He nods, that same brightness in his eyes that was there earlier coming back as he watches me. "Any time, Busy. Any time."

The next few days pass in a blink. Briar and I are hustling around getting final things ready for the store opening on the Fourth, setting out all the cute decorations and printing off the signage to go up around town. Now that all the shelves and books are in their permanent positions, I hop up on a ladder to add some last-minute paint flourishes to the walls to really make the forest vibe pop.

All the while, the stuff Reid said at Ugly Mug on Sunday is percolating in the back of my mind, ideas for how I might get myself back into the creative space I love and miss so much. When I got pregnant with Junie, I knew my whole life was going to change, but I didn't realize how much of myself I'd be giving up in order to put her first. Gone are the days when I could lie in bed all morning, thinking about the projects I was working on, imagining all the different things that would go into bringing the picture in my mind to life.

Now, I'm lucky to have the time to *look* at art, let alone create it myself. My brother Bishop's fiancée is an artist, too—she does ceramics—and I'm pretty sure snooping through her social media posts has become my own personal masochism. I could only *wish* to have the kind of time she has to pursue the passions that fill my heart.

When I finally graduated—a full year after the cohort I began with my freshman year—I knew that was it, knew I'd need to set my camera on the shelf and admire it from afar, maybe pick it up here or there to take pictures of our family. I knew I wouldn't have the time to do anything larger than that.

Another stark reality is, even though Briar is paying me well, and even though I have free childcare, I'm still struggling to keep my head above water. My student loans are looming, the amount absolutely staggering when considering the fact that I'm now working at a bookstore for an hourly wage, and the cost of raising a child is far more than I think anyone understands when they're preparing to have a baby. Just thinking about my financials—something I've always been horrible at managing—makes my throat tight and my palms sweaty.

But Reid's right. There has to be *something* I can do that pushes me back into a creative space that doesn't rob me of all my time and money.

I just have to figure out…what.

"I can't believe we're opening tomorrow morning."

I nod, exhausted and completely spent, knowing the anxiousness I feel about it probably pales in comparison to Briar's. She's been dreaming of opening a bookstore—something this town has always lacked—since she was a teenager, volunteering at the library.

We're lying on the floor in the middle of the store, staring at the leaves on the ceiling, knowing we still have a few things to get done but in desperate need of a break.

"And I *really* can't believe there aren't any more books to shelve. You must have come in for *hours* on Sunday to get that done."

Briar rolls to the side and wraps her arm around me, the moment uncharacteristic of my sister, who tends to keep her emotions close to the vest.

"Thank you. For all your hard work," she says, her voice soft. "I hope you know how much it means to me."

I lift my hands and rest them over Briar's, patting them gently.

"As much as I'd like to take the credit, I had some help. It wasn't *all* me." I turn my head so I'm looking at her. "But it did take *forever*, even with two people."

Briar smiles. "Really? Who helped you? I need to get them a bottle of wine or something."

"Reid Cohen."

When my sister is quiet for a long moment, I look her way, finding her watching me with a curious expression. But when she opens her mouth, nothing comes out.

"What?" I say, chuckling lightly. "Do you not want him... touching your books or something?"

"No, it's nothing like that," she says, an embarrassed smile on her face. "Are you guys like…dating?"

"Definitely not."

My response comes out firm, and maybe a little more intense than I mean it to, and Briar's smile dims. "Oh, okay. Just curious."

I sit up, tugging the hair band off my wrist and pulling my hair up into a messy mop at the top of my head, trying not to think too hard about Briar's question.

"Well, if you *did* decide to date him, you should know…"

I glance at Briar as she sits up next to me, wondering what kind of bomb she's about to drop on my lap. What did he do? Something horrible? Is he an asshole in disguise? It would make sense considering the shitty men I've dealt with in the past.

"…he's actually one of the *sweetest* guys I've ever known."

My brow furrows, surprise rippling through me.

"Maybe a bit old for you, but"—Briar shrugs—"Bellamy and Rusty have a similar age difference and they're doing just fine. And my guess is you need a man with more life experience and maturity."

"I didn't realize you and Reid were friends."

Briar shakes her head. "Reid was a year ahead of me in school. He was on the swim team, so he was friendlier with Boyd's crowd, you know? The athletic types. But teenage boys can be dicks, so it's hard not to notice the nice ones."

I snort. "It doesn't really change as you get older."

My sister rolls her eyes and pushes up so she's standing then holds her hand out toward me. "You are so right. Unfortunately."

Briar gives me a tug and I pop up then glance around at the trash scattered on the floor that we still need to pick up—empty tape dispensers, cardboard boxes, tons of plastic and cellophane—knowing we probably have another hour of work before we get to call it a night. Or at least when *I* get to call it a night. Not sure about Briar, though.

"We haven't really talked about guys at all," Briar says, her tone cautious as we begin breaking down the cardboard boxes. "Or even that much about Junie's dad."

"No need to start now," I reply, giving her a cheesy smile.

"Oh, come on. That's no fun."

I pin her with a look. "Talking about all the ways men let you down is *never* fun."

That shuts her up, and honestly I don't even feel that bad because the last thing I want to do is talk about Jay with Briar. My sister dated a horrible man before she met her husband, so it might seem normal to gab with her about toxic men and the things they do that drive us insane. But Briar ended up falling in love with and marrying a man who treats her like a fucking queen, whereas I am going to be alone and loveless for the better part of the next two decades. It doesn't feel quite tit for tat.

"I'm sorry for bringing up Jay," Briar says as we're pushing out of Happily Ever After and onto Main Street once we've finished up. "You've said before you don't want to talk about him, and I should have respected that boundary instead of being nosy."

I shake my head, watching as she locks the front door then gives it a tug for good measure.

"You don't have to apologize, Briar. You weren't being nosy, you were being…a sister."

Her lips tilt up at the sides, and she loops her arm in mine as we walk down the street, heading toward where both of us have our cars parked in the lot at the end of the block that's reserved for Main Street shop employees.

"Can I ask you one more thing and then I promise I'll drop it?" she asks once we've come to a stop behind my car.

Sighing, I nod, knowing I'll probably regret it.

"Is there a reason you don't want to date Reid? I mean…I feel like you guys would be so cute together."

Licking my lips, I can't help but let out an uncomfortable laugh. "Reid and I are just friends, Briar. I've told you that."

"Right, but…I mean, that doesn't mean it couldn't become something more, right? I bet he'd be an amazing dad. Are you not attracted to him?"

At that, I laugh again, shaking my head. "That is definitely not the problem," I reply, maybe a bit more honestly than I should.

I think back to that night when Reid and I almost kissed, to the night where I thought about him in the shower. Mixed in with those memories are the ones of him with Junie in the lake, eating mac and cheese with us against his better judgment, the hike, sitting on the patio drinking wine together.

Of course I'm attracted to Reid. Of course it would be amazing to have a man like him to wake up to every day, to be a father to Junie, a partner to me.

But life isn't a fairy tale. Forevers are hard to come by, and I knew long ago—maybe even before Junie—that it probably wouldn't happen for me. It's safer to just accept that. For both of us.

"It's just…not a good idea, Briar," I say, shrugging my shoulders, not wanting to get into all that. "And that needs to be good enough."

Her eyes search mine for a long minute before she nods. "Alright. That's fair."

Then she reaches out and tugs me in for a hug.

"But you *do* deserve a happily ever after, Busy. Everyone does," she says before pulling back to look at me. "It took me a long time to learn that lesson, and I hope one day, you learn to believe it, too."

chapter twelve
reid

Summer crowds in Cedar Point are always a lot to handle. Families, singles, groups, kids at summer camp, people towing boats and jet skis...it's an eventful time around town.

The fireworks show in our little community is recognized throughout the region—hell, throughout the state—for being one of the best. A massive floating dock is motored out to the middle of the lake, manned with about a dozen or so pyrotechnics experts and a few firefighters, and at nine PM on the dot, once the sun has finally fully set behind the crest of the mountains, the sky gets set on fire for about fifteen minutes. It's bright, powerful, and loud as hell as the booms ricochet off the walls of trees and reverberate around the lake.

Understandably, a show of our caliber is an even larger draw than any other period during the summer, resulting in almost every hotel, B&B, campsite, and guestroom completely maxed out and the city pushed to capacity when it comes to resources. Residents are warned weeks in advance to have a spare tank or two of gas and to stock up on grocery necessities. Some locals even go out of town to avoid the masses, not wanting to deal with the traffic or congestion that happens in almost every corner of Cedar Point.

As exhausting as the holiday can be, I never complain, because from a business perspective, it's the most profitable week of the year. From the moment we open the door at eight in the morning until we shut down at eight PM—an intentionally long day to capitalize on the foot traffic around Main Street—we have customers. And not just people wandering around to escape the heat. They're active, interested, paying customers. Something about visiting a small mountain town turns everyone into a rustic furniture connoisseur, imagining their own fireplaces back home bookended by two leather chairs made from locally sourced wood.

"Heather, can you write up an invoice for that gentleman looking at the bookshelf against the wall?" I ask, digging around underneath the register, looking for a pen. "I have to help a customer load up a chair into their RV back at the shop."

She nods. "Can do. Also, I think it's time for Jen to leave for the day."

"Ask her to stay another hour and I'll pay her time and a half?"

Heather smirks. "You're already paying us time and a half."

"Double time, then. You're the best!" I toss over my shoulder as I hustle through the back door that exits to a small alleyway behind the row of shops along Main Street.

The shop where I design and craft the furniture for the storefront is only a few minutes' walk, and in almost no time, I spot the obnoxiously oversized RV parked outside.

"Thanks so much for sorting this out today," the guy says.

"My wife and I have to head back home really early tomorrow, and I know she was just so in love with that loveseat."

I grin at him. "No worries, man. Happy to help."

It doesn't take much time for us to hoist the piece from where I stored it a few days ago, when this gentleman and his wife first visited the store and reserved it, and get it tucked in through the side door of his RV. Once it's done, we shake hands and he heads out, leaving me with a few blissful moments of quiet alone in my shop before I lock up and head back.

Technically, it's more direct for me to take the alley all the way back to Cohen Custom, but I glance at my watch, knowing I made quick work with that load-up, and instead head out onto Main Street to take in the crowds. It's just as busy at the south end of the street, away from the lake, as it is near my end. The brewery is packed with customers filling the patio to the brim. There are pop-up tents in the street, which has been closed off to cars and limited to just foot traffic. It smells like sunscreen and popcorn and beer and hot asphalt, and I smile as I stroll slowly through the crowd.

When I get to Happily Ever After Bookstore, I stop, stepping up onto the curb and over to the small shop, glancing through the door as a customer exits, a bag of books in hand. Then I give in to the desire to poke my head in, stepping through the door and into the shop itself. I immediately spot Busy, standing at the register and chatting with a customer, a smile wide on her face as she rings up a purchase.

"Misery!"

I laugh when Junie suddenly appears at the back of the store, waving wildly. I wave back just as wildly, and she sprints my way, launching herself into my arms as if she's jumping off the dock back at the lake.

"Hi, Miss Junie," I say, lifting her up and giving her a hug.

"Is my birfday!" she says loudly, raising her arms in the air, her hands in fists, an almost maniacal smile on her face.

I spin her around in a circle. "It is! Happy birthday! Are you *two* today?"

She nods dramatically.

"You are such a big girl!" I tell her, just as dramatically, then turn, looking toward where I know Busy is standing behind the register. "Did you know Junie is turning *two* today?"

Busy rolls her eyes, but her smile is stretched wide across her face as she puts a stack of books into a blue tote bag then thanks her customer.

The woman grins at Junie and me before she says, "Excuse me," and slides past us toward the door.

"Could you two be any louder?" Busy jokes, rounding the counter and walking our way. She tickles Junie's bare foot where it dangles. "Huh?"

Junie squeals with laughter again, and I crouch down, setting her on the ground where she promptly races off through the store, toward where I can see Patty Mitchell talking with Briar at the back. I wave when they spot me, and they both wave back before returning to their conversation.

"So, how's the day going?" I ask, glancing around, spotting at least five…no, six customers looking at titles on the shelves or flipping through open books in their hands.

"Really good, actually. Briar said we've already surpassed her stretch goal for opening day sales, so…we'll see how it looks when we tally the final number."

In my peripheral vision I see Patty and Junie walking our way, with Junie dragging her grandmother by the hand as fast as she can.

"Goodness, this one has already had too much sugar," Patty says as they come to a stop next to us.

"She's going to be a nightmare later, I'm sure," Busy jokes, bending down and picking her daughter up then placing her on one hip. "Because *someone* is getting a special chocolate cake for her birthday!"

Junie starts clapping, that slightly loony smile returning, and I can't help but laugh.

"We're having a party today at six," Patty says. "You're welcome to join us. We're doing a barbeque and cake."

I open my mouth, but before I can say anything, Busy interjects.

"Mom, Reid has more important things to do than eat chocolate cake." She laughs as she says it then looks at me with an apologetic expression. "Don't let her guilt you. She's very good at getting people to do things they don't want to do."

There's nothing sassy in the way she says it, but it still strikes something in my chest.

"Oh, honey, if that were true, my days mothering five teenagers would have been a lot easier," Patty says, giving me her own look of exasperation as she takes Junie out of Busy's arms. "Alright, well…if you change your mind, you know where we'll be. Say goodbye, sweetheart."

"Bye Misery!" Junie says, waving wildly again.

"Wish us luck as we brave Main Street," Patty jokes, winking at me before the two of them leave the store and head outside, disappearing into the crowd.

"I seriously love that she calls you that. I laugh almost every time."

I nod. "I do, too."

"So, how are things at *your* shop?"

"Good. I actually have to get back, but I hope the rest of the day goes great," I tell her, backing away and heading for the front door.

Her smile dips slightly before it reappears like nothing changed. "Thanks for coming to say hi."

I wave then step out into the thrall, rubbing at the center of my chest as I walk the short distance to my own shop a few doors down. Patty was just being kind, inviting me, and Busy was just trying to protect my free time, assuring me I didn't need to go. Still, hearing her imply that Junie's birthday isn't something I want to go to…it didn't sit right.

I watch the clock for the rest of the afternoon, as the day ticks along and the store stays busy. At quarter to five, I flip the sign at the front, making decision in the moment. Then I spend a few minutes letting the customers wandering around know we'll be closing at five.

"We're closing?" Heather asks, her eyebrows high on her head.

I nod. "Yeah. If you want the hours, you're welcome to keep working. There's some paperwork and inventory that needs to get done, and I know holiday pay isn't something a lot of people want to miss out on, but…" I shrug. "I think it's time to close for the day. Besides, I have somewhere I want to be."

It might be ridiculous, closing several hours early for a two-year-old's birthday party, but I don't feel even the tiniest bit guilty. Even if it impacts the bottom line, I know I'm making the right choice.

Once the store is empty and Heather has taken off—gleeful about her suddenly free evening—I shut off the lights, lock up, and hustle home to grab the birthday gift I made for Junie last week. I planned to give it to her at some point this weekend, but this will be even better.

I do my best to ignore the voice that says I hope Busy likes it, too.

Even if it *is* the truth.

Growing up, I was kind of peripheral friends with the eldest Mitchell kid, Boyd. Friends of friends, sometimes overlapping hangouts. Which is why after thirty-two years in this small town, I've only been over to their house once or twice.

So when I pull up out front a few minutes after six, parking in the grass next to the driveway alongside several other cars, I take a long minute to just...look at it. It's massive, far larger than the three-bedroom I grew up in, though that makes sense when considering there had to be enough beds for seven people. There's a four-car garage and a detached in-law unit, and I can see the lake stretched out behind it.

This. This is the kind of house I wanted as a kid.

I hoist Junie's present out of the back seat and sling it over one arm then head to the gate on the side, figuring based on the music and laughter I can hear that everyone is out back. Once I push through, my guess is proven accurate when I spot the dozen or so people scattered around holding beers or hanging out near the barbeque. Junie is down at the dock, sitting between Patty's legs, her feet dangling into the water.

My eyes scan over everyone until I finally spot Busy, emerging from the house with a bag of hot dog buns and crossing to where her dad is manning the grill. God, she's gorgeous. Not for the first time, I watch her from afar, taking in her sweet smile and casual beauty. Everything about her is effortless.

Of course, it's as I'm admiring her that her eyes find mine. She freezes.

Suddenly, I feel self-conscious showing up unannounced, like maybe I overstepped somehow. There aren't a ton of people here, and the ones who *are* have a very clear connection to the Mitchell family. I don't really know how I fit into that. Or if I do at all, in truth.

But then she changes course, heading my way, hot dog buns still in her hands.

"What are you doing here?" she asks as she approaches, a wrinkle in her brow, and from this distance, I can't tell if she's happy to see me or not.

I shrug. "Just wanted to make sure Junie got her present on her birthday."

Busy's eyes flick to where I have the wooden rocking horse under one arm. I set it down in the grass, the weight beginning to be too much to hold on my own any longer.

"If you want, I can just drop it off. I don't have to stay."

As if my words have tugged her out of a trance, she takes a few more steps forward and envelopes me in a hug, her arms wrapping around my middle and her face tucked against my chest.

I only delay for a second, having been caught by surprise, before I wrap my arms around her as well, reveling in the way it feels to finally have her petite frame tucked against mine. I could stand here all day, holding her like this, and the most natural thing in the world would be to dip my head and press my lips to the crown of her head, to inhale the sweet smell of whatever that jasmine stuff is that she wears.

But then I glance around, and I realize there are more than a few pairs of eyes aimed our way.

Clearing my throat, I release Busy and take a step back. She does the same, though when her gaze finds mine again, I imagine the slightly dazed look on her face matches my expression.

"I'm glad you could come," Busy says, licking her lips and taking a deep breath before letting it out in one go. Then she motions in the direction of the grill. "We're just finishing up the hot dogs, if you want one."

Another food I haven't had in forever. Who knows what goes into the making of a hot dog, anyway? I chuckle internally, acknowledging that at least it's not neon.

"I'd love one," I tell her. "Is there somewhere I can put this for now? Until I can give it to Junie?"

Busy nods, taking a few steps back, in the direction of where she was walking toward the grill a few minutes ago. "Yeah, you can just take it inside. Through the sliding doors and anywhere in the living room is good."

"I'll be right back."

She smiles then spins around, and I do the same, heading in the opposite direction. When I lug the rocking horse off the grass and onto the porch, I nod hello at Busy's sisters where they're sitting together on the patio.

"Let me grab that for you," Briar says, hopping out of her chair and crossing to slide the door open for me.

"Thanks."

I step into the blissfully air-conditioned home, wishing not for the first time that my cabin had a window unit or *something* to keep me somewhat cooler during the summer.

"You don't realize how hot it is until you step into somewhere that doesn't feel like the face of the sun," I joke to Briar as I cross through the kitchen and set the rocking horse down in the corner of the living room.

"My friend Abby and I used to live in the cabin Busy's in now, before you moved into the other one. I do *not* envy the way either of you are probably absolutely baking right now."

I grin, resting my hands on my hips, my eyes darting around briefly and taking in the photos on the walls and the lake life décor scattered about.

"Can I ask you something?"

My eyes return to Briar, finding her watching me with a curious expression.

"Something very personal?"

I squint slightly, considering, and then I nod, crossing my arms.

"Sure. Doesn't mean I'll answer, though."

"That's fair." Briar's lips twist slightly and she rests her hip against the couch, watching me intently. "Why did you and Sarah get divorced?"

I blink, my eyebrows rising. "You're right. That *is* a personal question."

"And if I wasn't wondering what you're doing with my sister and my niece, I wouldn't have asked it."

"Busy and I are just friends," I tell her, the words feeling wrong on my tongue. "That's all."

Briar nods but then glances at the rocking horse before her soft gaze returns to mine, waiting for me to answer her question.

Licking my lips, I tuck my hands into my jeans and shrug my shoulders. "It just didn't work out."

"Why?"

Chuckling uncomfortably, I shake my head. "Because…

Sarah and I wanted our future to look a certain way, and when that reality changed, it wasn't fair to her for me to hold her in a relationship anymore."

"That's incredibly vague."

"And more than I've ever said to anyone about why we got divorced, so it'll have to do."

She hums quietly, and I wonder what she's thinking. Does she think I'm full of shit? Or that I'm a cheater? That's always been my biggest fear, that people in town will think I did something bad or hurt Sarah in some way, and that's why we split. In reality, it's the exact opposite, though I can't really control what other people think. A hard truth to learn as you get older, but one you become more accepting of.

"We're just friends, Briar," I repeat. "That's all we can ever be."

Briar assesses me for another beat before she nods, and I can tell when whatever kind of interrogation hat she put on temporarily has been removed. Her shoulders ease and her arms drop from where they were crossed in front of her.

"Well, then. If that's really all it is...I'm glad she has a friend like you." She turns, heading back toward the sliding doors leading out to the porch. "Let's eat, yeah?"

I let out a long breath and follow in her wake, though I come to a stop when she pauses just before opening the door.

"But if you *did* decide to be more than friends, I think a man like you could be exactly what Busy needs."

I blink, surprised by her approval, though I don't say anything in response as she pulls the door open and steps outside. It takes me a few seconds to follow behind her, and when I emerge into the unforgiving sun and humidity, I find that everyone is surrounding a table on the deck, putting together their plates of food.

My eyes find Busy's immediately, bright and happy to see me, before they lock on Junie, who is snacking happily on a hot dog bun as she sits on Busy's hip.

Just friends.

Just friends.

Just friends.

I repeat it over and over in my mind, like a mantra, a reminder I need to live and breathe for as long as I am lucky enough to be in Busy and Junie's lives.

I wasn't lying when I told Briar friends is all Busy and I can ever be. The smarter thing would be to not even allow that, because I can't be around Busy and not be just...overwhelmed by her. Fascinated by her. Captivated with her.

The truth is I wish what we had was more.

The truth is if I could give her more, I would do it in a heartbeat, would give *her* my heartbeat, my very last breath.

But I can't. I can't do that to her.

It wouldn't be fair.

chapter thirteen
busy

After everyone has eaten, we bring out Junie's birthday cupcakes and sing to her. She claps and laughs, and then we stick a big candle with the number two on it on her own cupcake to blow out, which she figures out after a few tries. Then she absolutely demolishes the treat.

When Junie turned one last summer, it was just the two of us in our apartment near campus, and after she went to bed, I cried as I picked up the mess of her cake smash from the floor. It was partly because I was so, so exhausted. But it was also because we were alone.

Mom was on the Fourth of July committee last year and Bellamy and Rusty were visiting a friend in Seattle. Bishop and Gabi and Boyd and Ruby live clear on the other side of the country. Briar offered to come, but honestly, I was doing summer school and the idea of having anyone come visit felt chaotic and stressful, so I told her to stay in town and enjoy the holiday at home.

In the end, that meant it was just me and my Junie Bee,

which didn't feel like a big deal until it suddenly was, until the loneliness of what it's like to handle everything on your own as a single parent felt like too much to just barrel my way through.

I had just curled up in bed, crying quietly and trying not to wake Junie, until the fireworks did the job. Then we sat outside together, headphones over her ears, watching the sky erupt. I promised her then that it would be the only birthday she would ever spend alone for as long as I could help it.

And now...

I've felt on the verge of tears all evening watching everyone rally around Junie at my parents' house, making her feel special, like it's *her* day, and not just a holiday. From the décor—unicorn themed to strike a stark contrast to anything red, white, and blue—to the food to the most thoughtful gifts.

Not that gifts are the way to show someone you love them. But to see her surrounded by toys that were bought with her in mind warmed something in my heart. Mom and dad got her this cushy chair that looks like a couch for a toddler. Bellamy and Rusty went in with Andy and Briar on a kitchenette play station, though Bellamy wanted to assure me she wasn't 'sending my daughter to the kitchen', which made me laugh.

And then there's the gift from Reid, a wooden rocking horse he made himself. An oak body, yarn for the mane and tail, and tiny leather ears.

"It might be too big for her," he says, crouching down and hoisting her onto the seat, showing her where to grasp the handles. "But I figure it's a toy she can grow into. And I left the wood unvarnished in case you want to paint it. Give it some more...personality."

Reid looks up at me then, his eyes soft.

"You know...get back into the water."

My throat grows tight, and after instructing Junie to thank Mr. Reid—"Thanks, Misery!" she says, to a chorus of laughter from my family—I excuse myself for a moment.

To catch my breath.

To calm my heart.

To still my shaking hands.

Only then do I return to my family, a smile on my face as we all head back out onto the deck to hang out until the fireworks start. After a while, we take chairs down to the water, lining them up in a row facing south, towards where the motorized dock is floating. I have Briar on one side and Reid on the other, Junie in my lap, and it's *so* much better than last year. So, so much better.

At nine sharp, the fireworks begin. Junie oohs and aahs and claps her hands, her little face lit up and her eyes huge as she watches explosions fill the sky.

I can't help but watch Reid, too. The way the reds and blues and whites pop color on his face, his head tilted back, that perpetual stubble in ever deeper shadow tonight. His friendship has become so important to me since I moved home, but I would be lying if I kept trying to deny that there isn't more to how I feel about him. From the moment he caught me trying to break into his house, my heart has thumped an uneven rhythm. Tonight, that beating has grown louder, harder to ignore, and has rattled something free within my chest that I didn't know was there.

Love.

Not lust, the way I've felt about other boys in the past, where it's all butterflies in your stomach and a tingling under your skin, but love. The kind of devotion you read about, the kind that happens to other people, but never to you.

Maybe...maybe there *is* room in my life for a forever kind

of love. Something profound and unexpected and…fulfilling in a way I didn't know love could be.

In the past, the only kind of love I had experienced was the selfish kind, the kind that was about what you could get, not what you can give, and that was enough.

Until it wasn't.

Now, I can't imagine ever giving those boys a second look when I know there are men like Reid, though that thought has me shaking my head. There are no other men like Reid Cohen. I'm sure of it. He stands apart. Strong, sturdy, steadfast.

As the fireworks show rises into its climactic finish, Reid looks my way, his eyes bright and his expression easy. He's not smiling, but I can see that dimple on the left side of his face that tells me he's happy.

And then he looks at me, too.

For a long moment, we just stare at each other, as the last of the fireworks pop off in the sky. He searches my face, though I'm not sure what he's looking for, then opens his mouth, like he's going to say something. I wait with bated breath, desperate to know what's on his mind, wondering if his thoughts might mirror my own.

But then the sky goes dark, the show concluding, and Reid looks away as my family begins to applaud. We can hear cheers from neighboring homes, other families and friends gathered on docks and in back yards to watch the spectacle as well.

Just like that, the moment—whatever that moment was—is lost.

I pull to a stop on the parking pad outside my cabin and sit there for a moment, leaning my head back against the headrest, my eyes closed.

What a night that was.

I'm pretty sure *unicorn* is going to be Junie's entire personality for the foreseeable future. She still had glitter on her face as I carried her upstairs to put her to bed in my childhood bedroom, and she didn't stir at all as I got her tucked in.

She had way too much sugar today and was bouncing all over the place...up until she crashed almost the minute after the fireworks show ended. Mom suggested setting her up in my old room for the night, since I have to be at the store bright and early—*day two!*—and it didn't make sense to take Junie home, waking her up, disrupting her sleep, and then bring her right back at six in the morning tomorrow.

I hope Junie gets some good sleep, because I'm not sure I will. It's my first night away from my baby—ever—and I'm not exactly sure how I feel about it. Before my mind can wander too much, a pair of headlights flash as they turn the corner behind me and begin to pull down the lane toward the cabins.

Reid.

He left only a few minutes after I did, offering to load the rocking horse back up in his truck to bring home because I have a bunch of shit in the back of my SUV for the bookstore. I shut off my engine and step out, stretching slightly before I head over to where he's coming to a stop.

"Thanks again for bringing this home for me," I say as he opens up the back seat and tugs out the rocking horse.

"No problem. Originally, I planned to just give it to her here, which probably would have been easier but a whole lot less fun."

Junie *loved* her gift from 'Misery.' He was right…it *is* a bit too big for her, but it's going to be an amazing toy for her to enjoy for a few years.

I grab one end, prepared to help Reid carry it inside, but he shakes his head. "I got it." Then he hoists it over one shoulder and begins walking, leaving me to admire his muscles as he goes, his strong, broad shoulders and the biceps that flex with the effort.

As he sets the rocking horse down in Junie's room, my mind scrambles, searching for something to say. I'm not ready for him to go yet.

"I'm thinking about enjoying my freedom tonight and jumping in the lake for a night swim," I say, the idea coming to me suddenly. "Wanna join me?"

Reid rubs at the stubble on his face for a minute, and I wonder if he's going to say no.

Then he nods, his lips tilting up at the sides. "Actually, yeah. Gimme a second to change and I'll join you."

A bubble of joy begins to swell in my chest, and I nod as Reid turns, heading out the door, his feet thudding on the deck outside before disappearing as he steps down to the grass. I sprint into action, dashing into my bedroom and digging around through the clean clothes that are still in a hamper in the corner, next to my bed that's still on the floor. It would be nice if I could get all my shit finally set up and furniture in this place so it doesn't look like a bachelor pad, but that will come in time, I'm sure. I just have to be patient.

Eventually, I find my navy blue swimsuit, the only two piece I own that makes me still feel sexy even with the stretch marks that never really faded after Junie was born. I wear them like a badge of honor—they are a mark that at one point, my body did the hard work to make space to protect my baby—but every so often, I can't help but wish it were still the cute thing it was pre-pregnancy.

Sighing, I aggressively shove all those thoughts into a box in my mind and seal it tight. There's no room for any of that tonight.

Once I've changed, I pop into the bathroom and take a look at the light layer of makeup I've had on all day, then do a little sprucing, wiping away the mascara that has smudged slightly before swiping on more and adding a dab of concealer over a few red spots around my temples. Then I grab my towel and my phone and head out to the dock.

I stand on the edge, waiting for Reid to join me, thrilling when I hear the subtle squeak of his screen door in the distance and a few beats later feel his footsteps on the dock as he comes up behind me. Turning to say hello, I about choke on my tongue when I see him, my eyes traveling the length of him as he strides my way.

Then I spin back around, wishing I wasn't so damn obvious. I've already seen Reid without his shirt, but that doesn't mean it's any less delicious the second time around.

"I thought you'd already be in the water," he says, dropping his towel on top of mine.

"I'm always a bit scared to jump in by myself," I share honestly. I glance back at him. "At night, I mean. I know it's kind of ridiculous."

"Maybe a little," he teases, bumping me gently with his shoulder as he steps up to the edge next to me. "But really, who knows what's in there? All kinds of creepy things. Could be like…the Loch Ness monster or something."

I snort and roll my eyes. "Now who's being ridiculous?" I

ask, bumping him back, the skin of his bicep soft and warm as I graze lightly against him.

"Hey, I'm just trying to be good company," he replies, shrugging his shoulders. "*You're* the one who's afraid to jump in."

At that, I giggle, enjoying this round of flirty banter.

"Is that why you invited me?" Reid asks. "Because you wouldn't be able to jump in if you were alone?"

I shake my head. "Nah. I just like seeing you without your shirt on."

Reid raises his eyebrows, surprise rippling through his expression at my bold comment, but before he can say anything in response, I let out a cackle and jump into the water, one hand plugging my nose and my eyes scrunched tight.

The cool water envelopes me, the chill providing relief to my warm skin. I'm unsure how deep this part of the lake is, but it's enough that I don't feel even a hint that the bottom is near as I sink low into the cool darkness then kick myself up to the surface. When I emerge, I wipe the water from my face and look to Reid, who is still standing at the edge of the dock, a smirk on his face.

"You coming?"

He chuckles. "Just wanted to make sure you scared off Nessie before I join you."

My laughter turns into a squeal as he launches off the dock and plunges in just a few feet away from me, water splashing me. When he emerges from below, he tosses his hair out of his face and grins.

"God, this feels amazing," he says, rotating so he's floating on his back. "I feel like I need to do this every night."

I follow suit, and then we're both staring at the sky, at the stars just beyond the tree line.

"Yeah, it's pretty dreamy."

We drift like that for a while, not saying anything, each of us just enjoying the sensation of weightless buoyancy.

"I've missed being able to see the stars like this," I tell him, my memory taking me briefly back to my childhood and teen years when I spent countless nights lying out on the dock next to Bellamy, staring at the sky. "In LA, there was too much light pollution. You'd be lucky to see *anything* in the sky other than smog."

Reid chuckles. "That's what I hear."

I turn, glancing his way. "Have you never been to LA?"

"Nah. I've done plenty of traveling to big cities, and they're fun, but not for me. I'm a small-town boy through and through." He pauses. "Even if I don't know everyone's names."

My eyes return to the sky as I giggle to myself, and we float in silence side by side for a few minutes, just enjoying the peacefulness of nature. Every so often I hear the faint pop of fireworks being set off or the thump of music as cars pass in the distance. But thankfully, it's pretty quiet on this end of the lake, considering it's still a holiday.

"So…looked like Junie had a great time tonight," Reid says after a few minutes. "Was the party a success?"

I grin. "A *resounding* success. The *most* successful."

"Good. I'm so glad."

"Nights like tonight make it all worth it, you know?"

"Makes what worth it?"

"The move. Coming here. It was for this, the chance for her to be with her family. Surrounded by people who love her, who want to…*celebrate* her, because they know she deserves it."

"She *does* deserve it," he tells me, his voice so certain.

I hum in acknowledgment then spread my arms wider,

moving my exhausted limbs in gentle circles.

"She's staying at your mom's tonight, right?"

I sink down into the water, submerging my body up to my shoulders.

"Yeah."

Reid chuckles. "You sound so sad about it."

I laugh, too. "I'm not," I say, though I know it's not true as soon as the words are out of my mouth. "Okay, maybe I am. Part of me feels like I *should* be ecstatic to have a night completely to myself, but...I've never been away from Junie like this before."

Reid sinks into the water as well, giving me a sweet smile. "You freaking out a little bit?"

"A little bit. But it feels...ridiculous."

"Hey." He swims closer to me so we're just a foot or so apart. "It's not ridiculous. That's your kid. It's okay to be nervous for something like this."

Taking a deep breath, I nod. "Thanks."

I don't know why, but it felt like I needed that, needed permission to miss her.

It's only one night, but it's still new, still a transition. And one we didn't plan for, either. I didn't even have time to worry about all the things because it was just...happening, me tucking her into bed at my mom's and kissing her forehead then driving away.

I dunk my head under the water and scrub at my face, refusing to let myself cry, then break through the surface again.

"So how about you?" I ask, shifting the conversation away from me and anything else that might bring up emotions I'd rather not focus on right now. "What did *you* think of the party?"

Reid grins and grips the dock with one arm. "It was great.

I've been to a few kid parties in my day with Leo and Nina, but this one was pretty spectacular. I mean, there were fireworks."

I roll my eyes at his tease and swim over to the dock as well, grasping the ladder and hoisting myself up before plopping down on the edge, my feet dangling in the water.

"But you're glad you came? To the party?"

Reid's head tilts to the side, eyeing me. "Of course."

"I just...you took off work, so..." My voice trails off, and I hope I don't sound as needy as I feel.

Thankfully, Reid chuckles briefly before his tone becomes more sincere again. "Busy, life is too short not to do the exact thing you want to be doing," he tells me. "I wanted to be there, so I made it happen."

He says it like it's the simplest thing in the world. Like it didn't just...heal something in my heart to see him put my daughter first, especially when he has *no* obligation to do that.

When I don't respond, Reid climbs up the ladder and takes a seat next to me, his thigh pressed against mine, our arms grazing.

"It was fun visiting your parents' house. When I was a kid, I always wished we had a spot like that, on the water."

I tuck my hands underneath my thighs. "And now you do."

Reid chuckles. "The cabin's great, don't get me wrong, but it could use a few more square feet, maybe some a/c."

I pin him with a look. "My freshman year of college I didn't have air conditioning in my hall and I promised myself I would never do it again." I shake my head. "I forgot how miserable it is. When we had that heat wave last week it made me wish I'd moved in with my parents instead. And trust me when I say that was the absolute *last* thing I wanted."

"They wanted you to move in with them?"

I nod. "Yeah. They said it was a waste for me to spend money on rent when they have a hotel's worth of empty bedrooms available. And when I was lying in bed in my undies, sweating because it was 95 degrees at one in the morning, a tiny part of me wished I'd given in."

He laughs. "Well, if it's any consolation, I'm glad you're here."

I grin at that. "Yeah?"

Reid nods. "Yeah. I mean, before you it was just a bunch of partiers and weirdos next door. Now, I have a neighbor who brings me cheap wine and breaks into my house."

I can't help but laugh at his callback to our introduction. "You're gonna keep up with that bit, huh?"

He shrugs then bumps his shoulder against mine. "Maybe."

"For how long, you think?"

Reid hums. "Probably for the rest of our lives."

Something about the way he says it hits me square in the chest, all my reserves falling by the wayside, all my effort to keep myself from falling for Reid going to waste.

We watch each other for a long minute, our bodies pressed together, the night air warm, and when I see his eyes dip to my lips, I don't think, I just move. Reaching out, I place a hand on his cheek and then my lips against his. He freezes for a beat, and I worry for a moment that I took a misstep, that I completely misread…

But then his mouth opens against mine, his teeth nibbling my bottom lip gently, his hands coming to either side of my face.

I breathe a sigh of relief and he swallows it whole, his tongue dipping lightly, asking for permission that I willingly give, and then the taste of him explodes in my mouth. He tastes like birthday cupcakes and hops and warm summer nights, and I know somewhere deep inside of me that I could exist on nothing but that for the rest of my life.

I lean back, tugging him with me, my back flat against the wooden dock and Reid's body hovering over mine. He kisses me like he never wants to stop, like he can't get enough, like I'm the only person he ever wants to kiss for all eternity. It tastes so good, *feels* so good, as his hand reaches down and grips at my ass through my swimsuit then slides down my thigh to my knee and hitches me up so my leg is hooked over his hip.

His mouth begins to trail down my neck, sucking at my exposed skin, and then he shifts, pressing the hardness between his legs against me. I whimper at the delicious sensation, knowing I'm already growing wet and it has nothing to do with the lake water.

"Reid," I moan, my hands gripping his damp skin.

My use of his name brings him to a hard stop, his entire body stilling above me. I know almost instantly that he's calling it right here, my assumption confirmed as he pulls back slowly, and I find regret written all over his face.

"Busy, I…"

He pauses, maybe trying to find the right words. But I know, no matter what he says next, it won't be what I want to hear.

"I think you're great."

I laugh, though I can't keep the slight edge out of it or hide the way I feel irrevocably wounded, even though I wish I could.

"Always what a girl wants to hear." I push up and Reid leans back, both of us returning to the sitting positions we were in just a few minutes ago. "Especially when the next word is going to be 'but.'"

I look his way, an eyebrow raised, waiting for him to speak again.

"But…"

There it is.

"...it's complicated."

My laugh is caustic. "Isn't it always."

"I just...don't want to be in a relationship."

With me. That's the unspoken. He doesn't want to be in a relationship with me.

I nod, my smile tight. "I get it."

As I push up onto my feet, embarrassment courses through me. I knew it was a mistake to think there was something there, to think maybe this friendship could become something I never could have seen coming. Instead, I probably ruined whatever this burgeoning friendship was becoming as well.

"I'll see you later, Reid." I grab my towel and wrap it around my body, suddenly desperate to cover myself and my foolish attempt to...*what*...entice him?

"Busy..."

"Thanks again for coming to Junie's party," I say, giving him a pinched smile as I back away. "I'll see you later."

His face is pained, but I don't have the mental capacity to care about his feelings in this moment as I turn and walk up the dock, heading back to my cabin.

My empty cabin, and my no a/c, to wallow in the mess I've surely made.

chapter fourteen

reid

"This is…absolutely perfect. Everything about it."

I smile tightly at the blonde but keep my attention focused on the dining table I'm currently helping her husband hoist into their trailer. Once we've gotten it into place, I rotate my right shoulder, the sensation of strained fatigue a lot stronger than it was before. Hopefully just an overworked muscle and not something worse.

"I'm glad you love it," I finally say, hopping down off the trailer and watching as her husband covers it with a tarp.

Normally, I'd offer to help, but I'm feeling wiped, the exhaustion I've been experiencing recently surely not helped by the poor way I've been sleeping and the long hours I've been working.

"Well, Hannah, I hope you love the table, and if you need anything else or you're interested in custom work for your home, just give me a call," I say, digging a business card out of my wallet.

I pass it over and she takes a look. "Do you deliver? We're just here on vacation. We live in the LA area."

Nodding, I tuck my wallet into my back pocket. "I do. I work with a shipping company that can do door-to-door service, white glove and everything. They'll unload whatever it is and set it up for you and take all the packing supplies."

"That's what I told her we should have done this time," her husband says as he rounds the back of the trailer, tightening the cinches that will keep the table held in place.

Hannah rolls her eyes and looks at me, an amused smile on her face. "Anyway, thanks so much for your help. I can think of one or two things I might want for the house, so I'll definitely reach out once we're ready."

I nod then accept a handshake from each of them before they load up in their fancy truck and drive off. Sighing, I wipe the sweat from my brow and head through the back door, into the blissfully airconditioned space.

The heat this summer is unreal, and the reprieve we had a few weeks ago didn't last nearly long enough before temps started rising again. I've been running the fan on high, but it's been basically no help, the moving air doing almost nothing to relieve the sweltering warmth.

I've considered coming into the store and laying out blankets over one of the couches, just to get a good night of sleep, or asking Marie if I can borrow her RV for a few days. I heard a customer yesterday mention the exceptional a/c at the resort, and even shelling out a few hundred bucks for a night in a hotel room sounds preferable to how rough things have been.

But for whatever reason, I haven't pulled the trigger on any of those options.

I roll my eyes at myself as I head into the bathroom at the

back of the store to wash my hands. Like I don't know the reason I continue in my misery, choosing to return home night after night.

It's because of Busy, and Junie. Knowing the two of them are next door, likely also struggling with the heat, makes escaping it less desirable, like suffering alongside them somehow makes a difference. I know that's stupid, but I can't imagine booking a hotel room and sleeping in cool air knowing they're still wilting away.

So I stay.

Though it would feel a lot better if Busy would actually talk to me without that weird fake smile on her face. One that doesn't quite reach her eyes.

Something that's entirely my fault.

I grab a broom from the back closet and head to the front then begin sweeping the area where the table I just loaded up used to be. Time to do some rearranging then look at the pieces I have waiting in the shop to fill the empty space.

Out of my peripheral vision, I catch sight of a blonde head of hair walking past my window, and I jerk my head to the side, though my shoulders dip slightly when I realize it's the *other* super blonde Mitchell, Bellamy, walking down the street holding hands with Rusty Fuller. Sighing, I sweep up the collected dust and take it to the trash in the back then return the broom to its spot.

"Hey, Heather, I'm gonna head back to the shop," I say, looking to my store manager. "Gimme a call if you need anything before close, okay?"

She beams at me. "Sounds good. Thanks, Reid."

I spin and step through the back door, back into the alley that stretches behind all the Main-facing stores, heading back toward my warehouse. I spot Busy at the end of the path, walking away from me over to the trash bins at the end of the lane, carrying a stack of cardboard.

I've been thinking of nothing else but our kiss since it happened. The taste of her tongue, the plump heaven of her lips, the way it felt to hold her in my arms and press her against me. Kissing her was one of the most gratifying moments of my life.

And the greatest mistake I could ever make.

It's one thing to imagine how it would feel to hold a woman you have developed feelings for in your arms. It's quite another to hold her and then have to let her go.

Busy chucks the cardboard into a large green bin then dusts off her hands before she spins around to head back, her movements easy and relaxed, until her eyes lock with mine. She freezes for a second, like a scared cat, before she waves and gives me that fake smile.

"Hi, Reid. You surviving the heat?" she asks as we come to a stop right outside the back door of the bookstore.

I nod. "Barely."

Busy laughs. "Same. The forecast says it should dip again in a few days."

"I'm hoping for a summer storm to break the humidity some."

She clasps her hands together. "That sounds amazing. I hope you're right."

We stand there silently for a beat or two before she speaks again.

"Well, good to see you."

I nod. "You, too."

She walks past me and tugs open the door, heading back inside.

It's been two weeks since our kiss, and it's also been two weeks since things between us have felt the way they used to. Casual. Comfortable. Busy is friendly, sure—I think it's just in her nature—but the ease isn't there anymore.

Our interactions always feel a little forced, a little awkward, a little too much like friends who have caught feelings tiptoeing around each other for the sake of...something, though who the hell knows what. I want to say for the sake of the friendship, but I can feel that slowly sliding away from me. Like so many other things, it feels like it's slipping through my fingers, and I'm not sure there's much I can do to stop it.

When Nick invites me out for a beer with the guys at The Mitch on Friday night, I reluctantly say yes, knowing I need to get out of the house. When I sit down at a table with him, Jeremiah, Teddy, and Carlos, my hope is that I'll have a drink or two, laugh a bit, and break out of this weird funk I've been in for the past few weeks.

But two drinks becomes three, then four, and before I know it, my inhibitions are much, much lower.

And then Busy Mitchell walks through the door.

My eyes dip down to where she's wearing those cowboy boots and then slowly rise, taking in her frayed jean skirt and tight top that dips just enough in the front to hint at the tits I've been hyperaware of since that night on the dock. She doesn't see me as she strolls across the bar with both of her sisters, and for that I'm actually grateful. I don't know if I'd be able to handle seeing that fake smile aimed my way again. Not today.

It feels like my brain is split in two as I try to keep my attention at the table while simultaneously staying constantly aware of her as she moves about the room.

"Reid."

My eyes zip over to Nick, who is watching me intently.

"Yeah."

"You look like you're a million miles away," he says, chuckling, but I see the layer of concern there, too.

"Sorry, man. Just a lot on my mind," I say. And it's true. There's always a lot on my mind.

I try to shake it off and lean forward, pushing myself to focus more on the baseball game everyone's talking about. I mostly succeed, even if my eyes do flick Busy's way more than I normally would allow. Eventually, the other guys get up and head to the bar to order another round, leaving Nick and me at the table alone.

"So...what's going on with you and the Mitchell girl," he asks, leaning toward me on the table and—thankfully—keeping his voice low.

My brow furrows. "Nothing."

He pins me with a look.

"Seriously, nothing," I insist.

Because it's true. There is *nothing* going on between us, no matter how much I might wish that wasn't the case.

His eyes narrow and he takes a sip of his beer, then his eyes glance to the right, where I know Busy is posted up at the bar with Briar and Bellamy.

"It's interesting that nothing's going on when she keeps glancing over here."

Licking my lips, I debate with myself about looking over my shoulder to where she is. Eventually I lose the war and I turn, finding her glancing in my direction at the exact same time. Her eyes widen slightly and she gives me a tight smile then turns back around, facing the bartender who's chatting with Bellamy.

Nick scoffs, and when I look over at him, he's leaning back in his chair, his hands folded casually against his stomach.

"Sure. There's nothing going on. Not like she looked at you like she's seen you naked or anything."

"She hasn't seen me naked."

Nick watches me for a long beat. "But?"

Sighing, I lean forward. "We kissed on the Fourth of July."

One eyebrow rises high on Nick's forehead before a wide smile splits his face. "Holy shit. Nobody talks about a kiss like that unless the earth has fucking moved. You're falling for her."

I am. Which is what makes all of this feel…impossible.

"Just go for it, man. After that bullshit with Sarah, you deserve someone who will make you happy."

"Nick, I told you before. I'm not interested in starting anything up, with anyone. I wasn't kidding."

At that, he rolls his eyes. "And like *I* told *you*, there are plenty more fish in the sea. Hot ones. Frisky ones. Ones you take to bed and ones you take home to your mom." He shrugs. "But you can't just…be alone forever."

I take a long sip of my beer, wishing Nick knew the truth, wishing he understood the reason why I say I never plan to date or fall in love ever again. Nothing lasts forever.

"And once you hook a good one like her?" he continues, hitching his thumb in the direction of the Mitchell sisters at the bar. "You don't cut the line and let someone else go after her."

I look back at Busy at the bar. If only it were that simple.

Honestly, the best thing I can do for Busy is hope someone else *does* go after her, someone far better than me who can give her the kind of life she's dreamed of.

Not one…filled with complications and responsibility she can't even begin to imagine.

When Nick drops me off at home later, I'm what I consider to be just the right amount of buzzed. Just enough that I feel good, but not so much that I think I'll feel like trash tomorrow.

Perfect.

We'll see if I still feel the same way as I nurse my headache and achy body in the morning.

When I key in through my front door, I glance around, knowing instinctively that Sydney isn't in the house. I sigh then push out onto my deck and look over to Busy's, finding Sydney lying on the edge with her head resting on her paws, looking out at the water. Her head rises when she hears me, her tongue lolling out of her mouth.

"Am I ever going to be able to leave you at home without worrying you're going to escape?" I ask, dropping down into my seat and patting my lap. "Or are you just going to keep doing this for the rest of your life?"

Sydney pushes up—reluctantly, it seems—and slowly heads my direction. Once she's finally stopped between my legs, I reach out with both hands to scratch her head.

"Try to at least *act* like you're my dog, okay?"

My eyes flick up when a light comes on outside the green cabin, illuminating the red decking and spilling down the steps, fading as it gets closer to the dock. A few beats later, I hear Busy singing and Junie laughing, and I smile, imagining them dancing around in their living room.

Sydney's head perks up at the sound of Junie's voice, and she looks at me, silently asking for permission. I should take her inside. I should *also* do a better job of trying to find out how she's still getting out on the days I leave her at home, but I have remained almost gleefully ignorant.

"Go ahead," I mumble, watching as she leaps off my deck and heads excitedly over to Busy's, where she stands at their screen door waiting, her tail wagging.

I remain in my seat, trying to pretend I'm not itching for an excuse to go over there and bring her back home.

"Sinny!" Junie's sweet voice cries out, and then I hear the screen door open.

Busy steps outside, letting Sydney into the house, a smile on her face when she glances my way.

"She heard Junie and ran right over," I call out, chuckling. "I'm not even sure she's my dog anymore, to be honest."

"She's definitely Junie's dog now," Busy replies, letting the screen door close and crossing a few feet toward me. "Can't say I hate it, especially when Junie needs to run off some of her energy. Grandma decided to give her a sugar cookie about an hour ago." She holds up her hands, her fingers crossed. "Hoping it'll wear off any minute."

She turns and looks out at the water, tucking her hands into the back pockets of her skirt, and goddamn she's beautiful. I try not to notice. Really, I do. But it's nearly impossible not to see it on a regular night. With several more beers than normal warming my blood, I don't have a chance at keeping my eyes to myself.

God, I wish things were different, wish I could hold her and love her and protect her the way she deserves. I hate that I broke something between us, something I didn't realize I wanted or needed from someone until I had it and then it was gone.

I hate that I'm broken, too.

"I'm sorry," I say, just loud enough for her to hear it.

And I know she does, because her body grows rigid.

"You don't have to apologize, Reid," she replies, turning to give me that same tight smile.

"But I do. Because…things aren't the same, and that's my fault."

I feel like a whiny shit saying that, but it's the fucking truth. I want my friend back. I want those soft smiles and easy conversations and the laughter. God, I want the *laughter* back.

"It's nobody's fault, Reid." She shakes her head and crosses her arms, looking back out to the water. "It's just life. We're still friends."

Friends.

God, I fucking hate that word, hate it with depths I didn't know I had, but I can't be upset at her for it. She's doing what any woman in her position would do: protecting herself, walling off her heart from me because I made her believe she had to. In reality, as her *friend*, I should be proud of her for what she's doing.

Instead, I'm stewing in my own agony, my own desire, my own…fear.

That's really what it is: fear. It's fear of losing her as a friend because I can't provide her with more, and the worst part is there's nothing I can do to change it.

After a little while, when the giggles stop, Busy pokes her head back inside then disappears, only to reappear a few minutes later with Sydney trotting along at her side…and a bottle of wine in her hand.

"They were snuggled up in Junie's bed together," she says, crossing over to my deck then dropping down in the chair next to mine. "It was super cute."

Busy takes a sip from her wine bottle then extends it in my direction. I blink twice, wondering if maybe I had more to drink than I first thought. Is she really here right now, shooting the shit like nothing's wrong?

I reach out and take the bottle from her hand then tilt it back for my own sip.

"I'm thinking it might be time to get a couch," she says, settling into her seat and lifting her bare feet up to rest on the small coffee table, crossing her legs at the ankle. "I'm kind of done sitting on the ground, you know?"

Because I've had a few drinks, it takes a minute to understand what she's doing, what she's giving me. And when I realize, my heart breaks a little bit.

Busy is giving me her friendship. Opening up her heart to me again, even though I don't deserve it.

"I think that's a great choice. Especially because I'm starting to have a hard time getting up off your floor. These knees aren't what they used to be."

At that, her head falls back and she giggles, the sound one of the sweetest things I've ever heard.

"You're not *that* old."

I shrug, take another sip from the bottle, and pass it back her way.

It's hard to rein in my smile for the rest of the night.

chapter fifteen
busy

I scroll through the photos on my phone, marking a few as favorites that I want to get printed so I can put them up around the house. I've been considering pulling my camera out of the closet, where it has been collecting dust since the day we moved in, so I can start capturing things that inspire me. There's something inside me brewing, though I don't know what it is, and I think it might be time to *jump into the water.*

It's kind of scary, though, considering what that might look like. I'm sure there are plenty of people who would roll their eyes and tell me to get over it. Just grab your camera and start snapping. What's the worst that could happen?

But there are many worsts, in my mind.

What if my inspiration has been sapped, and I realize I can never create again?

What if I get distracted from Junie and something bad happens?

What if the skills I've been honing for years have somehow

disappeared?

What if I waste money on getting something printed and then I'm in a tight spot financially and the photo sucks anyway?

What if...

What if...

What if...

When I think about it too hard, for too long, it just feels really crippling. Debilitating. Like I'm frozen in indecision because of how many things could go wrong.

But then I remember the way Reid looked at me when he gave Junie her rocking horse, his thoughtfulness in leaving it unvarnished so I could add some *personality*, as he called it. Maybe I start there? Buy some wood paint and...but then I'd have to spend money. Maybe I take my camera out on a lunch break one day and see what happens?

I groan, my mind walking in a circle—the same circle I've been going over—for what feels like the millionth time. The bell on the door jingles and I almost sigh in relief, thankful to get a distraction from my own inability to make a decision.

And then I smile wider when I see who walked through the door.

"Hi, girl," Marie says, walking right over to the counter.

"Hey!"

I step out from behind the register and give her a hug, surprised at how easy and natural it feels.

"Good to see you."

"You, too," she replies. "I've been meaning to come by for a while and I've just been so swamped with summer activities it keeps slipping my mind."

I wave a hand. "No worries. Kids are distracting."

"Don't I know it." Marie laughs, then her eyes track around

the store briefly before returning to me. "Hey, I know things have been on the chaotic side since the store opened, but I was hoping you knew the Friday morning invitation is perpetual. We do Mom-osas every week, and I'd love for you to come again sometime if you can."

I don't mean to make a face, but Marie must see something in my expression that gives me away. "Unless you don't want to," she adds.

"No, it's not that I don't want to," I tell her, truthfully. "I just…sometimes get people-d out."

Her expression softens. "I get that. Maybe we could do something just the two of us, then, with the kids? Or without them. I hope this doesn't come across as aggressive, but…I just really like you, and I want us to be friends."

My lips tilt up at the sides. "I would love that. Truly." I glance at the clock on the wall. "You know, if you're not up to anything now, I was going to take a break and go grab a smooth-ie from that stand over by the marina if you wanna join me?"

Marie nods, and I make quick work of popping into the back to let Briar know I'm heading out for a few minutes. Then I grab my purse and we head out.

"So how are things going with the bookstore?" Marie asks as we sip our smoothies, strolling along near the marina, slowly making our way back to Happily Ever After. "It *looks* beautiful inside."

"It's going really, really well," I tell her, pride swelling in my chest at everything Briar has done to bring her dream to life.

"I'm so glad to hear that. I saw the sign about the kids story hour in August, and I'm excited to bring Nina and Leo for that."

"I know! I'm gonna have my mom bring Junie. I think she'll love it."

We stop for a beat before crossing the street, waiting at the crosswalk as a few cars go by, and that's when I see her.

Sarah. Coming out of Cohen Custom.

I feel stunned to see her, but I don't know why. It just feels… like a smack in the face, somehow. Blinking, I realize I've come to a complete stop and Marie has gone a few paces in front of me before seeing she left me behind.

She turns, laughing. "You coming?"

Nodding, I quickly catch up, and we cross the street. But I realize when Marie sees Sarah, too, because she also slows slightly then lets out a long, dramatic sigh.

"What's wrong?"

Marie groans. "Oh just…" Her head nods toward where Sarah is walking in the opposite direction, staring down at her phone. "Those idiots."

"Sarah?"

She nods. "And Reid."

I lick my lips, suddenly desperate for any information Marie might be willing to share.

"What happened there?" I ask as we continue walking, nearing Cohen Custom and the bookstore. "I feel like nobody knows."

"Because nobody knows," Marie replies, chuckling. "One day, they were happy, the next, they were getting a divorce and saying they were just better off as friends. Like, who does that?"

A question I've asked myself multiple times.

"And what's even *more* ridiculous is the fact that Reid told his mom he just wants to be a single guy, never wants to date or get married again."

She chews on her straw, and my brain scrambles over that information, trying to filter it into what I know about Reid. He wants to be single forever?

And then, a truly selfish thought...maybe him ending the kiss wasn't because he wasn't interested in *me*. Maybe it's because he's not interested in *anyone*. A mild balm on the wound.

But then I remember the kiss itself, how incredible it was, how it felt like he couldn't stop touching me until suddenly, it was over. I can't imagine him not being interested in someone, not dating or getting married. Maybe he just wants to be a bachelor forever, sleep around, have fun. Though I've never noticed any women coming or going from his cabin. Still, it wouldn't be unheard of, even though he doesn't exactly seem the type.

"I mean, he's my cousin, but even *I* know he's a catch. And he's great with kids and just...unendingly kind."

All things I already know. Things I'm beginning to love about him.

I clear my throat, trying to shake away that thought before it settles, with no luck. That's not what I need to be thinking about Reid. He's made it clear. He doesn't want anything else to happen. He's not interested. The reason itself doesn't actually matter. Our friendship is all I will get, and that has to be enough.

It just has to be.

Even if it physically hurts.

"I'm planning a family dinner for Sunday night," Mom says as she finishes packing up Junie's diaper bag a few days later. "Does that work for you?"

I nod. "Yeah. We can come."

"Great. I'll let your sisters know." She zips up the bag then passes it over. "Hey, did you ever end up going back to Marie's for those mom dates she does?"

Sighing, I tug the bag onto my back. "I already told you, I'm not sure it's for me. I just…don't feel like I fit with a bunch of moms, you know? They're all married and in completely different places than I am."

The way her mouth pinches makes me think she doesn't like my answer, but I don't know what else to tell her. She's asked me twice since the first and only Mom-osa thing I went to last month, and I don't know what to say to get her to leave me alone about it, to stop pushing.

"I did get smoothies with Marie earlier this week, though. I really like her."

Hopefully that's enough.

Of course, at that news, my mother's smile breaks free. "Oh, well that's great. I'm glad you're at least giving that friendship a chance." She reaches out and tucks a piece of loose hair behind my ears. "I just want you to have some *friends*."

I roll my eyes. "I have friends, mom. You act like I'm some kind of town pariah."

She pinches the bridge of her nose. "Stop being dramatic, Busy. That's not at *all* what I said," she says with a sigh. "I feel like you find any reason you can to be upset with me."

My head jerks back. "What?"

I can't believe she would say something like that. *Me?* The one who is always mad at *her?*

"What are you even talking about?"

"I'm talking about the fact that I can barely even say anything to you anymore without you being angry with me," she tells me. "At some point, you decided every comment I make is a dig at you. It's like you've been mad at me for so long you can't even remember why."

I'm so shocked by her statement that I'm completely silent, trying to understand what the hell she's talking about. She can't possibly think *I'm* the one who is causing this tension. Can she?

"I don't know when things between us changed," she continues, bracing herself on the kitchen island, "or what I did that was so horrible, but I wish you would just…tell me so we can put it behind us."

"Put it behind us," I repeat, staring at her. "I told you I was pregnant and you barely spoke to me for a month."

Her mouth drops open. "You didn't tell me you were pregnant until you were six months along!" She laughs, but there's no humor there. "It was like you didn't even need me! Excuse me for taking some time to lick my wounds."

What?

I try to mull her words over, certain I must be misunderstanding because…

What?

Something in my face must convey the shock at what she's said, because she lets out a long sigh then speaks again.

"Every mother wants her daughter to need her, Busy," she says, bracing herself on the marble countertop between us. "I've always been proud of you—how independent you are, how you've always blazed your own trail. You've never let anything stand in the way of whatever you want in life, but…" She pauses, her eyes dropping to where Junie is still sitting on the floor, playing with a stack of plastic blocks. "I guess I always assumed when you became a mother, that might be the time when you'd lean on me. I thought you might, I don't know, need me a little bit."

The vulnerability in what she says shakes me, and I drop down onto one of the bar stools at the island, feeling surprised and shocked and emotional in a way I wasn't expecting.

"You're my mom," I tell her, my voice quiet. "Of *course* I need you."

Her head tilts to the side, sadness in her eyes. "Sometimes, I'm not so sure."

I glance around, suddenly feeling desperate to explain this to her but worried I don't have the words.

"Do you want to know why I didn't tell you I was pregnant until I was six months along?" I ask, though it's more of a rhetorical question. "Why I waited to tell everyone? Because I couldn't muster up the courage to say I'd fucked up again, and this time, there was no going back. No 'fixing it'."

Her shoulders fall.

"I've always been the one getting in trouble or breaking the rules or screwing things up and I just…" I shake my head. "This felt too big."

My mom reaches forward and places her hand on mine. "Nothing is too big," she whispers. "Nothing is bigger than how much I love you."

I watch her for a long second before I speak again, and when I do, I can barely get the words out as tears threaten to spill down my cheeks. "It doesn't always feel that way."

It takes only seconds before my mom is rounding the island and wrapping me up in her arms, holding me tight in a way she hasn't done—in a way I haven't let her do—since I was a child.

"And that's *my* fault," she tells me, rocking us slowly back and forth as she holds me close. "That's my fault, Little Bee."

I cry into her shoulder, wishing I had just…talked to her

sooner so we wouldn't have this chasm between us, this open space we need to bridge. This thing has made us both brittle in how we talk to each other, how we act with each other for the past few years.

"I think I was so focused on what I wanted I didn't even think about what you were going through." She presses a kiss against my temple. "I'm so sorry."

We embrace for a long time, so long that eventually Junie walks over and wraps her arms around my legs. "I'n a hug," she says.

I let go of my mother and reach down to pick Junie up then wipe at my face, drying a few of the tears that have fallen free.

"Moms are imperfect," my mother says, tucking some of Junie's hair behind her ear, just like she did to mine a few minutes ago. "Even if we screw things up, we *never* stop loving you." She leans in and kisses my temple again. "That's a promise."

chapter sixteen
reid

"So what are you doing with this stuff?" Nick asks, grabbing one end of the couch and lifting it as I lift the other.

"Just doing a few deliveries."

I walk forward as he walks backward, moving the piece out to the trailer I have sitting outside the shop. Once we've gotten it in, I shift it slightly, adjusting the padding before scooting the couch snug against the railing.

"Since when do *you* do deliveries," he asks, chuckling. "I thought you hired people to do that."

I wrap the strap around the couch then begin to cinch it so everything is held snugly in place.

"Normally, I do."

Finished with the couch, I hop down from the trailer and head back into the shop, motioning to the coffee table that's sitting on one of the lower racks.

"So what's different about these?" he asks. "You sleeping with the customer or something? Providing a little...extra service."

He laughs, but when I pin him with a look that says I don't find it funny, his jaw drops slightly.

"Wait, *are* you? Because I was just joking, but…"

"I'm not sleeping with the customer," I tell him, rolling my eyes. "I'm not sleeping with *anyone*."

The last part I mumble more to myself, but I know Nick still hears it.

We pick up the coffee table and get it loaded into the trailer, but once I've finished getting it tightened up and jumped down, he asks again.

"So, what's the deal?"

I don't want to tell him the pieces are for Busy, because he's already highly suspicious of our friendship. Nick has made comments on more than one occasion about how much time Busy and I spend together, and I don't want to add fuel to the fire. But I know if I don't tell him, it'll become a thing, and that might even be worse. Besides, he's going to find out eventually.

"They're for Busy," I say, shutting the tailgate and dropping the pin in place to keep it secure. Then I glare at Nick, who is looking at me with his eyebrows high on his forehead. "Don't make it a bigger deal than it is."

He's quiet as I head back inside the shop and gather up a few tools to return to the toolbox in my truck then drop the wide rolling door and lock up. For a few seconds, I wonder if he might actually let the subject go. We hop into the cab of my truck and pull slowly out of the parking lot.

"Come on, man, *what* is going on with you two?" he asks, chuckling as we turn onto Fourth Street. "I mean, first you guys are eye-fucking at The Mitch, and I know you're hanging out a lot. You said you hooked up—"

"Kissed. *Once.*"

"—but what gives?"

I flick my blinker, staying quiet until we turn onto the main road.

"Look, I care about Busy. If I decide to give her a few pieces of furniture so she isn't sitting on the fucking floor of her living room anymore, that's what I'm gonna do. Is that okay with you?"

Sighing, Nick nods. "Yeah, yeah. Fine."

"I get that you're just looking out for me," I tell him, patting him on the shoulder. "And I appreciate it, but Busy and I are fine. Promise."

"Fine, man. If you say so."

We move on, shooting the shit about the recent A's game while we drive out to the cabins. We unload everything and bring the couch around to the back, where I know Busy keeps her screen door unlocked. Then we carefully maneuver the piece inside and get it set up in the center of the living room, facing the wall where most people would probably set up their TV.

"You're right. She *does* need some fucking furniture," Nick jokes, his eyes scanning around the living room. "You think she'll be happy about the fact that you're giving these to her or pissed?"

I chuckle as we begin walking back out to the trailer for the coffee table. "Oh, definitely pissed."

Nick laughs. "I'll be honest, I'm not sure I would want to see Busy Mitchell angry."

I think back to the night we first met, knowing it wasn't anger I saw on her face when I approached her in the dark, but fear. Sometimes the two can look fairly similar, though, so it's the only thing I have to go on.

"Well, I'll just remind her that she broke into my place and now I've broken into hers," I tell him as we get the coffee table set up in front of the couch. "So now we're even."

He shakes his head. "Do I want to know *that* story?"

I smirk at him. "Doesn't matter if you do. I promised her I'd keep it a secret."

"See, that's what I don't like," he says, crossing his arms as I close Busy's screen door. "You shouldn't be keeping secrets from me. I'm your best friend."

"And you don't keep secrets just between you and Claire?"

The question is out before I realize what I'm implying, but Nick catches it immediately, his head rolling back just slightly.

"You mean between me and my wife of eight years?" he asks, laughing. "Of course I do."

Sighing, I lead us back out to the front. "You know what I mean."

"Actually, I don't," he replies. "Because it sounds a lot like you're comparing your relationship with Busy—a woman you've known for a few months who you claim is just your friend—to the one I have with my wife." He pins me with a look that says he caught me.

And he did. He did catch me.

But what am I supposed to say?

I have feelings for Busy that are far more than the platonic ones I *should* have? I wish with everything inside of me we could have more than just friendship? Admitting those things out loud, to anyone, would be almost as bad as the fact that it's exactly how I feel.

"Maybe just think about it," he continues, tugging the passenger door open. "Dating her, I mean. Besides, what's the worst that could happen?"

I chuckle to myself, but it rings hollow.

Because the worst has already happened.

It's almost seven when I hear Busy's car pulling up on the gravel drive outside, her brakes squeaking just slightly as she comes to a stop. I lie stretched out on my couch, baseball on the TV, though now I can barely focus on it knowing she's going to walk into her house and see the furniture I set up. Honestly, I really have no clue how she's going to react.

Only a few minutes go by before I hear her screen door and then the heavy thuds of her footfalls first on her porch then mine. I know without a doubt those are not happy steps.

"Why is there furniture in my living room?" she asks, standing at my screen door.

I look over my shoulder, finding her with her hands on her hips, confirming my earlier assumption.

"When I told you I was considering getting a couch, I wasn't asking you to give me one."

Sitting up, I nod. "I know that."

"So then…what? What made you decide to give me furniture, and don't even try to deny it, because I *know* a Cohen Custom piece when I see one."

I have to work hard to hide my smile at that, because it was very much a compliment. Knowing Busy can spot my work—my family's legacy of work—bolsters something in my chest.

"I normally move a lot of pieces over the Fourth of July holiday and sales were just super slow this year," I tell her, having come up with this plan before I even asked Nick to help me load up the trailer. "These are some of the ones I was hoping to get rid of that didn't sell, and I was thinking maybe you and Junie might like to have them."

She's already shaking her head before I'm finished.

"I appreciate that Reid, really." She crosses her arms. "But I can't afford these, even if you do a wildly deep discount. And there's no way I would accept them for free."

I raise an eyebrow. "Why not?"

She scoffs. "Because."

"Because why?"

"What do you mean *because why*? Because…it's far too generous."

Sighing, I push up from the couch and cross over to the screen door. Then I shove it open. "You can come inside, you know. You don't have to stand out there."

"I'm serious, Reid," she continues, stepping in, her face awash with frustration.

"So am I," I reply. "You're doing *me* a favor. If you came to my shop, you'd see how many pieces there are that I need to unload. I need to make space for other projects."

Pinning me with a look, she rests her hands on her hips. "You're full of shit."

I laugh. "I'm *not*."

Nick said he wouldn't want to see Busy Mitchell mad, but I don't mind it all that much. She's fucking cute as hell, her fists clenched at her sides, the divot between her eyebrows growing more and more pronounced with each thing she says.

"Besides, the one I gave you is totally run down and I absolutely can't sell it."

Busy purses her lips, her head tilting to the side, clearly unimpressed. "Now I *know* you're full of shit."

At that, my lips tilt up at the sides. "Maybe a bit."

She sighs, rubbing her hand against her forehead, her eyes glancing around my cabin before finally returning to me.

"Will you let me pay you?"

I shake my head. "Not a chance in hell."

"Why are you doing this? Did you think I couldn't figure it out on my own?"

At that, my teasing expression falls. "Absolutely not, Busy." I step forward, wishing I could take her hands in mine. "This is not about thinking you can't do it. This is just...about wanting to help."

I don't like that she thinks this is some sort of charity thing, or that I don't believe she's a capable person, or worse, if she thinks I think she's a bad mom. That's not at *all* what this is about.

"I'm so tired of accepting everyone's help," she finally admits, her shoulders falling.

I wince, realizing maybe I've touched on a wound and caused more of a problem when what I was *trying* to do was solve one.

"Look, I didn't mean to upset you," I tell her. "If you want me to take the pieces back to the shop, I can. But when I tell you I want you to have them, I mean it. This isn't charity. This isn't me thinking less of you or not believing in you. This is just me, being your friend."

I pause.

"And selfishly wanting to come over without killing my knees."

Her lips tilt up at the last part, and I breathe a tiny sigh of relief, knowing I've at least made her smile.

"How about...you take the couch, and in exchange, I let you pay me for Junie's swimming lessons?"

At that, Busy makes a face. "That's not even close to the same."

"*But*, I'll let you do it and I'll stop arguing with you about it. And wouldn't that feel amazing?"

We've been in a major disagreement about Junie's swim lessons for at least two weeks, mostly because I've been refusing to let Busy pay me. I figure I've got the free time and it's getting me back into the water I've been avoiding for so long, but she doesn't see it that way.

She sighs. "You're not going to let me win this, are you?"

My nose wrinkles. "I'm not going to say *no*, but I'd say it's very unlikely."

Busy scratches at the back of her neck for a second, thinking something over before she sticks out her hand. "Fine, I'll keep the couch if you let me pay you for swimming lessons *and* you let me feed you once a week for the rest of time."

I chuckle at the dramatic stipulation, foreseeing a lot of blue box pasta in my future. Then I take her hand in mine and give it a shake. "Deal."

"*And*, I have a gift for you."

At that, my eyebrows rise. "What?"

She turns then and exits my cabin, the screen door closing behind her. After a few seconds, her face appears again. "Are you coming?"

Laughing, I follow in her wake, Sydney at my heels as we head outside then cross over to the green cabin.

"Misery!" Junie calls out when she sees me at the door. Then she puts her hands on her hips. "Where Sinny?"

Sydney runs inside and Junie squeals with excitement, the two dashing into Junie's room to play like they so often do.

"I'll be right back," Busy says, disappearing down the hallway toward her room for a beat and leaving me alone in the living room.

I drop down onto the deep green leather couch Nick and I delivered earlier today, sighing when I settle into it so comfortably. This might be one of my favorite pieces I've ever created— part of a line of green leather furniture I've been developing over the past year or so—and I can't imagine a better place for it than in Busy's home.

"Okay, so…now that I have it in my hands, it feels a little ridiculous," Busy says, walking out from the hallway and rounding to stand in front of me. She's holding something small and rectangular pressed up against her stomach.

"Well now I can't wait to see whatever it is," I tell her, grinning.

Busy sighs then looks down at the item before she hands it over, her cheeks turning pink.

It's a framed photo of me, Busy, Junie, and Sydney from our hike to Washburn Trail, a selfie she took with her phone while we were all sitting on the bench together, looking at the view. But it's not *just* a photo. She added to it, defining some of the negative space and painting pine trees and wild geraniums into the image in splashes of gold.

The imagery is stunning, and I have a feeling this is just a small taste of what Busy can do when she allows herself to jump into the water.

"If you don't like it, you don't have to put it up anywhere. I promise I won't be upset," she tells me.

I look back up at her, raising an eyebrow. "Are you kidding? This shit is going on my shelf."

It's hard not to miss the look of relief that sweeps over her at my words. My eyes drop again, and I look at the image, my thumb sweeping over it, tracing the image behind the glass.

"It's incredible," I tell her, my voice reverent. "Thank you so much for taking the time to make it for me."

When she doesn't respond, I look at her again, finding her watching me with a kind of glazed look for just a beat before she shakes her head slightly and takes a step back.

"I'm glad you like it," she tells me, rounding the couch and heading into the kitchen. "Now…I was going to make peanut butter and jelly sandwiches tonight, but I know you love mac and cheese. Any preferences?"

I chuckle quietly to myself.

"I'm down for whatever," I tell her, shaking my head, unable to erase the smile on my face. "It all sounds good to me."

chapter seventeen
busy

She's fucking swimming.

Swimming!

My Junie.

Okay, maybe not swimming like with backstrokes or anything, but she's learned to float on her back unassisted and knows how to doggy paddle over to the dock on her own from a few yards away.

Watching Reid with her went from one of the most terrifying things I've ever seen during that first session in the lake a few weeks ago to something that fills me with pride and joy every time I see her in the water. Obviously, being vigilant about Junie's safety is of the utmost importance, but I didn't realize how much anxiety I was holding on to by living near the water until I felt more sure that if Junie were to fall in for some tragic reason, she wouldn't sink like a stone.

And it's all because of Reid.

Junie launches herself off the dock and into the water. Unlike that first time we all got together, Reid is floating a foot or two away from where she lands, waiting for Junie to emerge with her goggles and begin paddling. Which she does, like the budding Olympian she is.

"Mommy, you see?" she calls out once she's in Reid's arms and he's hoisting her up so she's standing on his shoulders.

"I did see, baby!" I call out from where I'm seated on the dock, my legs crossed.

"I'n a big girl!"

"You are!"

She shrieks then jumps off his shoulders and into the water, emerging again, her tiny body bouncing rapidly as she treads water and makes her way back to Reid.

"I might have done something bad," Reid tells me, grinning sheepishly as Junie clings to his shoulders, trying to climb back up to her perch with little care about where she puts her feet.

I chuckle, watching the circus. "And what did you do?"

"I bought a window unit and installed it in my bedroom."

My mouth opens, my eyes wide. "Shut up."

Junie jumps again, making a big splash, some of which lands on me, but I hardly notice.

"Lois is going to chew me out, but I don't care," he says. "We're supposed to get another heat wave in the next week or two and I'm not going to lie in a pool of my own sweat again. I'm just not."

I give him an imaginary fist bump. "I'm so happy for you and not at all jealous."

Reid laughs. "You're welcome to come over any time."

I nod, though I doubt I'll take him up on his offer. As great as things have been over the past few weeks, I have to be careful about how closely I skirt that line that exists between us, the one that separates things that friends do and things that lovers do.

People who are dating hang out at their boyfriend's house. Friends sit on his porch.

People who are in love go out on dates in town. Friends go swimming then eat neon mac and cheese.

It's becoming a thing I ask myself any time we're together: Is this something I would do if I wasn't half in love with him?

Because, try as I might, I've realized I've been falling for Reid Cohen. If anything, it's only gotten worse over the past few weeks. I say worse because there is nothing more hellish than unrequited love, a new truth I've had to learn.

And the thing I keep going around and around in circles about is the fact that it doesn't *feel* unrequited in the slightest. It feels very much requited. In the way he talks to me, the way he looks at me, the way he smiles in my direction and how his eyes flick over me as I walk his way. It's been an infuriating reality I've had to come to accept even though I don't understand it, and that is my least favorite thing in the world. The last thing I am going to do is ask him about it. What am I going to say?

Are you sure we can't be together? Because you look at me like you want me.

Gag. Talk about desperate.

So I'm just trying to focus on how grateful I am for his friendship and how he treats Junie, even though each day is an exercise in ignoring how much I want to climb him like a tree. It doesn't help that I can't *handle things* on my own, either. And I have *tried*. Continuously. With practically no success. It makes me think I need to revisit the idea of going out and finding a one-night stand, someone who can just…handle things for me.

But then I see Reid with Junie and I realize some of what makes me want him so badly is just…*him*. I want *him*, not someone to *handle things*. And then starts the vicious circle all over again, and I shove my face into my pillow and scream because it's so infuriating.

God help me.

"Hey listen, my aunt and uncle are doing a barbeque at the beach park tomorrow to celebrate their anniversary, and Marie wanted me to invite you." Reid swims closer to the dock, Junie's arms wrapped around his neck as he drags her behind him. "Junie could play with Leo and Nina."

I lick my lips, thinking it over. Is this something people who are dating would do? Or something friends do?

What if it's both?

"Will it be weird for Lois since I'm her tenant?" I ask.

Reid scoffs. "Not at all. *I'm* her tenant, too."

"But you're family."

He shrugs as he helps Junie climb up the ladder. "So? Everyone in town is family. That's just what small towns are."

I purse my lips and give him a look. "You know what I mean. I don't want it to be weird." I pause. "Or for anyone to get the wrong idea."

I say the last part slowly, dipping my toe into the topic we don't address.

"I know, and it won't be weird." He shoves back from the dock, drifting a few feet away. "At least say you'll think about it."

"I'll think about it," I agree, just as Junie flies past me.

God, the girl has a never-ending energy source stowed in that tiny body.

"But if it gets weird I'm diffusing things by telling everyone you smuggled in an illegal air conditioner."

Reid gasps, his hands out as he waits for Junie to swim to him. "You wouldn't."

I cackle, unable to help myself. "I so would."

"Traitor," he grumbles, though there's no heat behind it. "Come on, Junie. Let's splash your mom."

My eyes widen, and before I can do anything about it, Reid is shoving a wall of water in my direction, the splash hitting me and drenching my clothes.

"We got her!" Junie calls out, raising her little fist in the air.

"Yeah, we did," Reid says, and then the two of them give each other a high five, laughing maniacally.

And just like every small moment that has come before, I fall a little bit more in love with him.

Shit.

When I pull my SUV into the parking lot at the beach park on Sunday afternoon, I expect there to be a pretty large group. If *everyone in town* is family, then *everyone in town* should be invited, right?

Clearly I'm mistaken, because even though there are plenty of people scattered along the shore, the only people hanging out around the pop-up tent are Lois and Paul's *actual* family. Marie, Craig, Nina, and Leo. Reid, of course, and Reid's mom, who I'm surprised to see since he speaks about her so rarely. The last time he mentioned her in passing, he said she was out in Hawaii with her 'new boyfriend', and by the way he said it, I assume he's not a fan of whoever the guy is. Though I don't see anyone else, so I'm also assuming the new boyfriend didn't come today.

Which makes me feel even *more* conscious of the fact that I'm here and definitely not part of the family. Before I can change my mind and hightail it home with a 'Sorry, not feeling great' text to Reid, he spots me and waves then begins to head in my direction, Sydney galloping ahead of him, her mouth wide and tongue flopping.

"I'm so glad you came," he says, holding my door as I step out onto the hot asphalt.

"Are you sure it's okay that we're here?"

"Of course."

He says it so matter-of-factly, like I should know how obviously normal it is for me and my daughter to come to a family beach day with the Cohens.

Reid flicks the wide-brimmed hat I have on, smirking. "Like the hat."

I roll my eyes. "I look like a Canadian Mountie, but I've had a few too many sunburns in my day to risk it."

I head to the back to grab my beach bag as Reid rounds to the other side of the car and tugs the door open.

"Hi Junie Bee!"

"Misery!"

I can't help but smile at the two of them, and I hoist my bag over my shoulder as Reid unbuckles Junie and helps her climb out of the car, where Sydney promptly licks her in the face. The three of us—four, if you include Syd—walk together over to the tent, and I get a round of hellos from everyone and several hugs. Then I set up my chair and drop down, tugging out some sunscreen and calling Junie over. She pouts and heads my way, standing between my legs with a sour expression as I slather every inch of her exposed skin.

"Trust me, baby girl, I know how you feel. But you will

thank me when you're older."

I remember my mother saying similar things to me and my siblings as she covered us in thick white sun protectant. It means almost nothing when you're a child. The second I'm done, Junie sprints off to where Leo and Nina are building castles down by the water.

"Beer?"

I glance up at Reid as he sets up his beach chair next to mine, and I nod, accepting the cold can he passes my way. Cracking it open, I take a long sip before tucking it in the cup holder in my chair.

"I can't wait for summer to be over."

"Same," I reply, leaning my head back and closing my eyes as I slip on a pair of sunglasses. "I wasn't built for the heat or the humidity or the sun. Give me scarves and hot chocolate and rainy days."

Reid hums. "Fireplaces and cider and a crossword puzzle."

"Bookstores and pumpkin patches."

We look at each other then lift our beer cans to cheers.

"But I will say, I *am* looking forward to Summerpalooza."

I scoff. "It's the best event in town." Then I gasp and grab Reid's arm. "I'll be old enough to drink this time."

His jaw drops and then he bursts into laughter.

I narrow my eyes. "What?"

Reid just shakes his head, still chuckling. "I just…keep forgetting how young you are."

"I told you, I'll be 23 in October…"

"23 in October, I know, you mentioned that," he says at the same time. "But in my head, you're closer to my age. Not…still excited to drink at a town event."

I roll my eyes. "I didn't come home at all last summer, and

that would have been my first summer when I was old enough."

"And you didn't do what every other kid did and just…sneak into the beer garden?"

"Mitchells can't sneak anywhere," I reply, smirking. "Everyone knows what we're doing all the time. I bet people are already talking about the fact that I'm here with you."

His brow furrows, like he hadn't ever considered that thought before. Before he can say anything else, Junie is racing over and grabbing his hand, begging him to go swimming with her.

"I'll be back in a few minutes," he says as Junie drags him off toward the water.

I watch for a few minutes, sipping my beer, then Tabitha drops down in the chair Reid just vacated.

"Good to see you today, Busy," she says, a bright smile on her face.

"Hey, Mrs. Cohen."

"Oh, honey, call me Tabitha, please."

I chuckle. "Okay, Tabitha."

She's already asked before, but my good manners will dictate that I refer to her as Mrs. Cohen the next time I see her. My mother drilled *that* into my head early.

We sit quietly, side by side, watching Reid and Junie in the water. She's doing their routine—climbing up on his shoulders, jumping off, then swimming back—and they both look like they're having a blast.

"He's good with her, your daughter." Tabitha glances at me. "You said her name is Junie?"

I nod. "Yeah. And he's great with her, actually. But the real star of the show is Sydney. Those two are besties."

She hums. "So…are you two…together?"

Internally, I sigh. I assumed there might be some confusion

about our friendship the more we spent time together, especially in public spaces. Reid seems to think it's not a big deal, and I'm trying to follow suit, but it's hard to get asked if you're in a relationship with someone you have feelings for who just wants to be your friend.

"No. We're just friends."

"Yeah, that's what Reid says, too."

I shrug. "Life's complicated, you know?"

At that, Tabitha chuckles. "Oh trust me, I *am* aware." Then she sighs. "But part of me hoped he would get over this...silliness of what happened with Sarah and find someone who loves him the way you're *supposed* to in a marriage."

Her words flutter around in my mind, and I try to plug them into the holes in what Reid has said to me over the past few months. I've never pressed him on why he kissed me then pulled away, why he's not interested in a relationship. That's *his* business. But I have always assumed it had something to do with Sarah and why the two of them got divorced. Now Tabitha's confirmed it for me.

I want to ask her about it. Something tells me she's one of the few people who truly knows what happened between them, a rarity in a small town where everyone knows everything. For whatever reason, both Sarah and Reid have been completely mum about why they split. The few tidbits I *have* picked up are all barely blips on the radar and mostly result in one thing: they just decided it was better to be friends.

That fucking word. My new least favorite in the English language.

"Marie said he wants to be single forever," I say to her, hoping she'll provide some further clarification without me appearing too...desperate. "That was surprising to me."

Tabitha nods. "It was surprising to me, too. In some ways." She sighs. "In others, maybe I get it. But I know my son. Once he's set his mind to something, there's no changing it." She chuckles. "If there was a way I could convince him to change his mind about anything, it would be this. And that's coming from a woman who is desperate for her son to like the new man in her life, too."

She sighs again and returns her eyes to Reid and Junie in the water.

"Motherhood is the hardest thing you'll ever do with your life," she tells me, a truth I become more aware of with each passing day. "Especially when you have to let your children make their mistakes."

Junie's still too young for that to be true just yet, but the sentiment isn't lost on me. Especially when considering my relationship with my *own* mother, the trouble she's watched me get myself into over the years. She's always been there to dry my tears and then spin me right back around to meet the consequences of my actions, face first.

I think about our conversation last week. Maybe I need to give her a bit more grace. We're all human, after all.

Tabitha and I move on to less emotionally laden conversation topics after that, thank god—the bookstore, her recent trip to Hawaii, the renovations at Dock 7. It's a really nice chat, and I have to say, I really like Reid's mom.

A while later, Reid and Junie plod up to us from the water, and I tug out a towel just in time to wrap Junie in it before she collapses in my arms.

Tabitha pats me on the arm as she prepares to stand. "Enjoy these days, sweetie," she says, a kind smile in her eyes. "They don't last nearly long enough."

She pushes up out of the chair and nods at Reid before heading over to sit next to Lois at the picnic table a few yards away.

Reid finishes drying off then drops into his newly empty chair.

"Have a good chat with my mom?"

He says it casually, but I can tell there's curiosity there.

"I did."

He pulls out a fresh beer from the cooler next to his seat. "Talk about anything fun?"

My mind flits over the beginning of our conversation—Reid's decision to be single forever, briefly touching on his marriage, watching your children make mistakes—and I shrug.

"Just mom stuff."

Reid hums, and part of me thinks he doesn't believe me. That he knows Tabitha and I got into some much deeper topics than I'm being completely honest about.

But then he smiles and tilts his head back against his seat, closing his eyes.

"I might want summer to be over, but right now? This feels really nice."

I nod, tilting my head back as well, my heart feeling full with Junie snuggled against me and Reid at my side.

"Yeah. It really does."

chapter eighteen
reid

"I like her."

I glance at my mother then back out at the water where Busy and Junie are playing with an inflatable alligator.

"I like her, too."

"You know what I mean," she says, patting her hand on my knee. "I like her for *you*."

"Yes, mom. I do know what you mean. I just wish you'd stop meaning it." I take a sip of my beer. "And you're sure you didn't say anything about…"

"I said I didn't, Reid. Do you not trust me?"

Shrugging, I set my beer back in the indention on top of my cooler.

"I trust you."

"Good." There's a long pause before she speaks again. "Though I think you're making a mistake by not talking to her about it."

Sighing, I scratch at the stubble on my face.

"I already explained to you why I'm not sharing this with anyone. Alright? And I don't want to argue about this *every* time I see you."

She licks her lips and crosses her arms, her way of saying *Fine* without actually saying it.

After I got back from swimming with Junie, Busy became more quiet and reserved, which of course just made me suspicious about her conversation with my mother. She said they talked about mom stuff, but I'm not so sure. Even so, Busy hasn't mentioned anything about…anything, so I guess I just have to accept what she's said.

As the sun begins to dip in the sky, we all start packing up. The tent comes down and the chairs and coolers get tucked into the backs of cars. Hugs are exchanged. Then Syd and I hop into Busy's SUV with her and Junie and she drives us all back to the other end of the lake, the windows down and the breeze blowing the wild tendrils of her blonde hair.

I get what my mom means when she says *I like her for you*. Because I do, too.

For a long time, I thought my life was going to end up pretty much like anyone else's. Grow up, find someone I like, get married, have a few kids. Up until a few years ago, that was the direction I was moving in.

Sarah and I met in high school when she and her family moved to Cedar Point in the middle of our sophomore year. We were friends for years before one day, I was standing across from her at the coffee shop—where she was a manager at the time—and it occurred to me just how beautiful she was.

I asked her out that day. We moved in together inside of a year, and before I knew it, I was proposing and we were having a small ceremony in my parents' back yard. We weren't that young at 26 and 25, but there was definitely still a youthful kind of energy about us. We dated for three years before we got married, and we were married for three years before we got divorced, something I've always thought was interesting. Like it took us just as much time to fall in love as it did to fall out of it.

Though I guess that's not fair. We didn't fall out of love. Not really.

Now, I can look back and see that…maybe we weren't ever really that in love to begin with. Maybe it was more that we were convenient for each other, or we loved the idea of what love *could* look like, even if neither of us understood what kind of commitment it truly takes.

There's no way you can know when you promise for better or for worse if you really understand what it means, and when Sarah was faced with the realities of 'for worse' far sooner than she imagined, she took the out I gave her. Ultimately, I know it was for the best, but the truth of what it feels like to be abandoned is difficult. Challenging on the good days, devastating on the bad.

"You want to come over and watch a movie or something tonight?" I ask as I hoist the cooler onto my front porch then return to Busy's SUV to grab her beach chairs. "I have that nice new air conditioning," I add, sing-songing the last few words to sweeten the deal.

Busy laughs.

"And before you say no, remember that Junie is going to sleep like a rock, and you're going to be literally fifteen feet away with the baby monitor on at full volume."

She licks her lips as she unbuckles Junie from her car seat and helps her out, and I can tell she's at least *considering* it.

"Let me think about it," she says. "I'll see how I feel after I've showered and changed and gotten this one to bed, okay?"

"Sounds good. Just text me."

We say our goodbyes and head to our respective cabins, and I spend a good fifteen minutes getting the sand and dirt off of Sydney before I head inside to do the same for myself. There's something exceptional about rinsing off your body and washing up after a long day in the sun. The air feels more crisp and clean.

I make a quick chicken salad for dinner then do a brief walkaround to pick up some loose things here and there. When Busy's text comes in, I'm almost embarrassed by how quickly I yank my phone out of my pocket.

Busy: So what movie are we watching?

I grin then send off a quick reply.

Me: Your pick
Busy: Well I'm in for a rom-com, so buckle up

I chuckle and send a thumbs-up then head into the kitchen to throw a bag of popcorn into the microwave. I'm just dumping it into a bowl when I hear Busy's gentle knock at the screen door.

"Come on in," I call out, and I hear the door squeak as she walks inside.

"God it feels *amazing* in here," she says. "You weren't kidding."

"Right? Total game changer."

I glance over my shoulder to tell her I made a snack, but the words die on my tongue when I see her.

Fuck, she's gorgeous.

She's wearing a loose tank top and a pair of cotton sleep

shorts—nothing too scandalous. In fact, I've seen her in less, but something about seeing her in the outfit she probably wears to bed makes my blood begin to heat in my veins.

"Ooooh, popcorn," she says, dropping a small bag on the couch and stepping up to the island, a smile on her face. She picks up the box off the counter and examines it. "No salt, no oil, no butter." Her eyes rise to mine, an amused expression flickering behind them. "Going wild tonight, *Misery*."

I smirk and pick up a few pieces, chucking them in my mouth and letting out a dramatic *Mmmmmmm*. Busy laughs.

Picking up the bowl, I exit the kitchen and head to the couch. "I'll ignore your veiled insult against my popcorn."

She snorts as we both take a seat. "Veiled? I was being as unveiled as possible."

"I'll just keep this delicious treat to myself, then," I joke, tucking the bowl in the arm furthest from her and shoving another handful in my mouth.

"How will I *ever* recover?" she asks, just before tugging a bag of M&Ms from her own bag.

"Alright, sassy pants, let's just pick a movie, huh?"

We spend a few minutes browsing around, ultimately settling on one that came out earlier this year about a singer falling for an older woman. Not necessarily the vibes I would go for if I were enjoying a movie night on my own, but for Busy? I've got nothing but time to watch any romantic comedy she wants.

As the movie progresses, I find myself increasingly distracted by the woman next to me. First by that scent she's always wearing—I've determined it definitely *is* jasmine—then by the way she puts her hair up in a messy bun on the top of her head, exposing more of her skin that's been gently kissed by the sun.

She's the most beautiful woman I've ever seen. But it's not

just that she's beautiful—because that will fade. So much about our bodies fades over time. I know that better than anyone. It's also how kind and warm she is, how she's an amazing mother to Junie.

And the way I laugh with her is…well, it's second to none. Because I'm not a guy who laughs often, but with her I feel like I can't stop smiling.

"Are you even watching the movie?"

I blink, realizing in my haze of internal thought, I've been staring at Busy, and she's now staring right back.

Licking my lips, I nod. "I am."

Her lips tilt up. "Really? What just happened?"

Looking to the screen, I try to assess what's happening. "They are…taking their relationship public."

Busy laughs. "Lucky guess."

"Okay, so…I might not have been watching."

"Knew it."

"I was just thinking," I say, wanting to tell her how important she has become to me in such a short time but struggling to find the right words, "how lucky I am to have you as a friend."

I'm rarely that honest. I can't remember a time when I've *ever* said something like that to anyone, let alone a woman. It feels like a big deal for me.

Which is why I'm surprised when Busy's smile slips and she quickly looks away, back at the screen.

"Did I…say something wrong?" I ask, feeling confused.

She shakes her head then looks back at me. "Not at all. I'm glad we're friends, too."

But that fake smile is back, the one I thought we'd gotten rid of, the one that says she's not really being herself, not being honest. And the worst part about it is that I see sadness there, too.

I hate it.

We sit in a stilted silence for the rest of the movie, and I couldn't tell anyone what happened if they offered me a million dollars. Instead, I'm hyperaware of Busy next to me, her breaths and the way she sits with her bare feet on the edge of the sofa and her arms wrapped around her knees.

When the credits finally begin to roll, Busy stands like she's been waiting for it to end for hours, shoving the M&Ms she's barely touched back into her purse.

"Thanks for inviting me over," she says, giving me a tight smile as I stand. "I need to get back to Junie, so…"

"Busy, what happened?" I need to know. "Why did you… shut me out like that?"

"I didn't."

I raise an eyebrow. A flat-out lie if I've ever heard one.

I've never been the type to push when someone isn't honest. I tend to be a 'live and let live' kind of guy. If you don't want to be honest or want to keep your thoughts to yourself, that's your choice. I rarely share exactly what's on my mind with anyone.

But I have a feeling if I let Busy leave right now, she'll shut me out again, become that version that's friendly but distant. And that's the absolute last thing I want.

"Tell me what's going on in that head of yours," I say, my words softer than I feel inside. "I don't want you to leave upset."

She looks at me, clearly surprised. "I'm not upset."

"Really? So that fake smile was because…what?" I ask. "You didn't want me to know you hated the movie?"

"I didn't hate the movie. It was actually really good."

"Was it? I have no idea because I barely watched it."

"And that's my fault?"

I grit my teeth. "I feel like you're trying to pick a fight, and

I'm not trying to fight."

"Then what *are* you trying to do?" she asks.

"I'm trying to understand."

She growls and takes a step forward. "Fine. You want to *understand*? Sometimes, I smile even though I don't want to, and I'm your friend even though I don't want to be. Every day, I have to act like I don't want more from you when I do. *That* is what's going on."

I swallow thickly, not feeling any of the relief I thought I would feel at getting her to open up and be honest with me. Because now I know for sure exactly what is causing her to be disingenuous with me, and it's all my fault.

"*You* want to understand," she continues, stepping close to me. "Well I do too. How can we have this kind of relationship that we do, where we spend all our time together…how can you look at me the way you do and we can have the chemistry we do…and you just want to be my friend?"

She swallows and shakes her head, looking up into my eyes with an emotion I think I might be able to name if I were brave enough to do so.

"I don't want to just be friends," she whispers, her hand coming out to rest on my chest. "And I don't think you do, either."

I watch her for a long moment, my heart and my mind at war inside of me. One says to take what we both clearly want. The other tries to remind me just why I've attempted to avoid things like this in the first place.

But tonight, I don't have the strength to listen to that rational voice. Tonight, all I want is her.

I dip down, pressing my lips to hers, the relief I feel at that simple movement staggering to the point where I feel like I might fall over. And I do. I tug her with me to the couch, stretching my long body out and bringing her on top of me, never breaking our kiss.

And god, what a kiss it is. Her tongue tangling with mine, her lips plump and delicious, the little movements she makes. It feels like we're dueling, and I really don't care who wins.

My hands slowly trace down her back until I reach her shorts, where I pause only briefly before they dip down and grip the meaty flesh of her ass cheeks, groaning as she shifts her body against me.

God, I'm so crazy about her, so turned on by her in so many ways. From the tiny freckles on her shoulders that I pepper with kisses as I tug at the strap of her top to the way I can feel her moan as I suck on her neck.

Fuck.

And the way it feels as she grinds down against my cock, which is hard and aching for attention…

My mouth returns to Busy's, my hands on either side of her face, then one travels into her hair, tugging it down from the bun it's wrapped up in. It spills down around me, and I catch another breath of that jasmine scent I crave. I just want to breathe everything about her into my soul, lick up every part of her until she cries out my name.

My hand slips beneath her shorts, gripping her ass again and grinding her center against my dick, reveling in how she tosses her head back, moaning. And when I bring my other hand slowly along the outside of her leg, her eyes glitter as she watches me then droop when I lightly graze that soft skin of her inner thigh.

She licks her lip and pants gently as I bring a hand between us and slip a thumb through the leg of her shorts, stroking softly as I make my way to her core. When I get there, her head falls back as I move small circles around her clit through her panties.

"Fuck, Reid," she whispers, her hips beginning to move.

But I grip her hip, stilling her movements.

"Don't move," I tell her. "Let me take care of you."

She blinks a few times, but then her eyes close entirely as I begin those soft, circular movements again, as I get so close to where I know she wants me to touch, but just barely not the right spot.

"Reid, please," she begs, the words making me groan.

"Patience," I reply.

Her hands come to my shoulders, bracing herself as I dip my thumb down to where—*fuck*—I can feel that she's drenched. Then I slip my fingers past the damp material and swipe that wetness back up, finally rubbing at that bundle of nerves. Her fingernails dig into me, her mouth falling open and her hips beginning to rotate again.

"I'm so close." She whimpers, the sound the most delicious thing I've ever heard. She bends forward, pressing her lips to mine briefly before whispering, "So fucking close."

"I want to know what you sound like when you come," I tell her. "Give it to me."

Her eyes open at my words, her face inches from mine. "I'll give you anything."

My movements stutter, something in my chest feeling cut wide open. But I catch myself, adjusting my hand and slipping two fingers inside of her.

Busy cries out, something wild and desperate about it, and I only stoke inside of her for a few seconds before I feel her clamp down on me, her inner walls pulsing angrily as she finally falls over that peak. It's the sexiest thing I've ever experienced, and I can't help but want to recreate this scene, over and over again, for the rest of my life.

She collapses against me, panting as though she's just run a mile.

"Fuck, that was…" She trails off, pressing her face into my chest before she laughs.

I grin and wrap both arms around her, holding her tight against me. Then I shift us so we're lying on our sides, facing each other.

She watches me for a long beat, her eyes searching mine. "Kiss me," she says, her words aching with something.

Leaning down, I press my lips to hers. As hard as I am right now, I try not to pay it any attention. Because as incredible as this was, I can't let it go any further. I already fucked everything up by letting it go *this* far in the first place.

We kiss like that for a long while, slow and lazy and unhurried. She feels sated and warm tucked against me, and I try to soak it all up while I can. I run my hands along the soft skin of her arms, twisting my tongue leisurely against hers.

Despite all my best attempts not to, I have fallen wildly in love with Busy Mitchell. And now I have to break her heart.

She rests her head against my chest, one finger tracing a pattern over my ribs.

"I have to go back to my house, but…I mean…do you want to come over there? Stay the night?" she asks, then she rests her chin against the back of her hand, her eyes searching mine. "I don't have the good a/c, but I figure it's not so bad to be a little sweaty."

I watch her for a long minute, trying to come up with the kindest way to turn her down.

But before I can even say anything, Busy must see something on my face, because that soft, content look begins to drain away.

"You still just want to be friends, don't you?" Her voice is a whisper, but it's not really a question, because somehow she has learned enough about me to know what I'm thinking even though I haven't said a word.

"Busy, I…care about you so much," I start, emotion welling inside me.

I want to tell her the truth—that I don't just care about her, I *love* her…her and Junie—but I know if I do that, it will make all of this that much more difficult.

"God, I don't…" Busy pulls back, shaking her head. "What the fuck was I thinking?" she says out loud, her question clearly rhetorical. "I can't believe I…"

She shoves off of me, standing quickly and adjusting her top and shorts that were tugged in opposite directions.

"Nothing has changed for you, has it?"

A beat passes before I respond. "Nothing has changed, no."

She stares at me for a long minute, and I swear to god I've never seen someone look so wounded and then blink it away in an instant.

"I need to go."

"Busy, can we talk about—"

"No. No we absolutely cannot." Her words are firm as she grabs her bag and stomps away.

"Please don't leave angry."

"Well, how am I supposed to feel?" she replies, spinning around and glaring at me.

When I don't have a response for her, she presses her lips together.

"Exactly."

And then she storms out the door.

chapter nineteen
busy

I sit on my knees on the floor, looking at the camping gear scattered all over my childhood bedroom, trying to figure out what I'm going to use and what I can get rid of so I can make room for the things I need to bring for Junie. The Kilroy trip at the end of August will be my first time taking my kiddo on a real hike and overnight camping trip, so to say I'm feeling overwhelmed is an understatement.

Which is why I'm here, snooping through all my parents' gear instead of just using the sleeping bag and backpack that were tucked in my closet.

Every year growing up, our family has done the six-hour hike into the surrounding mountains, up to the top of Kilroy, to watch the most breathtaking sunrise over Cedar Point. For many years, it was my favorite trip, and I was always careful not to plan anything that conflicted with it because I wanted to make sure it was a priority.

Thankfully, my siblings all really enjoyed it as well—except for Boyd, who seems to finagle his way out of it on a regular basis—and each summer when we'd converge in Cedar Point together during the month of August, Kilroy was the one thing consistently on the docket of family activities.

Until I became pregnant and didn't come home for two summers, I was the one Mitchell to do every single hike. So this year, it feels of the utmost importance that I go, even if I have to miss out on the first part and drive to meet my family halfway up. Because let's be honest, no two-year-old is going to be manageable for a six-hour hike.

Since it will be the first time in several years that our entire family will be doing it together, it feels supremely important that I figure out how to make it work with Junie, sooner rather than later.

"Remember that one year when your father brought the really high-powered flashlight and it looked like he was sending out the bat signal?"

I laugh at the memory. "I told Bellamy if we had two we could have swooped them around like a movie premiere."

Mom laughs. "That's right. I think we were all lucky to get out of that weekend without going blind."

"Speak for yourself," I reply, leaning forward and grabbing an older backpack that has seen better days. "I think I still have a bit of corneal damage from when Bishop turned it on in our tent."

Setting that backpack in the 'do not need' pile, I continue looking at the array of items strewn about the floor.

"I'm glad you're going to be coming this year," mom says after a lull of silence. "It hasn't been the same without you there."

I glance in her direction, wrapping my arms around my knees. "Really?"

Her brow furrows. "Of course, really. We've missed you around here."

Part of me wants to default to the way I've been feeling over the past few years and tell her it didn't seem like she missed me all that much, but then I think back to our conversation from a few weeks ago, and I bite my tongue. Even if I might have felt that way, I know my family loves me, and I know my mother wouldn't say something like that if it wasn't true.

"It'll be really fun for Junie to get her first experience camping," I end up saying instead. "Not that she'll remember it."

Mom shrugs. "It isn't always about whether your kids remember every detail, though. I mean, what are you supposed to do? Ignore them until they're old enough to create memories?"

I chuckle at that. "Okay, that's fair."

"And even if your kids don't remember something, that doesn't mean the memory isn't meaningful for *you*."

At that, I actually get sort of choked up, thinking about what it will be like someday when Junie's older.

"What's it like, watching your kids grow up?"

I'm sure my question is out of left field, but if there's anyone who can talk about the different stages of kids, it's my mother. Having raised five of us, with a ten-year age span between her oldest and youngest, I don't doubt she's been through it all.

"Talk about a loaded question," she says, leaning to the side on my bed and resting her head in her hand. She hums and seems to think it over for a second.

I lean back against the dresser behind me, just watching as she stares unseeing out the window, surely scanning through a million different memories.

"Well, it's a lot of things. First, it's incredible, because you get to watch these little monsters you created slowly grow and morph and change. And, I'm sure you're seeing it with Junie, but how quickly they learn things is just…amazing. You feel so proud all the time because you're the one helping them learn those new things."

She tilts her head from side to side, considering.

"But then it's hard, too. It's hard to stay sane when you're getting no sleep and there is just…constant noise. It's hard to teach your children *how* to be those kind, considerate people you want them to become. It's hard to begin backing off so they learn independence and how to take care of themselves. And then it's *really* hard when you watch them make mistakes."

Her words echo a sentiment similar to what Tabitha said at the beach park last week, and, not for the first time, I wonder if, when my mother looks at me, she only sees the mistakes I've made.

"What has it been like for you, watching Junie?"

I scratch at my chin, thinking it over, realizing almost immediately what my mother means when she says it's incredible.

"I'm just so…astounded by her. All the time. I mean, the things she says, the way her brain works, how curious she is." I shrug, my hand playing with the zipper on a two-person tent. "It's amazing."

"*She's* amazing," my mom says, and I look up to find her watching me with a sweet smile. "And that's because she has an amazing mom."

My throat grows tight at her words, the realization of how much I've wanted to hear them only just now hitting me. I open my mouth, wanting to say thank you, to tell her how much it means to me, but feeling too choked up.

So I just nod and lick my lips.

After a beat or two, my mom slaps her thigh and pushes up

from my bed.

"Alright, well…I'll let you finish this," she says, tiptoeing between things until she makes it to the door. "I'm gonna go check on your father and Junie. I think he said they were gonna go sit on the dock, so that's where I'm headed."

"Sounds good," I finally reply.

She turns, but before she disappears, I call out to her again. "Hey mom?"

Her face reappears in the doorway. "Yeah?"

"Thanks."

Her lips tilt up at the sides, and I hope she knows I'm actually thanking her for more than just the camping gear.

Maybe someday, I'll learn how to say exactly what I mean.

I jog up the front steps and key into my cabin, stopping briefly to grab a package leaning up against the door. Then I'm wandering through the house, having left work on my lunch break to search for Junie's blanket.

The thing about toddlers that nobody prepares you for is how batshit crazy your child will be if their routine gets thrown off. I know all too well if Junie doesn't have her blanket when my mom puts her down for her nap soon, she won't sleep at all.

With no luck, I fill up a glass of water and drink it slowly, leaning against the counter, my eyes scanning the living room for something I missed. As I'm dumping it out, I spot Sydney on the porch.

"Hi sweet girl," I say, pushing my screen door open. "You just out here enjoying the sun?"

Sydney's head spins my way, her tongue flopping out and her mouth wide as I crouch down next to her. She rolls onto her back, exposing her belly, and I laugh, giving her really good pets.

"Always looking for tummy rubs, huh?"

I sit outside with Sydney for a good ten minutes before I head back inside, deciding to try one more time to find the blanket before I give up. Miraculously, this time, it's found—tucked between Junie's bed and the wall—and I let out a dramatic, victorious sigh.

Then I give my mom a call.

"Hey."

"I found it."

"Oh, thank goodness." I want to laugh at the relief in her voice, but at the same time, I know exactly how it feels. I keep my giggles to myself. "Last time we didn't have it, it took two hours to finally get her down."

"I remember."

I tuck the phone between my ear and my shoulder then grab the package that was at the front door and slice it open with a knife.

"I'm just gonna make myself a sandwich and I'll be…"

My voice fades as I pull out a bottle of pills and spin them around. There's a label with the name of some kind of medication but no patient name. I look back at the box, cringing when I realize it says Reid Cohen in big fat letters.

"Busy?"

"Sorry," I say, shaking my head. My voice is distracted, my mind still focused on the orange bottle. "I'll be there in ten minutes."

"Sounds good. See you soon."

"See you."

I end the call, rotating the bottle and reading the complicated drug name a few times before tucking the pills back in the box then leaving it on the counter.

I drop the blanket at my mom's and get back to the bookstore, and as the day continues, I find it difficult not to think about that orange bottle. It feels ridiculous, because there are any number of reasons someone might receive medication in the mail. Simple things. Uncomplicated things. It's probably something for migraines or blood pressure.

Eventually, though, I succumb to my curiosity and look it up...only to then feel even *more* curious. Why is Reid taking something to manage seizures?

By the time I get home after closing up the bookstore and picking up Junie, it's almost seven, and I have to move quickly to manage dinner and bath time and get my girl tucked into bed. As soon as Junie is asleep, I grab the package off the counter and head next door.

Reid and I haven't done more than say hello to each other since the night we fooled around on his couch, and that was a over a week ago. It's been understandably awkward since he basically gave me an orgasm then said nothing had changed.

Not basically.

That's *exactly* what happened.

What I *wasn't* expecting was for Reid to be the one to pull back. He's been distant, more than I would normally expect from him, and in some ways, it has been a relief. But in others, it's been...well, maybe not a nightmare, but definitely far from a dream.

I knock on his door, and when he opens it, his brow furrows.

"Why are you knocking on my front door?"

I chuckle awkwardly. "I don't know. I just...felt like that was what I should do."

He nods, his eyes falling to the box in my hands. I see the shift in his expression immediately.

"Is that my package?"

I glance down at it then thrust it forward, like I did something wrong by opening it when really and truly, it was just an accident.

"It got left at my door by mistake," I tell him.

"And you opened it?"

I nod. "I did. I'm so sorry. I was on the phone and I wasn't paying attention..."

"Obviously, or you would have realized it says my name, right here, in huge letters."

Blinking, I take a step back, surprised by his bristly attitude. I've never actually heard Reid...angry before.

"I said I'm sorry."

He scrubs at his jaw, the irritation evident in his every movement. Then he sighs.

"Thanks for bringing it over."

We stand there for a minute, and I war with myself. Should I ask him? Part of me knows I shouldn't, knows I've already violated his privacy, first by opening the package and *then* by searching for information about its contents.

But I have to know.

"Do you...I mean...that medication is for seizures, right?"

Reid licks his lips then chuckles, but there's absolutely no humor in it. "I'm assuming that's what it said when you searched online."

My response is slow as I try to read his mood. "It is."

He shrugs, his expression flat. "So then why are you asking me?"

Before I can say anything else, he shuts the door in my face.

When the bell over the door rings at the end of the day on Tuesday, I groan. The last thing I want is a slow-moving customer right before I'm scheduled to close up the bookstore, especially on the first rainy day we've had all summer. For whatever reason, the people who come in five minutes before close *always* move as slow as molasses, and all I want to do is head home and revel in the fact the recent heat wave finally seems to be on the verge of breaking.

"Is anyone here?"

"I'll be there in just a second," I call out, climbing up my step stool to add a few more books to the top.

Happily Ever After has a mixture of used and new titles, but the ones absolutely flying off the shelves are the romantasy titles. It isn't surprising, but it has been wild. Sometimes we get in a new shipment and customers will have cleared them all out within a few days. A great problem to have, especially as a new business.

Once I'm done, I hop down and return the stool to the closet in the back before walking up to the front.

"How can I help you?" I ask the blonde looking at biographies against the far wall.

When she spins around and I realize it's Reid's mom, the

previous disappointment at a last-minute customer fades away, and I smile.

"Oh, hi Mrs. Cohen!"

She returns the book in her hand to the shelf, her eyes wandering around the store, taking everything in as she heads my way.

"This bookstore really is something special. I wish this was here during any of the forty years I lived in this town," she says, coming to a stop in front of me. "And it's *Tabitha*."

"Sorry about that," I reply. "It's good to see you again. I didn't realize you were still in town. I assumed you were only visiting for Lois and Paul's anniversary."

She lets out a sigh. "Well, that's why I *was* in town. But I had a conversation with Reid the other day and I felt it was really important for me to come back."

My eyebrows rise. For a split second, I think maybe she's talking about what's going on with *me* and Reid, but just as quickly as that thought comes, it goes. Because that would be ridiculous right?

"Really? I hope everything's okay."

"It's not. And I think, primarily, it's because of you."

I bring a hand to my chest, my brows coming together. Even though I just contemplated the idea that it would be about me and Reid, nothing could have prepared me for the fact that that's actually why she's here.

"Excuse me?"

Tabitha steps forward and takes my hands in hers, her aging hands strong and her grip firm. "I'm just going to rip the Band-Aid off because there's no use tiptoeing around everything. Reid is in love with you."

My shoulders fall, relief coursing through me. I thought

something was *seriously* wrong, but this is something else entirely.

"I told you, Mrs. Cohen—"

"Tabitha."

"—we're just friends."

She rolls her eyes. "Busy, please don't insult my intelligence. I know my son, and I know he is head over heels in love with you, even though he puts on a brave face and tries to pretend he's not. The reason I know is because my boy wears his heart on his sleeve for everyone to see."

I want to tell her that's not the truth, but at this point, who the hell knows *what* the truth is. The way Reid talks to me, looks at me, touches me would lead me to believe what Tabitha is saying, but all I can go on are the things he *actually* says.

"I can't force him to do something he doesn't want to do," I finally say, being maybe a little bit too honest. "Regardless of how either of us feel."

Tabitha takes my hands in hers again. "But you have to."

I chuckle uncomfortably. "I can promise you no woman wants to have to convince a man to love her." I shake my head, my mind briefly flitting to Jay, even though I know these situations aren't similar in any way. "It is…probably the last thing I would ever consider doing."

"You don't have to convince him to love you, Busy." She pauses, her face tight as she appears to deliberate on what she's going to say next. "You have to convince him that *you* love *him*—enough to weather any storm."

Something prickles at the back of my neck, then. A warning, maybe.

"What do you mean?"

Tabitha takes a deep breath and lets it out, long and slow.

I almost know it before she says it.

That something is wrong. Reid is pushing this *friends* narrative because of a bigger reason.

But in the end, when she finally does speak again, nothing can prepare me for what she says.

chapter twenty
reid

I barely hear the knock over the sound of the rain.

Setting my cup of tea and crossword on the coffee table, I pat Sydney's head where it's resting on my thigh before I push up off the couch and head to the front door. It's not a huge stretch for me to guess who might be there when I open it, but I'm shocked to find a completely drenched Busy when I do.

"Are you okay?" I ask, stepping back and letting her inside just as a flash of light streaks through the sky. A few seconds later the boom of thunder echoes around us, shaking the walls of my cabin.

"This was just from my sprint from my car to your door," she tells me. "I have *never* seen rain like that before."

"Global warming," I say, heading for the bathroom to grab a towel then returning to the living room to hand it to her.

She quickly dabs at her hair and dries off her face and arms.

I glance at my watch. "Are you just getting off work? It's almost ten."

Busy shakes her head. "No, I…finished work at six. I've just been driving around, thinking."

"Where's Junie?"

"At my mom's. She's spending the night."

My shoulders droop in relief, and I'm surprised by the slice of fear I felt, wondering where she was.

"Are you… I mean, you don't seem okay."

"Because I'm not," she replies.

The tension in my neck and back returns, worry coursing through me.

"Your mom came to the bookstore today." Her eyes, normally bright and filled with life, seem sad in a way I haven't seen before.

And that's when I know. My mother overstepped, finally shared information that wasn't hers to share.

"She told you."

"About your plan to be alone for the rest of your life because you're sick? Yes, she told me."

Whatever sadness was there a second ago is gone, and in its place is a woman filled with fire.

"And I have to say, I agree with her."

I scoff. "Well it doesn't really matter who agrees with who when the decision is up to me."

"It might be up to you, but that doesn't mean the people who love you can't weigh in."

It's hard to miss the fact that she used the word love, but I brush it aside. I know she just means it in the 'I care for you' kind of way, and it would be good for me not to confuse the two.

"Trust me, the people who love me have weighed in plenty."

"Can you at least explain it to me?" she asks, her hands tightly gripping the towel she's still holding. "Please? I feel like

I just got hit with this wrecking ball of information that I don't completely understand."

Sighing, I run my hands through my hair, tugging on the messy strands before letting them go.

"I thought you said my mom talked to you."

"She did, but she was vague. Said I needed to get the rest of it from you."

I grit my teeth, irritation rolling through me.

Thanks mom. Drop a bomb then leave me to clean up the mess.

I take a deep breath and let it out slow, then lean against the wall behind me, crossing my arms.

"I have something called Kennedy's disease," I tell her, hating the way the words sound as they come out of my mouth. I try to avoid saying them as much as possible, not because I can't admit the truth but because I just don't want a constant reminder that I have a disease that's slowly robbing me of my future. "It's a neuromuscular disease, kind of like MS." I pause. "It basically means at some point in the future, I'm going to struggle to take care of myself."

Busy slowly drops down until she's sitting on my couch, her eyes carrying that same sadness that was there when she first arrived. "Struggle to take care of yourself how?"

I tilt my head back and stare at the ceiling, pulling up the list from my memory. "Muscle twitching and weakness, issues with my reflexes, shaky muscles, tremors." I sigh. "I'll struggle to swallow and speak at some point, too, though hopefully that's further down the line."

"Do they...do they have a timeline? For what that looks like?"

I grit my teeth, hating how broken she looks.

This. This is why I don't tell people. Why only my mother

knows. And Sarah, but she's a different story.

"It varies by person. For me, I'm dealing with some hand tremors. That's what my pills are for."

"But online it said it was for seizures."

I shrug. "Doctors use the same drugs to treat a variety of different things."

We sit in silence for a while, and I can tell she's processing everything I've told her.

It's a lot. I get it.

It's just another reason why I wish nobody knew.

"Your mom said that your disease…Kennedy's…is why you and Sarah got divorced?"

God, she is just sharing everything today isn't she.

I guess at this point, there isn't much point in keeping things to myself. If she's going to know some of it, she might as well know all of it, so I tell her.

I tell her how I watched my grandfather get diagnosed and then re-diagnosed and mis-diagnosed until they finally got it right. How I watched him decline, watched my grandmother and my mother do everything they could to take care of him. The amount of work and energy and care that went into it once he got to the point where he couldn't control his movements anymore.

I explain how most men don't get diagnosed until they're in their late 30s and into their 50s, but I was one of the lucky few who found out early because we knew what we were looking for when I started to notice some of the early warning signs—fatigue and light muscle cramping.

And then I tell her about Sarah.

Even my mother doesn't know the full truth about Sarah, doesn't know what that conversation looked like. How I sat her down and told her about my diagnosis. How she cried. And then, when I offered her the choice, how she left. How she couldn't leave fast enough. How she *fled* away from me and the idea of being stuck with me and this disease.

If only I could run away, too.

"I'm not telling you this so you pity me," I say, once I've shared the worst of it. "I'm telling you because Sarah saw the end, with my grandfather. We were dating at the time, and she came with me to visit him often. Saw all the things my grandmother and mother had to do for him. Get him out of bed, take him to the bathroom, help him eat."

I clear my throat, becoming emotional at both the memory of that time for my grandparents, but also at the idea that it could be my future.

"She saw the end, and she knew she couldn't handle it. And she shouldn't have to. Nobody should have to. So when she left, I promised myself I would never put anyone else in that position. I knew it would be better for me to be on my own."

Busy's eyes are filled with tears, and as I finish talking, they finally break free, tracking down her face and dripping onto her still damp shirt.

"I'm so sorry," she tells me.

"You don't have to be sorry. But hopefully now you understand why something happening between us is just…a mistake. A horrible option for anyone, but especially for you and Junie." I shake my head. "You deserve better than a man who is just going to be a burden."

She swipes at her face, clearing away the streaks left behind. "Well I *don't* understand," she finally says, her tone shifting, that sadness from before beginning to fade.

I blink, surprised by the firmness in her voice as she pushes off the couch and begins to pace my living room.

"Let me just parrot back the information you've given me. See if I have everything right, okay?"

Before I can even say anything, she launches in.

"So you were married to someone who left you because there is something wrong with *her*. She signed up for a marriage that was until death do us part, for better or worse, and then she bailed when life became more complicated than just sex and giggles with her incredible husband."

My eyes widen at her description. "No, that is not—"

"And because of that failing on *her* part," she continues, cutting me off, "you've decided the best way to move on with your life is to sit in a hole by yourself and be lonely and alone and just…completely alone."

I sigh, realizing my very detailed story did *not*, in fact, convince her that I made the best decision for me.

"You're being a little dramatic, Busy."

"I'm *not* being dramatic," she insists, quitting her pacing and looking at me dead on. "I'm fucking pissed that you're not even going to give us a chance because you think I'm going to abandon you the way she did."

Shaking my head, I clench my fists, trying to keep my cool.

"I could never do that, Reid. Ever. I don't care what horrible thing is in your future. I don't care if I have to wipe your mouth or help you to the toilet someday. Those are the things you do for someone you love."

My throat gets tight, tears prickling my eyes.

"Why are you doing this?" I whisper, feeling frustrated and angry and wishing she would just leave me in that hole all alone. "Why are you pushing this?"

"Why *wouldn't* I?" she demands.

"Because it doesn't concern you!" I shout.

"Of course it does!" she shouts back. "How can I stand by and watch the man I love hide away because he's afraid?"

I scoff. "I'm not afraid, Busy. I know my fate and I've come to terms with it. This is not about fear. I don't want to be a *bur-den*—can't you see that?"

Busy shakes her head. "Of course it's about fear. I get that you don't want to be a burden, nobody wants that. *I* don't want to be a burden either, and I feel like that's all I am to the people in my life, someone who needs help and support and an extra hand *constantly.*"

It's not even close to being the same.

"But this isn't about burdening someone with future complications," she continues, her voice still firm but losing some of the edge. "This is about you being terrified that you're going to be abandoned again when shit gets hard."

Gritting my teeth, I spin around and stare out the window, at the rain that is still falling steadily but is no longer battering the house.

"There are a lot of scary things in this world, Reid, but I feel like living a life completely alone, without love, is the worst of them all."

"You wouldn't love me if you really knew what's coming," I say, my voice flat and devoid of the emotion roiling in my soul.

Busy sighs, and when I turn to look at her, the sight of her tears again sends nausea coursing through my stomach.

"I would love you until I took my last breath," she tells me. "And when it was gone, I would fight tooth and nail for just one more."

I turn back to the window again, but I can still see Busy in the reflection: her arms wrapped around herself, watching me just as intently as I watch her.

I would give anything for this thing between us to have a future, but the only one I can give her is filled with promises I'll eventually have to break. How am I supposed to promise to protect her and support her when I could end up in a wheelchair? How am I supposed to be there for *her* in sickness and in health if I'm the one who always needs to be cared for?

No. The best thing I can do for her, the best way I can love her, is to give her a chance to be with someone who *can* give her those things.

"You should be with someone who can give you everything you want, someone who can give you the kind of life you deserve."

"And who says you aren't that man?"

I scoff and spin around to look at her again. "I think we've gone over that, in detail."

"Do you even *know* what I want?" she asks, and her question gives me pause. "Do you know what kind of life I want? The future I picture for myself and my daughter?"

I watch her as she walks over to the bookshelf in the corner, where I have all the pictures of my family. I know them all so well. Each moment. Each memory. There's one from the Cohen family reunion a few years ago when my Uncle Paul arranged for all of us to go on a harbor cruise in San Francisco and my cousin Ruben jumped into the water. There are a couple from high school—me with Nick, me with Rusty and a few other guys from the swim team, me at graduation with my parents. Several with me and Leo and Nina. And my favorite, a photo of me and my dad, fishing off the dock at the marina.

Busy reaches out and pulls the one she gave to me from our hike off the shelf then holds it up for me.

"This. This is what I want." She looks at the picture again, one finger stroking gently across the glass. "I have spent years of my life feeling like an outsider, like I don't belong...anywhere. But when I'm with you, I feel like I finally fit. That's what I want."

Her eyes flick to mine, still watery but sure.

"I want to belong, and I want to belong to *you*." She smiles as a single tear tracks down her cheek. "It's really as silly and uncomplicated as that."

Busy turns then and sets the picture back on the shelf, wiping at her face before looking at me again.

"You think what will happen to you someday should be enough to keep me from loving you now, but that couldn't be further from the truth," she tells me, shaking her head. "The downside to forever is the grief that comes when you lose the person you love, but that pain is the price you pay for the life you're lucky enough to share until that day comes."

My chest grows tight as I listen to her, emotion pouring from her every word.

"Do you think your mom wouldn't have married your dad if she knew she'd lose him?" she continues. "Or do you think she would still have loved him with every breath, knowing what was to come?"

I swallow thickly, knowing the truth even though I don't say it aloud. That she would choose my father over and over, regardless of what the future held.

I want to tell Busy that it's not the same. That what my future holds is a completely different situation.

But is it?

"In the end, I'm just looking for someone who can hold my hand when things are hard," she continues. "Can you do that?"

I don't respond, because I know she doesn't need me to. She already knows the answer.

"Because everything else is just circumstance."

We stand there for a long moment, just staring at each other. I don't know what to say to her, how to process all the things she's said.

"I don't know where to go from here," I finally say, feeling like I've lost my balance.

I've spent the past several years convincing myself that being alone is my best choice, and in one conversation, Busy has come in and taken a sledgehammer to nearly every argument I've had in my pocket.

She surprises me when she steps forward and slips her hand in mine.

"Let's go…jump in the water."

My brow furrows and I look back toward the window, where I can very clearly still see rain.

"It's raining."

She shrugs, laughing quietly even through her tears. "Sounds fun to me."

I almost want to laugh at the idea of leaving behind this very serious conversation and running out into the storm. But then again, maybe that's the point.

I squeeze her hand, and her smile grows, and then we're sprinting out the door, still fully clothed. Onto the deck, down the grassy path and then out to the end of the dock, almost completely drenched by the time we get there.

Neither of us slow. We just launch ourselves into the water, me with a shout and Busy with a peal of laughter.

And then we're plunging into the abyss.

Together.

We don't spend too long in the water, the fear of lightning returning enough to pull us out after only a few minutes. But we do sit at the end of the dock together for quite a while, my arm around Busy's shoulders, her petite form tucked snugly into my side.

It feels so good to hold her, and even though there are a million unanswered questions, a thousand decisions to be made, I can't bring myself to ruin this moment by talking. Instead, I just enjoy what it feels like to have her in my arms.

Neither of us mentions the rain. Instead we just sit in it together, the air around us noticeably cooling. Hopefully, this storm will bring some relief to the heat that has been pummeling Cedar Point all summer.

"Doing anything fun this weekend?" Busy asks a while later, snuggling closer to me.

I shake my head, wondering where she's going with this. "Not particularly. You?"

"We're hiking Kilroy," she says. "It's the big family trip."

"That'll be fun. Short route or long route?"

"Everyone else is doing the long route, but I know Junie will be hard to manage on a six-hour hike, so we're meeting them at the midway point."

I nod.

"I was wondering…any interest in joining us?"

I blink, surprised at first.

But then I smile, imagining me, Busy, Junie, and Sydney, hiking the trail together, camping at the top, enjoying nature.

"Yeah," I say, before I can get in my head about it.

Her eyebrows rise and she pulls back, her smile wide. "Really?"

I nod. "Absolutely. Misery loves company."

Busy laughs, her head flying back, her eyes bright. And then I do the most natural thing in the world.

I lean in and press my lips against hers.

chapter twenty-one
busy

I fling my hiking bag over the edge of the truck and into the bed then hoist Junie up to stand on the bumper.

"Your turn, little miss."

She tugs off her own small pink bag—filled with snacks and crayons and a few toys—and chucks it in next to mine and Reid's.

"I think that's everything," Reid says, resting his hand on the tailgate. "Unless you want to go over your list again."

I smirk at him. He's been giving me shit about my list since he first saw it typed in the Notes app on my phone.

"You mock me, but just know my list has been the savior of all on more than one occasion."

His eyebrows dip. "The savior of all?"

I shrug. "Okay, maybe not *all*, but it's definitely come in clutch. Just ask Bishop about the time he ran out of toilet paper."

Reid laughs. "I think I'll pass on that story, but thanks."

I get Junie set up in her car seat as Reid opens the door on the other side, allowing Sydney to hop up into the cab next to her. Then we're climbing in as well and pulling down the gravel path out to the highway.

It's only been a few days since our conversation about what's going on with Reid, and things have been in this kind of limbo space. We both know we still have things to talk about, know our conversation from Tuesday night was too important not to revisit. But we are also both strangely okay with letting it breathe for a minute, like we both know we don't need to rush it. There's a certainty I have that we'll come back to it once we've both had time to sit with…well, with everything.

And there is a *lot* to sit with.

Even though nothing between us is clearly defined, something has changed. I can feel it in the way he looks at me, the way he touches me. Like now, as we drive up the highway, heading out of town, his arm stretches along the back of the seat. His hand rests on the back of my neck, stroking my skin gently. It feels far less cautious and much more intimate, as if he has given himself permission.

I like it.

It takes about 30 minutes to drive to the outskirts of Belleview, which is where the midway point of the trail begins. Once we've parked, we tug Syd and Junie out of the car and unload all of our gear. My family left at six this morning from the base of the trail, and if we've timed everything correctly, they should be stopping here soon to use the bathrooms and refill their water bottles before we all continue up together.

"What did your family say when you told them I was coming?" Reid asks as he fills up his own water.

When I don't answer, he looks at me then frowns.

"You did tell them I was coming, right?"

"There hasn't really been time."

His eyes narrow. "Busy. Are you serious?"

"It won't be a big deal at all."

"Then it shouldn't have been a big deal to tell them."

"Except they'd have a bunch of questions I don't have the answers to." I cross my arms and narrow my own eyes. "Because we haven't finished our conversation from the other night."

Reid tips up his chin, still giving me the stink eye. "Okay fine, that's fair. But next time, warn me, alright? I don't like to be unprepared."

I gently kick his foot with mine. "Sorry."

He wraps his arm around my shoulders and tugs me into his chest then presses a kiss to the crown of my head.

"I'n a hug!" Junie shouts, jogging over from where she was plucking leaves off a nearby bush.

Reid bends down and picks Junie up. "Oh, do you?" he asks, hugging her tight then twirling her around, making her shriek with laughter. Sydney barks a few times and prances around them, clearly wanting in on the action, too.

"Reid?"

I turn at the sound of his name, my entire body growing tense when I see who it is.

Sarah.

She stands completely still, her eyes evaluating Reid where he stands, holding Junie. It's hard to miss the very visible shock painted all over her face.

"Hey, Sarah," Reid says, his voice easy—far easier than I feel, that's for sure. "How are you?"

"Good." She pauses, her eyes dropping to mine for a beat before returning to his. "What are you up to? I thought you were working this weekend."

I swallow thickly, not liking the way she says it. Or maybe not liking the fact that she thinks she knows what she's talking about.

"We're doing the back half of Kilroy," he replies, lifting Junie so she's sitting on his shoulders. "Hiking and camping overnight."

He doesn't address the work comment, though my mind still flitters over her words, trying to dissect them.

"We, meaning…"

"My family," I interject. "We do it every year."

She nods then tugs a piece of hair out of her mouth. "This is my friend Cindy. I think you guys met when we went to…"

"The Cedar Cider opening, yeah I remember," he says, giving her a friendly nod. He pauses, his eyes connecting with mine briefly before he looks back at Sarah and Cindy. "Cindy, this is my friend Busy and her daughter Junie."

I wave, trying to keep a friendly smile on my face, but all I can focus on is the fact that he called me his *friend*. Again.

Is that still all we are?

Thankfully, at that exact moment, I spot my sister and her husband emerging through the trees. I breathe a sigh of relief.

"My family is here," I say to Reid, before I turn to Sarah and Cindy. "Nice to see you. Enjoy the rest of your hike."

I jog over to where Briar and Andy are walking in my direction, meeting them in the middle. I fling my arms around my sister's shoulders, and she embraces me right back.

"Hey!" she exclaims, laughing lightly. "Everything okay?"

When I don't respond, she pulls back, a concerned look on her face, then her eyes slide past me to where Reid is still talking.

"Is that…Reid? And Sarah?"

I nod.

"Is he going on the hike with us?" Andy asks, tucking his hands into his pockets. "Because I don't know how I feel about you two sharing a tent."

Briar smacks him in the arm, and he chuckles.

"Everything's fine, it's just…weird, seeing him with Sarah." I glance back in their direction. "I think they still talk pretty regularly."

"I mean, does that matter?" Briar asks me. "You guys are just friends, right?"

My eyes connect with hers, and then her mouth forms a small 'O' as she nods.

"Gotcha. Well, he's walking over here, so we'll talk more about this later."

I spin around, giving Reid a smile as he approaches, Junie still on his shoulders. A quick look at his face says he feels just as uneasy about that conversation as I did. Which is, frankly, a relief.

"Hey! Glad you're joining us," Andy says, sticking his hand out. "It's been a while."

Reid shakes it and nods. "It has. Good to see you."

"Where is everyone else?" I ask.

"Here we are!"

I beam as the rest of my family emerges through the trees, the mass of them sweaty and dusty, but with big smiles on their faces. Along with Briar and Andy are my oldest brother, Boyd, and his wife, Ruby; my sister Bellamy and her boyfriend, Rusty; my brother Bishop and his wife, Gabi; and my parents. There is a chorus of hellos and hugs, especially with Bishop and Gabi, who just got in yesterday from North Carolina.

"Hey, Little Bee," he says, wrapping his sweaty arms around me and giving me a good squeeze.

I grin at the nickname. "I'm surprised they let you take days off."

"They don't," he replies, chuckling. Then he pulls back to look at me. "I'm not actually supposed to be here. I'm supposed to be on a plane heading to Seattle, but…" He shrugs. "I'll be there for the game on Monday. They don't need to know every single thing I'm doing."

I laugh and look at his wife, Gabi, who I've known since we were teenagers. "I still can't believe you put up with him."

She raises an eyebrow and gives Bishop a once-over. "Me neither."

They all make quick work of filling water bottles and using the bathroom while Reid and I load up our packs. Then we surround the trailhead sign and ask another hiker to take our picture before we begin making our way back over to the path.

"Just a reminder that we'll probably be moving slower than everyone else," I call out.

"I don't know, Boyd's been pretty slow so far," Bishop says. "My money's on him for caboose."

Boyd wraps his arm around Bishop's shoulders and tugs him in then gives him a quick tap in the nuts.

I roll my eyes. I guess it doesn't matter how much older siblings get. We're always just a bunch of kids when we're together.

"Alright, Mitchell family. Let's head out!"

Dad's announcement is the indicator that it's time to stop fucking around and get a move on, and we all fall in line behind him and begin making our way up the trail.

I've never been particularly active, not like Boyd or Bishop were with soccer and baseball, so long hikes like this are normally outside my comfort zone. But the thing I've always loved about this trek in particular is that the ascent might be long, but it isn't crazy steep. Instead of short stretches of uphill climbs, it has long stretches of gentle incline, which is much easier on my calves that have always been on the weaker side.

It's also one of the more scenic hikes in the Tahoe National Forest, which makes it so much more enjoyable. Creeks and streams that lead into the lake down below pepper the landscape, and there are at least a half dozen outlooks that showcase the entire valley. The trees stretch high into the sky and sit densely packed together, creating a canopy of shade that protects us from the hot sun.

Reid and Junie and I stop often, pulling out snacks and letting Junie pick flowers. Sydney stops to sniff everything and pee on as many trees and bushes as she can. We fall quite a ways behind the pack, even though Boyd and Ruby move the slowest to make sure we don't get completely separated. Eventually, we just wave them on, letting them know they should feel free to keep going.

"I haven't done this hike in years," Reid says when we reach a sign that says we have one mile left. "I forgot how long it takes."

"And we started at the halfway point," I remind him.

He chuckles. "Even worse. I did it with my dad a few times and I was a lot faster back then." Reid's smile slips, and I can only imagine what he's thinking about.

"You don't have to put on a brave face for me," I tell him, my voice quiet.

His eyes connect with mine before they look forward again.

"It's not a brave face," he says a few minutes later. "It's just... sometimes I forget it's not just about getting older. It's because there's this thing inside me, actively working against me, every single day."

We stop for a second, tugging out our waters and taking a

sip. I crouch down and beckon Junie my way, handing her the water as well.

"Well…when you're thinking about that, what can I do?" I ask, standing and screwing the lid back on. "Do you want me to bring it up? Stay quiet? Listen if you want to talk?"

He considers me for a minute, his hands on his hips, looking at the path that lies ahead of us. "You know, I've never had someone to talk to about it, so…I'm not really sure. But, I'll let you know."

I nod. "Sounds good."

"Junie, wanna shoulder ride?" Reid asks, crouching down.

Of course, my girl lets out a squeal and races his way, grabbing his hands as he flips her up onto his shoulders.

"She can probably walk the rest of the way," I tell him, somewhat concerned he's going to wear himself out.

Reid turns my way and gives me a look I'll never forget. "I only get so many days in my life when I'll be able to do this kind of stuff. Today is one of those days."

I take a deep breath and nod, and then we keep walking.

I slink to the back and take out my phone, capturing a picture of the two of them, with Sydney trotting at Reid's side.

Kilroy Camp is a small campground and not super popular, but my dad always books the same site each year just in case. When we get there, I don't even need to wander around to find our crew, I just lead Reid to site three.

This spot is about a mile from the outlook that has the view of sunrise, and tomorrow morning, while it's still dark, we'll make our way out there. For tonight, we're tucked into a mostly wooded area a little ways off the trail.

"There they are!" my mom calls out, waving with both hands over her head like we can't see them in the wide-open space. "Just in time—we're roasting hot dogs!"

Reid chuckles next to me. "They brought a grill?"

I pin him with a look. "A grill, chairs, tons of food, games… one year, my dad brought a telescope. When we were younger, Bishop would bring a hitting net and bat so he could get in some practice." I shake my head. "This hike is executed with an almost militaristic efficiency."

"Clearly."

"How did Junie do?" Dad asks from his spot at the grill.

"She was a trooper," Reid says, hoisting her off his shoulders and setting her on the ground.

Junie immediately races over to Briar and crawls into her lap, which makes my heart swell.

"Not surprising," Mom chimes in. "She has more energy than any kid I've ever met."

I laugh. "Ain't that the truth."

Glancing around, I take in the tent situation before pinpointing a spot for us to set up.

"Briar…" I start, but she waves me off, her arms wrapped around Junie, a tender look on her face.

"Do your thing. I got her."

I smirk then look at Reid. "You know how to pitch a tent?"

He snorts. "Only been doing it every day of my life since I was in junior high."

At that, I burst into laughter, and the two of us wander over to the empty spot near the back of the site to set up our tent. It doesn't take long, but by the time we're done, the sun has mostly set, and we return to where everyone is sitting in small clusters around the campfire, eating their hotdogs and chatting in a variety of different conversations.

Before long, it becomes clear that Junie's energy has finally reached its max capacity, and I carry her sleepy body over to our tent, unzipping it and crawling inside to get her settled in her green sleeping bag.

When I begin to crawl out, she peeks her eyes open.

"Where Sinny?"

I glance over my shoulder, spotting the pup a few feet away, watching us, her tail wagging.

"Sinny!" she calls out, putting her hands in the air.

Ever the faithful girl, Sydney runs right in and snuggles up next to Junie, her head resting on her stomach. I chuckle quietly then finish crawling out of the tent, zipping it up before returning to the fire.

"Everything go okay?" Reid asks.

I nod. "Yeah. Sydney went right in and snuggled up next to her."

He laughs and shakes his head. "Of course she did. I'm not even sure that dog belongs to me anymore," he says before taking a sip of his beer.

"I think she belonged to Junie the minute they met."

Reid glances at me then, his lips parting slightly like he's going to say something, but before he does, Briar announces that it's time for Earn Your S'more, and the entire group erupts in lively conversation.

"What's happening?" Reid asks, glancing around as everyone chatters excitedly, adjusting their chairs into a full circle around the fire.

I grin. "Only the best game to ever come out of the Kilroy hike. If you want a s'more, you have to pay the price."

"It was my claim to fame—*you're welcome*—and I brought pens and scraps of paper for everyone." Briar walks around to everyone, passing supplies out.

"I've been brainstorming mine for literal weeks," Bishop says, instantly scribbling on his slip.

"Okay, so how it works," Briar says, looking at Reid, "is you write down a task that someone in the group will have to complete in order to earn their s'more. It can be anything you want—within reason—but it's something you have to be willing to do yourself because you might grab your own out of the pile."

Reid rolls his pen back and forth between his palms. "Interesting. Very interesting," he says, eventually jotting something down.

Before long, we've all dropped our slips into Bishop's hat, and then Briar mixes them all up inside.

"Who's the brave soul that's going to go first?" she asks, glancing around.

"I'll do it."

I blink, surprised, watching as Reid stands, crosses over to Briar, and grabs a slip out of the pile.

"Oh, come on," he says, grinning wide. "*Read the ingredients on the hotdog package as seductively as you can.*"

Everyone bursts into laughter, and even in the low light of the campfire, I can see the way Reid's cheeks flush slightly pink.

"Get to it, Mr. Cohen," I say, smirking.

Reid grabs the plastic package out of the trash and looks at the label for a long minute before he spins around and looks at me.

"Kosher beef," he says, biting his lip. "Delicious, nutritious water."

I cover my mouth with my hand, barely able to contain my laughter.

"Sodium lactate and paprika," he continues, dropping the package on the ground then bending slowly to pick it up. "Hydrolyzed soy protein."

The laughter around the fire is so loud I can barely hear the rest of the ingredients, and when Reid finally finishes, he gets a standing ovation from the entire family and a few pats on the back.

After Reid breaks the ice, the rest of the game goes pretty quickly with some well-thought-out tasks:

Bishop acts out the *Titanic* scene with dad, though dad tries to convince everyone that by obligating him to participate, he's off the hook to draw his own slip of paper. Nobody else agrees.

Boyd has to do the worm and can barely manage once or twice because he can't stop laughing.

Gabi has to give her best impression of Rusty, which she does by sitting there with a frown, glaring at everyone and rolling her eyes before finally bowing.

Ruby has to bite into an onion like an apple, which Bishop brought with him on the hike just for this moment.

Bellamy howls like a wolf for a full minute, which is a lot longer than you would think.

But there are also a few duds:

Mom sings Happy Birthday to herself.

Rusty has to walk the runway like a model but kind of half-asses it and everyone boos and chucks marshmallows at him.

Dad has to wear his socks on his hands for the rest of the game, which feels particularly unsanitary.

Andy has to give his worst pick-up line to mom, which ends up being, "Need help with those groceries?" Everyone gags a bit.

And mine is to catch three marshmallows in my mouth.

Then it's Briar's turn, and she pulls out a slip of paper from her pocket, clearing her throat dramatically to get everyone's attention.

"Make a baby." There's a collective pause before she shrugs and says, "Oh, well I guess I get a pass then because I'm already doing that."

"Shut the fuck up!" Bishop shouts.

"Wait, what's going on?" Mom asks, sitting up straighter, her eyes wide.

Briar's smile stretches wide. "We're pregnant!"

The campfire erupts as all of us fly out of our chairs, hugging and laughing and crying and expressing our excitement. When I finally get my chance to hug Briar, I can't hold her tight enough.

"Junie's gonna have a cousin!" I say, my arms wrapped around her, feeling an emotion I can't exactly describe.

"I know!" she shouts, and then we're jumping up and down, laughing and hugging at the same time.

"Alright, y'all, someone get this pregnant lady a s'more," Dad shouts.

And then we're all laughing and digging into the bags of supplies, the evening taking on a new life—literally—that none of us expected.

chapter twenty-two
reid

"What time are we heading out in the morning?"

Busy yawns. "Around four. We have to pack up and walk the mile to the lookout, and the sun rises at five, so…"

I nod and glance at my watch, knowing we need to crawl into our tent soon but not wanting to go. What I *want* to do is stay here, chatting with Busy. We're the last ones up, everyone else clearly familiar with the drill and getting to bed early so they aren't completely delirious in the morning.

Not us, though. We've been sitting out here talking quietly, adding wood to the fire for the better part of two hours.

"I can't believe Briar's pregnant," Busy says, though it's probably the third or fourth time she's said it tonight. "Junie's going to be the best big cousin, I think."

I hum in acknowledgment, my eyes beginning to grow heavy as I stare at the flames. I'm incredibly exhausted, and the hike took a lot out of me. More than I normally try to give of myself.

It felt important today, though, to use my body while I still can. The specialist I see has made it clear that, for the most part, I need to be gentle on exercise and exertion, because overdoing it can cause a lot of fatigue on muscles that are already beginning to struggle. But I figure one intense day can't hurt.

"Can I ask you something?"

When I look at Busy, I find her watching me with a curious expression. Part of me wants to say no, because I have a feeling it's about my health, but I shove that default reaction to the side and nod.

"Sure."

Busy licks her lips and tilts her head to the side. "Earlier today, while we were hiking, you said you haven't ever had someone to talk to about your health stuff. Did you...not ever talk about it with Sarah?"

I lick my lips, considering her question. Did I ever talk about it with Sarah?

"Not really. I mean, I shared the original diagnosis, but that was pretty much it before we talked about getting a divorce."

Her shoulders fall and she shakes her head. "I'm so sorry."

"I told you, Busy. I gave her the out." Shrugging, I bend forward, pick up a twig off the ground, and chuck it into the fire, watching it singe and disappear immediately.

"I get that, I just...I'm sorry you got this crazy, life-altering information and didn't really have anyone to talk to about it." She reaches out and places her hand on mine. "You don't *have* to tell me anything you don't want to, but I hope you know you can share anything you do."

I swallow thickly, blinking hard as I stare at the fire.

"Well, thanks," I murmur, not sure what else there is to say.

If I have to be completely honest, I feel sick to my stomach.

The things Busy says are so simple and yet so surprising at the same time, like she's revealing things I didn't know I wanted with every passing remark.

How was I to know someone you love would be willing to hear all the shitty things going on with you? How was I to know having someone in my corner would feel this way? That I don't have to keep the worst to myself, bottled up inside of me?

My mom and dad were great people, and so are my aunt and uncle and my cousin and her family. But your partner is supposed to be just that: your partner, the person by your side through anything. Somewhere along the line, as I was making allowances for Sarah and trying not to be upset at her for taking the out I offered, I forgot that's what marriage is really supposed to be.

It's late when we crawl into the tent, each of us collapsing on opposite sides with Junie and Sydney snuggled in the middle. But I stay up long into the night, staring at the sky through the open netting at the top, thinking about the woman who has blown my carefully crafted life apart in just a few months.

Or, maybe that's wrong. Sarah blew up my life. Busy is helping me piece it back together.

I rest my head in my hand, propped up on my elbow, watching her as she sleeps, her soft breaths filling the tent. I didn't know it was possible to love someone like this, like it's the only thing that matters.

I know it's unfair of me to continue to compare how I feel about Busy with how I felt about Sarah, especially when I realize now that Sarah barely even registers on the meter. But at the same time, how can I not? How can I not use the way my marriage crumbled like a sandcastle under a wave as a reference point? Especially when I'm quickly realizing the kind of stronghold Busy has claimed on my heart could weather any storm.

Busy and I still have some things to sort through, still have plenty of uphill battles ahead. But god, how much easier it is to scale those walls when you have a helping hand, when the person at your side wants the best for you as much as you want the best for them.

I reach out my arm above Junie's head and take Busy's hand in mine. She startles briefly, her eyes opening and searching the tent. Then our gazes connect, and she settles, entwining her fingers with mine.

This is what I want.

What I need.

For the rest of my life—whatever that life might look like, however good or bad, easy or difficult, short or long it is—I want to be the one to hold her hand, like she said that night in my cabin.

"In the end, I'm just looking for someone who can hold my hand when things are hard. Can you do that?"

As we lie there, Busy and Junie and Sydney dozing next to me, I know I've never felt as happy or as content as I feel in this moment.

So, yes, Busy, I can do that. As long as you're there to take my hand, I will hold it tight in mine.

The sunrise is breathtaking.

I've lived in Cedar Point my entire life, and never have I seen a sunrise as glorious as the one I witness with the Mitchell family the following morning.

Though, to be honest, part of me wonders if that has to do with my own realizations in the tent last night, if my feelings for Busy have cleared away some of the cobwebs so I can see things in a new light. I think whatever went through my mind is reflecting on the outside, because the way Busy looks at me, her eyes soft and her smile sweet, makes me think she knows where I'm at.

By the time we make it back to the house, I can barely go a few minutes without taking her hand in mine, the act suddenly feeling so natural.

"Come on, Junie Bee," Busy says, carrying her daughter into their cabin. "Let's get you a bath and then a nap. How does that sound?"

"No nap."

Busy giggles, and I love the sound of it as I follow behind them, carrying some of her gear.

"No nap, huh? Alright, well we'll see about that."

We're hit by the heat as soon as we walk in the door, and Busy groans.

"I should have left all the windows open." She leads me into the living room, where she sets Junie down then turns to take the bags from my hands. "Thanks for this. If you want to leave some of our crap in the back of your truck, I can come out and unload it in a little bit. I don't want you to have to do it all."

I shake my head. "Nah. You take care of your monster, and I'll leave the rest of your things on your porch."

She takes a deep breath and lets out a long sigh, her entire body tired but her smile still genuine. "Thanks. And thanks for coming, too. I'm really glad you were there."

"Me, too."

We watch each other for a beat before an idea comes to me. "Hey, why don't you and Junie come over tonight," I say. "We can set up a movie for her, I'll cook dinner. And when Junie needs to go down, we can set her up on my bed and then you and I can talk." I take her hand in mine, twisting our fingers together. "About everything."

Busy's eyes brighten and she nods. "That sounds really good."

I step forward and pull her in, my arm around her shoulders, then I close my eyes as I just hold her there for a minute. I breathe her in, that familiar hint of jasmine mixed with the dust and sweat from our long hike out of the mountains.

I don't mind.

I want every part of her.

"Text me later," I say, pressing a kiss against her forehead then taking a step back, keeping hold of her fingers until the last second.

She nods. "Sounds good."

I turn reluctantly, wishing she were coming over right now, and head outside to finish up unloading. There isn't a ton left, but what's Busy's I leave on her porch and what's mine I set outside my own front door. I'll need to do a thorough clean of the tent and some of my other gear before I store it away, but for now, I just want to take a shower and rinse off all this dirt.

After I've scrubbed up, I check my phone, which died at some point overnight, surprised to see several text messages from Sarah.

Sarah: It was nice bumping into you yesterday
Sarah: Give me a call when you're home
Sarah: It's important

My brow furrows, a tiny thread of worry rolling through me.

Me: Hey, I'm home. Everything alright?

I finish changing, throwing on a pair of basketball shorts and a loose tee, then return to my phone when I hear it ring.

"Hey," I say, answering when I see Sarah's name. "You okay?"

"Yeah, I'm good," she replies. "You at home? I was thinking about swinging by. Or we could meet on Main. Maybe grab lunch."

Sighing, I take a seat on my couch, rubbing at the stubble on my jaw. "I don't think that's a good idea."

"Why? Are you busy with Busy?" she says, a joking intonation to her voice. Then she laughs.

"Not right now, no, but I have plans tonight and I don't really have the time right now."

What I want to tell her is it's not a good idea for us to spend time together anymore, but that feels harsh to do over the phone. Sarah and I might not be married, but I still care about her, and the last thing I want to do is cause her any pain.

"You're serious." She sounds shocked. "Are you guys like… dating or something?"

I waffle with how much to tell her. Things between Busy and I feel…tentative. Like there's a foundation of something strong and sturdy being laid, but it's still setting. I don't want to get into that with Sarah, because…well, because it's none of her business.

"You *are*," she replies when I take too long to respond. "What are you doing, Reid? I thought you told me you weren't ever going to be in another relationship."

"I did. But things change."

It's all I can think to say, because I don't *want* to talk about this with Sarah. I want to talk about it with Busy. I want to tell *her* the reasons why I'm going to let go of my decision to be alone. I want to talk to *her* about the way my heart has changed since we met, why I'm going to stare my own fears in the face.

"What things have changed?"

It barely takes me a second to respond. "Everything."

Sarah is quiet, and I wonder if maybe we *do* need to talk today, hash out a few final things before we both well and truly move on from each other.

"Look, Sarah…" I start, licking my lips and trying to figure out exactly what to say, how to say it in a way that doesn't hurt her.

Though I'm not sure that's possible.

"Can I just…come by?" she asks. "Please?"

Her voice sounds shaky, something I've rarely heard from Sarah in all the years I've known her. So I relent.

"Yeah." I nod my head, though she can't see me. "We can talk when you get here."

"I'm leaving Main now. See you soon."

Fifteen minutes later, I open the door and let her inside. I'm ready to get this over with, put the chapter of Reid and Sarah firmly in the past. Talking to her and getting lunch occasionally always felt like it wasn't a big deal, but now it does. Now it feels like a desperate attempt to cling to the past.

Sarah stalks into my living room then leans on the back of the couch, looking at me with frustration, her arms crossed. "What's going on, Reid? Something feels really different between us, and I don't like it."

"Something *is* different, Sarah."

"Busy Mitchell, you mean."

I rest my hands on my hips. "Yeah, she's part of it, but it's not just about her. It's about…a lot of different things."

"Like?"

I sigh, knowing I need to just rip the Band-Aid off and get to the point. I don't want to hurt her, but there's no use beating around the bush.

"I think there was a time when seeing each other felt good. Like we were still going to be friends in spite of the fact that our marriage was over, and wasn't that mature of us. Still loving each other, but in a different way." I pause, knowing this is the hard part. "But it doesn't feel that way anymore. At least not for me."

Sarah shakes her head and stands, walking over to the bookshelf against the wall where all my family photos are. She stares at them for a long time before plucking one down—the one Busy gave me from our hike together.

I put that photo on the shelf the minute I got home that night, knowing it deserved a place of honor. I knew, despite my best efforts, Busy and Junie had carved a space for themselves in my heart that only they could ever fill.

"Do you ever regret it?" Sarah asks me, her voice quiet. "The divorce?"

I blink, surprised. "What?"

She slowly sets the photo back in its place then turns around. That's when I see that her eyes have grown glassy.

"Because I do." Her eyes close, and her tears fall down her face. She shakes her head. "I regret it all the time."

I lean back against the kitchen island before I drop down onto one of the stools, feeling shock roll through me in a wave.

"Reid, I think I made a mistake," she says, taking a step toward me. "I think I was so…devastated by your diagnosis I didn't know what to do. It just made sense to do what was easiest."

I watch her as she crosses toward me, her hands twisting together in front of her, her face a wash of distress.

"Then you told me you were just going to be single, said it was easiest that way, and I figured we were the same, figured we both just wanted to avoid the pain the future would cause each other."

Sarah comes to a stop just in front of me.

"But I miss you. I miss what we used to be," she whispers, reaching out and taking my hand in hers. "Do you think we could get back to what we were before? Think you could forgive me?"

A million things run through my mind in that moment, appearing and then vanishing in a blink, but the one thing that stays at the forefront is Busy. The woman I love.

"I *do* forgive you, Sarah," I say, my voice soft, my heart sad. "But our time has run its course. There is no *us* anymore to return to. I've found…"

My voice trails off as I try to communicate what Busy and I have. When Sarah first got here, I wanted to shield all my feelings from her, not share them at all. But now, knowing she's entertaining the idea of getting back together, it feels important that I be as clear and transparent as possible.

"I've found the other half of my soul," I continue, hating the way she flinches at my words. "You and I shared something special, and I will always care about you. Always. But when things got hard, we gave up. Both of us, not just you."

I squeeze her hand, which is still in mine.

"So, no. I don't think we could get back to what we were before. Because my heart has found a new home."

Sarah watches me for a long minute before she pulls her

hand back and clears her throat, her eyes flicking around the room like she's desperate to get out of here as quickly as possible.

"Besides," I add on, wanting to lessen the blow, even just a little, "I think we both knew you always wanted to marry someone who makes a lot more money than I do."

Her head jerks back, but when she sees the smile on my face, her shoulders fall, her lips tilting up at the sides.

"I would make an *excellent* trophy wife," she replies, laughing quietly as she wipes away the last of her tears.

"Alton seems like a good man," I offer, trying to be kind. "You both seem happy."

She shakes her head, a tight smile on her face. "We're not long term. I know that. But…I'm sure there's someone else out there for me. Somewhere." She glances around and moves to grab her purse from where she set it on the couch. "So I guess… this is goodbye, then?" she asks, pulling her shoulders back.

I nod. "I think so."

I *know* so, but there's no reason to say that out loud. I can see that Sarah understands where I'm at. Where my heart is at.

The heat is stifling as we step out onto the porch, and I'm reminded of the fact that Busy is currently roasting in her cabin in temps even warmer than this. I'll need to crank the a/c when she comes over later.

"Hey, Reid," Sarah says, turning around to look at me. "I love you a lot, you know? I always have."

I nod. "I know. I never doubted that."

It's not a complete truth. I've never doubted that Sarah loved me, but from the minute she said she was leaving, I knew the love she had to give me wasn't enough, knew it wasn't *true* love, the kind you can't live without, because otherwise she never would have left.

"I guess I just want to make sure you don't hate me."

Shaking my head, I pull her in for one last hug. "I could never hate you, Sarah. Ever."

When I pull back, she gives me a watery smile then leans in and presses her lips to my cheek.

"You've always been one of the best men I know," she whispers. "I hope you and Busy are very happy together."

I smile, knowing we will be, feeling sure about it with every bone in my body.

Sarah turns to walk down the steps, which is when my stomach falls through the floor. Busy stands a few yards away from my porch, watching us with wide eyes.

"I just… You gave me one of your bags," she says, raising the backpack in her hand slowly so I can see it.

My heart begins beating rapidly as my mind scrambles over what she must think, seeing me on the porch, hugging Sarah, and *fuck*, Sarah kissing me.

"Busy, we were just—"

"You're fine, you're fine," she says as she steps forward and sets the bag on the steps, a tight smile on her face.

A fake smile.

"I'll just leave this and get back to Junie." She glances at Sarah then at me again. "See you later."

Then she spins around and hurries back to her own cabin, leaving me and Sarah behind.

chapter twenty-three
busy

I'm not an idiot.

At least I don't think I am.

Sometimes I make foolish choices, but it's rare for me to be in a situation where I'm completely in the dark. Which is why finding Sarah and Reid wrapped in an intimate embrace on his front porch was so startling. In no world did I see something like that coming.

I stand at the kitchen sink, washing a stain out of a pair of Junie's shorts for a few long minutes, trying to place how I feel. Before I can do too much reflection, I hear Reid's footfalls on the deck. He passes by my window, his eyes catching mine as he comes to the screen door.

"Can I come in?"

His words are gentle, tentative. He knows I'm upset.

"Yeah," I finally call, wringing out the shorts then laying them on a hand towel on the counter.

Reid steps into the living room, the height of him dwarfing

the space like it always does, and then he's standing at the counter across from me.

"Busy…"

"What did I walk in on?" I ask, not giving him a chance to speak first. "Because I felt like that's what it was, something intimate that wasn't meant for my eyes. And that doesn't feel very good."

Reid braces himself on the island between us, letting out a long sigh. "Sarah wants to get back together."

My head jerks back, surprise rolling through me. Again. "What?"

"She texted me when my phone was dead, so I didn't see it until we got home. When we got on the phone, she wanted to get lunch, but I told her I had plans, and she started asking about you. She seemed upset so I figured it couldn't hurt for her to come over so we could hash some things out."

Of course, I have a million questions, but I keep my mouth shut, knowing I should let him finish before I interrupt.

"She asked me if I regret the divorce because she does, said she wants to get back together, she misses what we used to be."

I hate it. Hate her.

She had her chance and she fucked it up, big time. Now she wants him back?

Well tough shit.

I cross my arms and glare at Reid. "And what did you tell her?"

He leans forward, his eyes pouring into mine. "I told her my heart already has a home."

My eyes narrow. Well isn't that fucking romantic.

I tilt my chin up. "You said that?"

Reid's lips tilt up on one side and he nods. "I did."

"In those words?"

"Verbatim."

I watch him carefully, looking for any signs that he isn't telling the truth but seeing none. That's something I love about Reid; there isn't a dishonest bone in his body. A refreshing change from the men in my past.

"Sarah and I are friends, sure," he continues. "But there isn't anything in me that wants to get back together with her. I've *never* wanted that. From the moment she said she was out, I knew that was it for us, knew any trust or love we shared was shattered beyond repair."

Reid clears his throat, and I see emotion rolling through him.

"You can't abandon someone in their darkest moment and believe you can come back to them later like they'll be unchanged."

My heart aches, knowing what he's been through. I can't imagine what it was like for him, finding out his diagnosis and then having his wife want a divorce so immediately. Like he was somehow defective, and now that she knew, she wanted a refund.

"I'm so sorry you went through that with her," I tell him, reaching out and placing my hand on his cheek.

He closes his eyes, his head tilting to the side, leaning into my caress.

"I'm sorry you saw us like that," he says, opening his eyes. "I hope you know we were just…saying goodbye. I told her we needed to move on from our friendship, told her it felt right at one point but doesn't anymore. Not now that I have you."

Reid pauses then chuckles, my hand falling away from his face.

"Not that I *have* you. But now that…you know, we're figuring things out."

Licking my lips, I step back from the island and lean back against the counter behind me.

"I appreciate that. I do," I tell him. "But I feel like if I hadn't walked over and seen you guys together, I wouldn't have gotten any of this information. Were you planning to talk to me at all about this?"

His head tilts to the side. "Honestly, I didn't see the point."

I nod, crossing my arms. "Maybe it's unfair of me to expect this from you, considering the fact that we haven't established what we are yet. But…" I pause, shaking my head. "I've dealt with secrets in the past, and they're something I can't handle. Earlier this summer, I talked with Sarah. I met her at Marie's. And she made it sound like you guys talk regularly or get together often."

Reid watches me, an unreadable expression on his face as I dump out all this…shit I've been carrying around for months.

"It bothered me then, but I kept it to myself because it felt like it *shouldn't* matter. Like I didn't have a right to wonder what was going on between you, because you and I weren't together. But now it feels like it matters. Now it feels like it should be something we talk about, like there shouldn't be these types of secrets."

Before I'm even done speaking, he's rounded the island and stepped close to me, taking my hands in his.

"I don't *ever* want to keep secrets from you, Busy," he says, his eyes searching mine. "For a long time I've lived a life where I kept things to myself because it didn't feel safe to trust someone else. But I feel safe with you. I feel like I could talk to you about anything and you…won't leave."

His words shock me. Not only because of how honest they

are, how vulnerable, but also because it makes it clear that he's been thinking about our conversation from the other night. He was so sure, then, that he had closed himself off from loving again out of some self-sacrificing motive. Now, it seems like he's accepted that it might be more rooted in fear of being abandoned again.

I step forward, wrapping my arms around his waist, sighing deeply as he brings me in tight against him. His hands gently caress my back, and I feel him place a kiss at the crown of my head.

"I'm crazy about you, Busy," he says, his voice quiet.

He pulls back, bringing his hands to either side of my face. "I didn't know love could feel like this."

I shake my head. "Me either."

Then he dips down and presses his lips to mine. It's gentle and sweet as he kisses me once, then twice. On the third, he nibbles at my lower lip, and I moan, opening to him, his tongue dipping in and tangling with mine.

God, I love the way he tastes, love the way it feels to be held in his arms, arms I know will hold me close even when they fail to hold steady.

My phone beeps with a chime that comes from the baby monitor on my phone, and a few seconds later I hear Junie call out for me from her room. I slow the kiss, wishing we had all the time in the world, right now, to kiss each other.

"I'll be right back," I tell him, stealing one more quick kiss before I head to Junie's room.

When I emerge back into the kitchen, Reid smiles at Junie and gives her a goofy wave.

"Misery!" she shouts, as if she didn't just see him an hour ago.

Then she's clambering out of my grasp and tottering across

the room to him. I understand the urge to race into his arms, and I laugh as he crouches low to pick her up then hoists her high up in the air. Junie squeals and laughs, and Reid brings her down and presses a bunch of kisses against her cheek.

My chest feels tight, and I rub against it, my palm moving in gentle circles as I watch them. It takes me a few minutes to realize what it is, and when I do, I smile.

I don't think my heart has ever felt so full.

When the door opens, my dad beams at me. "Hey, Little Bee," he says, embracing me like he hasn't seen me in weeks. "How many times do we have to tell you not to knock?"

I shrug and slip off my shoes as I step inside. "I don't know. Another thousand, probably."

He chuckles, closing the door and following me in. "Here to get your girl?"

I nod. "Yep. We're heading to the school to meet up with Marie and her kids."

"Oh, that'll be nice," he says. "She and your mom are outside. And just so you know…"

I grab the handle on the door then turn to look back at him.

"…she makes chicken piccata every Monday, hoping you'll stay for dinner."

My smile slips, and I glance over at the kitchen, spotting the bag of flour and containers of olive oil and chicken stock sitting out, surrounded by lemons and garlic and a few other ingredients.

"She does?"

He nods. "But she kept asking and you kept saying no, so…" He shrugs. "She didn't want to keep pestering you."

My throat grows tight, and I turn to look outside where I can see my mom and Junie sitting on a blanket in the shade.

"I know things have been…off between the two of you," Dad continues, coming up to my side and looking out with me. "But maybe some time, you could say yes? Might make her happy."

We stand there for a long minute before he pats me gently on the shoulder then walks away, probably heading back to his office on the other end of the house.

Things *have* been off between us, and even though we've touched on some of the reasons why, I've been careful not to address it again, not wanting to dive in too deep. Maybe it's time to stop avoiding the conversation.

Years ago, if I'd witnessed a man I was talking to embracing another woman, I would have shut down. No conversation, no explanations, no 'hashing it out'. But when I found out I was pregnant, I started going to therapy, knowing I needed to sort through some of my own issues if I had any chance of being a decent mom to this little girl.

It's the main reason why Reid and I were able to sort through what happened without it being so much worse. The reason why I didn't immediately jump to the worst-case scenario when I saw them. Why I was able to believe Reid when he told me what happened.

Maybe I need to do the same with my mom. I think, with her, the reason I avoid the difficult conversations is the same reason Reid was shutting out the idea of love: fear. I'm afraid she'll realize I'm too much trouble, the thing I've kind of always been waiting for. It might not be rational, but it's there just the same.

I watch them outside for a few more minutes before I slide my phone out of my pocket and call Marie.

"Hey! We're just loading up. Should be there in twenty minutes," she says, the sound of kids yelling and laughing in the background.

"That's actually why I'm calling," I tell her. "Can we raincheck for another day? I'm thinking about staying at my parents' for dinner tonight."

"Oh, no problem!" she says. "We're still heading over because these monsters need to run around and get some of this energy out. But just text me and we can try again soon."

"Thanks for understanding. Sometimes you just need…time with your mom," I say, something like relief settling in my chest.

Marie laughs. "Girl, my mom and I get together every week. I completely understand."

We exchange goodbyes and get off the phone, and then I tug open the door and head outside over to where they're sitting in the grass.

My mom turns and sees me then smiles wide. "Look, Junie! Mom's here!"

Junie giggles and climbs off her lap, tripping over her shoes before she stands again and begins racing toward me. My girl loves to run. I crouch low and accept a big hug, falling back into the grass with a laugh. We snuggle for a second and then I sit up, looking at my mom, who is shaking out the blanket they were sitting on.

"How'd she do today?" I ask.

"Good. Slept well, ate well." Mom shrugs and gives me a smile. "No complaints. How was work?"

"Also good. I think Briar is already considering hiring a new employee."

"Oh, wow. Things must be going really well, then."

I nod, staying seated as she approaches, her blanket flung over one arm.

"Hey, I was thinking, if you don't have plans tonight, maybe we could stay for dinner?"

My mom's eyebrows rise, but then she beams at me. "I would love that. I'm making chicken piccata."

I stand, hoisting Junie with me, something inside of me knowing that everything is going to be just fine.

"Really?" I say, following behind her as she heads for the door. "That's my favorite."

chapter twenty-four
reid

There are lots of things to take into consideration when deciding on what kind of wood to use for a project.

Appearance is the most common care for customers and guides a lot of the decision-making processes, things like grain patterns and color and how well the wood absorbs a stain. Cost is the next most important, followed by durability—how much damage can it sustain? How well does it withstand scratches and other wear and tear?

But the thing people don't think about, almost at all, is maintenance. The kind of work that goes into keeping your piece looking new and beautiful for years, whether it's for a table or a bookshelf or a chair or anything else.

Of course, on my end, those are things I think about constantly. When I'm making a piece, I try to use the type of wood that most closely aligns with the purpose. For example, I rarely use red oak for a table top, unless a customer specifically requests it, because the grain has a lot of open pores that make it easy for crumbs to get trapped in the surface.

The hardest part is taking two completely different woods and merging them together. Each type requires different care, can carry different loads, and handles wear and tear in completely different ways. Sometimes, though, what comes from finding two pieces that are different but well matched is truly beautiful.

I cross my arms, staring at the new slabs that were just delivered. They're leaning up against the wall of my shop, and I make mental notes about each one before I hoist them up onto the rack where I let new wedges sit for a few days before I get started. Then I return to the project I'm currently working on: finishing up the last elements of Ellis' chairs for the buildout at Dock 7.

"What do you think, girl?" I ask Sydney, spreading my arms wide once I've finished joining the last pieces together, the beautiful white oak and cedar pieces merging together to form a truly beautiful final product. "Think she'll be happy?"

Sydney whimpers and rolls over, putting her belly in the air.

"Well, that's not a good sign." I laugh, taking a step back to examine my work.

I don't often use dovetail joints on chairs, but I felt like it would be perfect for this project. It's decorative but still understated, and with the colored leather Ellis selected, it should provide a nice compliment.

She agrees when she shows up midday to take a look at it.

"Oh, Reid, it's beautiful," she says, clasping her hands together and circling around the chair, examining it from every angle. "You've really outdone yourself."

"And all the leather covers came in earlier this week," I say, stepping back into my office to grab the sample cushion I set up. "What do you think?"

Ellis gasps again, reaching out to touch it then taking it in her hands. "Wow." She rubs her hands across the soft material, humming softly. "It's perfect."

I smile. "I'm so glad you like it. If you don't want any changes, I can take the second deposit and get started on the remaining chairs. I'll have more than enough time to get them to you before the buildout is completed in October."

"Please consider this my official thumbs-up," she says, laughing. "I can't wait to see them all together."

We head to my office to handle payment, but when we're done and I expect Ellis to head out, she settles more comfortably into the chair on the opposite side of my desk and gives me a cheeky smile.

"So, Reid, is it true you're dating Busy Mitchell?"

I chuckle awkwardly. "Why do you ask?"

Ellis shrugs. "Well, I'm a woman who likes her gossip," she says, honestly. "And it would be nice to have something to share with the ladies at The Pines when I head over for my weekly bridge game tomorrow."

My lips twist as I try to hide my own smile. "We're spending time together," I reply, trying not to share too much without having cleared it with Busy first. I know she's a little self-conscious of everyone in town talking about her business, and I don't want to be the cause of that.

"What does that mean?" Ellis asks, with a titter of a laugh.

It's been almost two weeks since our hike to Kilroy, since our conversation in her kitchen, and we've spent almost every evening together, sitting out on the deck or snuggled on the couch, just talking about life and diving into the deep with each other. I feel like Busy and I have talked about things most people don't get into until they've been together for months, if not years.

I've cherished every single moment, even the hard ones,

when we've discussed what *my* future looks like and the pain both of us have been through in the past. It feels real and honest and true, and it makes me fall more and more in love with her every damn day.

But I'm not going to say that to Ellis.

"It means...Busy is very important to me," I answer.

More than just important. Busy is everything.

"Well, I know how you young folks like to pretend you're not dating. My granddaughter calls it 'hanging out', which is ridiculous," she says, rolling her eyes.

I can't help but laugh.

"But while you're 'hanging out', don't forget that every girl wants to feel like the most important woman in the room every once in a while." She pats my hand and stands. "Don't forget to woo her."

Ellis takes a few minutes to admire her chair one more time before I walk her out. But when we get to the door, she stops again and gives me a kind look.

"I just wanted to let you know," she tells me, "I've seen your grandfather work this shop, and I've seen your father work this shop, and I think both of them would be really proud of you and what you've done with this place over the past few years."

I give her a quiet smile. "Thanks, Ellis."

"Have a good day, sweetie. And keep me posted on my chairs."

She puts on a huge pair of sunglasses and struts through the door, and I can't help but smile to myself. She really is something else.

I spin around, looking back at the handful of half-finished projects I need to work on before admitting I need to get some admin work done and heading back to my office. I think about what Ellis said for the rest of the day, her words ringing more and more true as the hours pass.

By the time I'm ready to close up for the day, I'm like a man on a mission, and after I lock up, I head over to Main Street and down to Happily Ever After. I spot Busy through the window, her eyes connecting with mine. She grins at me as I pull the door open and walk right over to where she stands behind the counter.

"Hey, you! What are you—"

I slip my hand into her hair and tug her forward, pressing a kiss to her lips. When I pull back, her eyes are soft.

"What was that for?" she whispers.

"Busy Mitchell, will you go on a date with me on Saturday night?"

Her lips tilt up on the side. "Like out to dinner?"

I nod. "Yeah. Like out to dinner."

"Only if you promise to kiss me like this while we're waiting for our table."

Chuckling, I kiss her again. "More than happy to do that."

I release my hold on her neck and take a step back, and Busy's eyes glance around the store behind me. When I turn around, I spot a woman standing in the romance section, holding a book against her chest and staring at us with a gooey smile.

"I just have to see if my mom or Briar can watch Junie," Busy says, adjusting the postcards and flyers I bumped when I pulled her over the counter.

"Okay. And if they can't, Junie can come on the date, too."

Busy laughs. "You don't want a two-year-old at a restaurant. Trust me. It takes a lot of work."

"Well, since I'm gonna know that kid for the rest of my life, and I intend to take you out to dinner on a regular basis, we should probably start practicing. Make sure she learns."

Her nostrils flare, and her eyes get glassy. "You just know how to say all the right things, don't you?"

And then she laughs and rounds the counter to kiss me again.

When my phone rings on Saturday night when I'm getting ready for my date with Busy, I consider ignoring it, but when I see it's my mother, I answer.

"Hey, mom."

"Well, hello there, son of mine," she says, and I can hear the smile in her voice through the speaker.

"What are you up to?"

"Oh, just lounging by the pool at our hotel. We've been in New York City for the past week. But that's not why I'm calling." She pauses. "A little birdie told me you're dating Busy Mitchell. Is that true?"

I finish trimming up the edges of my mustache then slather some lotion on my hands and moisturize my face.

"It *is* true," I reply, leaning toward the mirror and giving myself a long hard look. "And even though I *should* be pissed that you talked to her without my permission, I guess I have you and your meddling to thank for it."

"Well, I've never been so glad to have my meddling pay off, because I was prepared for you to cut me out of your life forever."

I grab the phone and head into my room, tugging my closet door open.

"I would never cut you out of my life, mom. We have our disagreements, and…I've had to process a few things, but I love you. That will never change."

She clears her throat, a telltale sign that she's trying not to cry.

"So…how's New York?" I ask, selecting one of my few dress shirts and slipping it on. Then, after a pause: "How's Vance?"

There's a beat before my mother responds.

"It's amazing. We've been bouncing around from restaurant to restaurant, trying all the best, most delicious meals. I swear, Vance is going to have to roll me onto the plane when we leave in a few days."

I chuckle, finishing up the last few buttons on my shirt. I honestly can't remember the last time I got dressed like this—maybe for my dad's funeral two years ago—and I'm wondering if I should do it more often. I clean up nice.

"We're having a great time," she says with a happiness in her voice that I haven't heard in a long time.

"Well, I have to admit, I'm a little jealous," I tell her. "I've always wanted to go to New York."

"Maybe we can plan a trip there together someday," she says, sounding hopeful. "The four of us, or maybe five, if you two want to bring Junie along."

I nod, though I know she can't see me. "That might be fun."

There's a long pause on the other end of the line, and then my mother clears her throat. "Well, baby, I don't want to keep you. I know you have a *busy* night ahead of you…"

I groan, and my mother laughs.

"…so you go have fun."

"Thanks, mom. Love you."

"Love you, too."

chapter twenty-five
busy

I lick into Reid's mouth, moaning when his hand grabs my ass. My hands tangle into his hair, gripping tightly and giving a gentle tug, then I shift my hips as he presses me down against him.

We're sitting in the cab of his truck, my legs straddling his, making out like teenagers who don't want to get caught, and it's the most frustrating and delicious experience I've ever had.

"Fuck, Busy," he whispers as I kiss down his neck and suck at the skin, my tongue pulsing and my teeth grazing.

His hands slip through the leg of my shorts, grasping my ass, and I move my hips again, lifting slightly, hoping he'll slide his fingers between my legs like he did on our last date night.

We've been playing this infuriating game for weeks. We go out to dinner, wander around town—getting ice cream, coffee, walking the marina, any number of things—and then he brings me home and we make out in his truck. Then he adjusts himself and walks me to my door, where he usually kisses me again before sending me inside to where Briar or my mom are hanging out on the couch, keeping an eye on Junie.

I have never felt so sexually aroused in my entire life, desperate for his hands on me at any given moment, and yet he's been continuously slowing us down, putting on the brakes right before things get hot and heavy.

Like I said, infuriating.

I get why he's doing it, keeping us moving slow. He's worried we'll run hot and fast and burn out just as quickly, but there's no way that will happen. Not a chance in hell.

So I wait. Desperate. Needy. Wanting.

Reid's fingers swipe against me and my head tilts back as I moan, already wet.

"You gonna make me come?" I ask as the tip of one finger dips into my opening.

"Nothing I want more," he replies.

But then, instead of slipping those fingers into me, he pulls back, his hands sliding out of my shorts. Then he pats my ass twice.

"Do you wanna head inside? With me?"

I blink, surprise and elation soaring through me—until reality sets in.

Leaning forward, I rest my forehead against his. "I wish I could, but my mom's inside with Junie." I chuckle. "And I can't go fool around with you at your house knowing she's next door, watching my kid."

Reid kisses me, nibbling lightly on my lower lip, the way I like it. Then he pulls back. "Good thing she's at her house, then. With Junie, for the whole night."

I sit back, my ass resting on his thighs, confused.

"What?"

He smirks. "I might have asked your mom if she could watch Junie overnight for us. So after we left, she loaded up her car and went home." Reid leans forward and kisses my chin then my neck. "They've been there all night, and Junie's asleep at her house."

I must be quiet for too long because Reid speaks again.

"If you don't want to, we can head over and get Junie right now, bring her home. But if you *do* want Junie to spend the night at your mom's, we can head inside, have a night to ourselves."

I plant a hand on his chest. "Do you mean to tell me...you *planned* this? And we've been wandering around town all night chatting when we could have been in there, getting it on?"

Reid chuckles, his head falling back against the headrest, his fingers pressing at his eyes and the bridge of his nose before he looks at me again. "Maybe."

"Why did you keep this a secret?" I ask, my voice far too loud for the interior of his truck. "Why didn't you tell me earlier?"

"If I had told you about this, that I planned to leave Junie with your mom, what would you have done?"

Scoffing, I wave a hand around. "I would have wanted to skip dinner, obviously."

"Exactly." He smirks at me. "And I was in the mood for steak."

I burst into laughter and fall to the side, slipping off of him and onto the bench seat. I reach down for my shoes but pause when a thought occurs to me.

"Wait a minute, does this mean you and my mom conspired so I could get laid tonight?"

Reid winces. "It sounds a lot worse when you say it like

that."

I wave at him, dismissing what he just said.

"I'm not worried about it. She's always known I'm a troublemaker, and I have a child—there's no misconception that I'm still a virgin."

At that Reid barks out a laugh, and we both slip out of the truck and head inside his cabin. The early fall temperatures are far cooler than what we were experiencing all summer, so he's removed his air conditioning unit and returned to just keeping his windows open. A brisk autumn breeze wafts through, causing his wooden blinds to dance gently as we cross through his living room and over to his kitchen. He puts his leftovers in the fridge then lifts up a bottle that's sitting out on the counter.

"Do you want a glass of wine?"

I shake my head, stepping toward him and playing with one of the buttons on the dress shirt he wears every time we go out to dinner. "I don't want anything else tonight except you."

Reid's lips curve, and then he dips down to kiss me. It starts slow, even though we were already hot and heavy in the truck, and as much as I wish he would step on the gas, I also love that he's taking his time. You only get one first time with someone, and as much as I want to jump into bed and get to it, there's something romantic and special about savoring it.

He presses me up against the kitchen counter, his mouth on mine, his hands touching and gliding before they move to the buttons on my shorts. He undoes them then crouches down, slowly sliding them off my legs, his fingers grazing my overheated skin as he reveals my tiny black panties. Then he slips his fingers under the straps and slides those off as well.

Every movement is slow, leisurely, almost calculated, which is why it's such a surprise when, without so much as a warning, he presses his mouth against me, his tongue licking into the slit between my legs and pulsing against my clit.

I gasp, my hands flying to the top of his head, my fingers tangling in his hair, but he doesn't let me control him. Instead, he grips one of my ankles and slides his hand up, shifting my leg so it's hitched over his shoulder, opening me to him.

"God, you taste so good," he says, right before his mouth latches onto me again, his tongue swirling around my clit before licking down and thrusting into me.

"Shit," I moan. "Oh, god."

He groans against me, his head shifting from side to side as he eats my pussy like it's the only thing he wants to do with the rest of his life.

"I want you to come at least once," he says, looking up at me, his tongue still pulsing against my clit and sending delicious sparks through my veins. "Maybe twice."

Then he slips one finger inside me, followed quickly by a second. I cry out, knowing I'm barreling toward that first orgasm he's promised, my hips gyrating against him as he flicks his fingers against a spot deep inside of me.

"Come on, baby," he says, watching me. He uses his other hand to spread my lips apart, his tongue swirling around and around my clit but never touching it.

"Fuck, fuck, fuck," I whisper, the cord of tension within me pulling tighter and tighter and tighter…

Then he flattens his tongue and licks my clit again.

…until it snaps.

I go flying over the edge, prickly heat racing through my veins as my entire body shatters into pieces. I can barely manage to brace myself against him, and I slump down against the wall. Reid's arms brace me, catching the weight of me as I join him on the floor.

"That was so good," I whisper, my eyes closed, a smile surely stretched across my face. "So, so good."

He chuckles and presses his lips to mine, where I can taste the hint of me. "I'm glad."

We sit there for a minute until I get my bearings, and then we both stand and I pick my panties up from the ground.

"You won't be needing those," he says, slipping them out of my hand.

I smirk. "Feeling confident?"

Reid's eyes flit up and down my body. "Hopeful."

His response makes me smile, and I bite my lip, following behind him as he leads me into his bedroom, where we climb onto his bed and face each other.

"You should know, it's been a few years since I've had sex," he tells me, his hand reaching forward as he plays with the stud in my ear.

I take his hand and kiss it, and his eyes connect with mine. "I'm not worried." Then I take the two fingers that were just inside me and suck them into my mouth, watching as his eyes go dark.

"You do something like that again, and it might be over far too fast."

I shrug. "We'll figure it out."

He chuckles, sitting up on his elbow and looking down at me. "Feeling confident?" he asks, echoing my earlier words back to me.

Lifting my hand, I run it through his hair, pushing it back so it's out of his eyes. "Absolutely."

He smiles then presses his lips against mine before pulling back and reaching into his wallet to grab a condom. Then we're kissing and tugging at each other's clothes. I feel desperate to get naked, to be pressed against him, skin to skin. When we're finally undressed and I get a look at what he has going on below the belt, I sigh, licking my lips.

"I want to fuck this pretty mouth," he says, coasting his thumb over my lips. "But if I do, that'll be it for me tonight, and I'm even more desperate to be inside you."

I nod, but my head falls back on a moan as his mouth comes down on my chest, his tongue teasing my nipples. He plucks at them, nibbles at them, until I'm writhing again, my earlier orgasm long forgotten.

And then he's sliding the condom on and settling between my legs. His lips press to mine, kissing me gently, sweetly, lovingly, before he notches his cock against my opening and slides home.

I cry out as he spreads me wide, as my body makes room for the length and width of him, and I claw at his back.

"Fuck, you feel so good," he says once he's fully seated. "So wet." He draws back slowly before slamming into me again. "So warm."

"Oh my god, Reid." I can't keep my eyes open, can't do anything but cling to him as he draws back then spears forward again, desperate to anchor myself for fear of flying away.

"I love you, Busy," he groans, thrusting in then drawing back, again and again, his cock hitting some delicious spot inside me that has me on the verge of tears. "I love you more with every breath. With every blink. With every second."

We kiss, messy and sloppy and desperate for each other, as he fucks into me.

But it's not fucking. Or maybe it is. Maybe it's making love, too.

Maybe it's fucking love.

I begin to climb to the peak again, but slower this time, my body taking longer to get me there, already depleted from my earlier orgasm. Reid keeps at it, his hands coming down to stroke at my clit, his mouth dropping to suck at my aching nipples.

And then, just when I feel like I might sit at the precipice forever, he shifts just slightly, presses in just a bit more, and I fly over the edge.

"I'm coming," I cry out, digging my fingers into his back again.

My eyes slam shut and I see stars as lightning ripple through me.

"Oh, fuck, it's so good."

"Yes, baby, yes," he groans, his hips shifting faster. "Come for me."

He stills, his mouth dropping against my neck, where he sucks at the skin as he pulses within me. We lie there for a long moment, unmoving, exhausted, completely ruined, before he rolls off to the side.

"That was…" He pants, trailing off.

I nod. "So good."

We look at each other, and he smiles then takes my hand and kisses the back before he yanks the covers over us and tucks me into his side, where we very blissfully fall asleep.

I wake in the morning to the smell of something delicious—coffee and breakfast, if I'm guessing correctly—and I stretch my entire body out, flinging my hands above my head as I sink further into the covers.

What a fucking night.

Fooling around in the truck and then that delicious orgasm in the kitchen...I bite my lip thinking about it, the memory then rolling into what it felt like to have him between my legs, thick and hard and hot. I nearly groan just thinking about it, and I allow myself a few minutes of lying in Reid's bed before I hop up and slip on my panties with one of his shirts.

"Good morning," he says as I emerge, grinning at me from where he sits at the counter, sipping a coffee and...

"Are you doing the Sunday crossword?" I ask, stepping up to his side and looking down at the newspaper in front of him.

He nods. "Yeah. It was something my grandfather and I used to do together when I was a kid. Well, *he* would do the crossword and I would sit next to him, guessing wildly inaccurate words."

"That sounds fun," I say, giggling. "Are you any good at them?"

At that, he shakes his head. "Not in the slightest."

"Oh good, because I would be absolutely no help." I drop onto the stool beside him and take a sip from his coffee.

He watches me for a long minute before he leans in and presses his lips to mine. "I'm glad you stayed over last night."

"Me, too." I kiss him again. "We should do that more often."

"Count me in."

We laze around, nibbling at the biscuits he made and tossing around hilariously bad words for his crossword before we hop into the shower together. I drop down to my knees, taking Reid in my hand and stroking as he leans back, watching me with unrestrained desire. When I lick at him, swirling my tongue around his cock then sucking him in hungrily, his lips part, his eyes flashing.

And then he makes good on his promise to fuck my pretty mouth, my name a reverent prayer he chants over and over again as he comes down my throat.

chapter twenty-six
reid

When I step into the small building a few blocks away from Main Street, I'm nervous as hell. Maybe more nervous than I was when I went to the doctor's office to get my official diagnosis for Kennedy's, and that day was one of the more difficult ones in my entire life.

The receptionist is nice, a girl maybe close to Busy's age, and she gets me checked in and hands me a clipboard to fill out with some basic information. I wait until the doctor comes out to greet me and calls me back into her office.

She motions for me to take a seat, which I do, and then she sits in the chair across from me and grabs a notebook to place on her lap.

"Hi, Reid."

"Hi, Dr. Green."

"How's your day going so far?"

I shrug. "Pretty good, I guess."

Dr. Green nods. "I'm glad to hear that. Why don't you tell

me a bit about why you've decided to start therapy?"

"I filled out a questionnaire with that, I thought."

"You did, and I read it. But I always like to hear it in my patient's words."

I take a deep breath and let it out long and slow. "Right."

My eyes flit around the room, taking in the minimal décor and—I laugh—the gray walls.

"What's funny?" she asks, her lips tilting up at the sides and her eyes scanning the room as well.

"Just…the wall color," I tell her. "My girlfriend said you'd probably have gray walls. She calls it millennial gray."

Dr. Green laughs. "I've heard that before, about the color, not my walls specifically." She makes a quick note on her notebook. "So your girlfriend knows you're doing therapy?"

"She does. It was her idea, actually."

"And why is that?"

"Probably because it was so helpful for her. She went when she found out she was pregnant a few years ago, said she wanted to work through some things to be a better mom."

The doctor smiles. "That was brave of her. There are many things parents think to do to get ready for a child, but it takes a really smart person to realize they have some inside work they need to do as well."

"She's a smart woman."

Smart enough that I listened when she said I needed to consider talking to someone.

"So, then, tell me why you're here."

I sigh, looking down at my hands, roughened from the work I've been doing for most of my adult life.

"I have a disease that's going to eventually make it really hard for me to take care of myself, and my doctor recommended seeing someone to talk about things as my body begins to decline." I pause. "Said it might help to process it all, instead of just carrying it alone."

Dr. Green bobs her head, makes another note or two on her pad.

"And has something happened that makes you think your body is beginning to decline?"

I tilt my head from side to side. "Yes and no. I dropped a sander I was using a few weeks ago. I work with wood and do a lot of work with my hands. It was an easy mistake, a simple slip…"

When I trail off, she smiles gently. "But it didn't feel that way to you."

I shake my head, my chest tight as I admit something I don't want to. "No. It didn't feel that way to me."

We talk for the full hour, a miracle considering I only promised Busy I'd come to introduce myself. Thankfully, we don't talk *just* about the incident with the sander. We touch on my grandfather and what it was like to watch him go through this disease, on my dad passing away and some of the struggles I've had with my mom.

And we talk about Busy. A lot. About how incredible she is. Her and Junie. How much I love her. How thankful I am that she came into my life and fought for the us I didn't realize we could be, fought for us when I didn't even know how to.

When our hour is up, I don't necessarily feel like bouncing out of here the way some people talk about feeling after a therapy session, but the pressure in my chest feels like it's been released some. A surprise, to be sure, enough that I book a second appointment for two weeks from today without even dreading it.

"I'm proud of you," Busy says as we walk down Main Street

holding hands, her fingers twisted with mine.

I shrug. "I didn't really do anything. I just…talked."

"Exactly," she says, pulling me to a stop in front of Happily Ever After. "Talking is a hard thing to do. Especially for someone who is so used to keeping all his feelings tucked away inside this sexy chest."

She pokes me with one finger, and I laugh.

"Besides, you said you'd do something hard for you if I did something hard for me, and I did," she tells me, tilting her head to the side, in the direction of the gallery next door.

I glance to the side, the information taking a beat to settle until…my eyebrows rise. "Did you send them your portfolio?"

Her face twists, and she nods. "It was horrible and I'm never doing it again, not ever ever. But…I did it."

I yank her against me and wrap my arms around her, careful not to spill the coffee she's holding in one hand.

"I'm so proud of you," I say, pressing a kiss against the crown of her head. "Seriously. So proud. No matter what they say."

"They're going to say no," she mumbles into my chest. Then she pulls her head back and looks up to meet my eyes, even though the full weight of her still leans against me. "Or if they *do* say yes, it'll just be because I'm a Mitchell."

"Hey," I say, my brow furrowing. "That is definitely not at all true."

She raises an eyebrow.

"Okay, so the second part might be a little bit true, but that doesn't mean you're not incredibly talented."

Busy laughs and tucks herself against me again before letting out a long sigh.

"If nothing comes from it, it's okay," she tells me. "I just want to know I tried."

I nod and kiss her head again. "Exactly."

We continue strolling down the block toward one end of Main Street, admiring all the Halloween décor in the front windows of each of the shops before crossing the street and heading in the opposite direction. Junie is on a playdate with Leo this morning, so we have a blissful few hours just the two of us and nowhere in particular that we need to go. We've just been drinking coffee and wandering around downtown after my stupid therapy appointment ended.

Okay, maybe it wasn't stupid. It was actually a lot better than I assumed it would be, and I have Busy to thank for that, for pushing me for the past few weeks, ever since that incident with the sander. It's something she's been bringing up regularly ever since we first started dating back at the end of summer, saying how important it would be for me to process all the emotional and physical challenges that are coming.

"But I don't want to just constantly worry about the future," I told her one day. "If I'm always talking about what's going wrong, it's all I'll think about."

Busy pinned me with a look. "But isn't it all you think about anyway?" When I didn't respond, she gave me a pinched smile. "At least if you tried going to therapy, you'd feel less like you were carrying it all alone. And maybe you'd have someone giving you a better perspective on things as they change."

She doesn't realize that I have *her* for that. That *she's* the one who makes me feel like I'm not doing it all alone.

We've only been together for a few months, but the way having her and Junie around has completely reshaped how I feel about each and every day is just…mind-blowing. My shoulders don't feel so weighted down with the worries I carry. I didn't know I could experience this much joy on a regular basis, assumed it was only for obnoxiously positive or rich people.

But apparently, it's also for me.

"Have you decided what you want to be for Halloween yet?" I ask her, my eyes snagging on a sign for the annual Halloween Spooktacular.

"I was thinking I'd go as a cat."

I chuckle. "Where did that come from?"

She shrugs. "I love cats, and it's the easiest costume in the world. Wear all black, put on some makeup for the nose and whiskers, buy ears and a tail. It'll take me five minutes."

"You're ridiculous."

"No, I'm smart. The last thing I want to do is spend weeks planning a Halloween costume. I don't have the time for that."

When I don't say anything, she stops and stares at me.

"You're one of those people, aren't you? How long have you known what you were going to be for Halloween?"

I rub my tongue along the ridges of my teeth. "Since last year."

At that, Busy tosses her head back and laughs. "Oh my god, I love it so much. What are you going to be?"

"Nick and I are going as Harry and Marv from *Home Alone*."

"That is incredibly niche."

I chuckle. "It is, but it's going to be amazing." I tug out my phone and show her photos of the costume inspiration.

"It really *is* amazing," she says, giggling as she scrolls through the images I have saved. "How did I not know you're into this stuff?"

Shrugging, I tuck my phone away then take her hand. "We still have plenty of stuff to learn about each other."

At that, her smile softens. "Yeah, we do." Her fingers twist in mine as we continue walking down the street. "I can't wait."

...one year later...

I take a long, deep breath when we finally reach the lookout, soaking in the view of the lake below, the sun bright in the cloudless sky.

It's a perfect day for a quick hike up to Crestline Outlook, the autumn leaves at their most luscious and just on the verge of dropping, the air crisp and cool but not so cold that we need gloves or a heavy coat. It takes about an hour each way, just enough that it's a workout, but not so much that Junie can't come with or it overworks my body.

"I always love views like this of the entire town," Busy says, crouching down to pet Sydney, her eyes fixed on the lake where it stretches out into the distance. "And there are so many of them. I feel like I've only done half of the hikes that show most of Cedar Point, you know?"

I nod, the nerves racing through me keeping me from saying anything.

"Do you think this is a good spot to sit down for lunch? Or should we keep going? I feel like there might be one more spot about ten minutes that way."

I shake my head then pull off my backpack and begin pulling out supplies. "This one's good."

We take a few minutes to lay out the blanket and unpack the food—sandwiches and fruit and sparkling water, plus a juice box for Junie—before we're stretching out and enjoying lunch with a view.

"This was a great idea," Busy says, taking a bite of her sandwich. "I don't know why I never think of these things."

Junie tugs open her bag of chips and pops one in her mouth, crunching loudly before she looks at me.

"When are you going to ask to be my daddy?"

I freeze, my eyes flicking to Busy, whose face has flushed bright red as she chuckles.

"Junie, why would you ask something like that?" she says, glancing at me and shaking her head. "She doesn't know what she's asking."

"No, Mr. Reid's gonna be my daddy," she insists, and I feel a pang for the days when she used to call me Misery. "He told me."

Busy laughs awkwardly and looks my way. "I'm sorry, I don't…"

She trails off, though, when she finds me holding a small wooden box.

"I originally planned to ask you after lunch," I say, clearing my throat, realizing I need to go off script a bit. "But when you ask a three-year-old if it's okay if you marry her mommy, I think you take the risk that the surprise might get thrown slightly off course."

Her hands come up to her mouth, covering it as she watches me. I shift my position so I'm no longer sitting on my ass but instead on both of my knees—both because I will worship her for the rest of my life, if she'll let me.

"Busy Mitchell."

Her hands drop to her chest, and her eyes connect with mine.

"Before you, I had no clue what love really looked like. The kind of love I knew was shallow in its depth, and selfish in its execution. I've been afraid to open myself up to anything else, believing that protecting my heart was the only way to keep from getting wounded again."

Her eyes grow watery, and I resist the urge to reach out and pull her in to my chest.

"But, like I said…that was before you. Before I knew the truth. That love can reach depths I've never searched, be selfless and sacrificing even in the most difficult moments. The way I feel about you is more than I ever believed love could be, and when I think about 'forever', all I feel is joy and hope," my voice chokes as I pause, "even in the face of what's to come, because I know I'll get to spend each of my days at your side."

A single tear tracks down Busy's face, and she bats it away, but not before Junie notices.

"Don't cry, mommy," she says, getting up and walking toward her mother, hugging her tightly.

Busy embraces her daughter, but her eyes never leave mine.

"When I think about the future, there's nobody else on this earth I could ever imagine standing next to me, holding my hand. On good days, and bad. I want to hold your hand for the rest of my life," I continue. "And Junie's, too. And I hope you know that when I ask you to marry me, I'm asking you both. Because I'm not just asking you to be with me forever, I'm asking you to let me become a part of your family. To be your husband, to be Junie's dad."

At that, Junie smiles.

I open the box, showing her the silver band I bought for her, with the row of inlaid diamonds.

"Busy Mitchell, will you marry me?"

She turns to Junie. "What do you think, Junie Bee? Should we say yes?"

Junie nods. "I already said yes. He asked me yesterday."

At that, Busy bursts into laughter and scoots toward me, wrapping her arms around my shoulders. "Yes," she whispers. "Yes, I'll hold your hand for the rest of my life."

She presses her lips to mine, kissing me once then twice before pulling back so I can slide the ring onto her finger. She examines it for a long minute. "It's beautiful."

"And I have something for Junie, too, if that's okay?" I ask, tugging the other box out of my pocket.

Junie races over from where she'd begun eating chips again, her mouth opening when she sees the small bracelet, a silver chain with three bands looped together.

"Does this mean I'm getting married, too?" she asks, sticking her arm out and waiting for me to put the bracelet on her wrist.

Busy chuckles. "You're not getting married," she says, tugging Junie into her lap as I adjust the clasp. "But we *are* going to be a family. So that means Mr. Reid is making a commitment to both of us."

"What's a commetent?"

She laughs again. "A commitment is a promise." Her eyes meet mine. "And he's promising that he's going to love us forever."

Junie bounces up and down. "And he'll be my daddy?"

I nod. "If you want me to be."

She giggles and flings her arms around me. "Can I call you daddy *now*?"

This kid. My heart swells with love for her. It's been the most incredible thing, watching her grow over the past year, how she's changed and learned and turned into this...*child* when it feels like she was just a baby when I first met her.

Busy shrugs, her eyes connecting with mine. "I'm okay with it if you are."

"I can't wait to tell my friends I have a daddy," she says, climbing out of my lap and walking back over to where she left her bag of chips.

"It's pretty cool," Busy calls over to Junie, but her eyes are on me.

"It *is* pretty cool."

She shifts over so she's sitting between my legs, her back resting against my chest, and then glances down at her ring again. "It's beautiful, Reid."

"I'm glad you like it," I say, kissing the side of her head. Then I lower my voice. "And just so you know…*you* can call me daddy, too, if you want."

Busy barks out a laugh and elbows me gently in the ribs.

"Or…husband," I say, wrapping my arms around her. "Maybe hubby."

"Or best friend."

"Partner in crime."

"Soulmate."

I hum, my lips tilting up. "I like that one." I press a kiss to the top of her head with a smile. "I think I like that one the best."

Busy squeezes my hand with hers. "Me, too."

epilogue
busy

"I know you're planning something," Reid says as he steps up behind me at the mirror, his arms sliding gently around my waist and pulling me snug against him. "You've always been a horrible liar."

"I don't know *what* you're talking about." I smirk as I put on my second earring, a simple gold hoop set that Junie gave me for my birthday last year. "Besides," I continue, my eyes connecting with his in the mirror, "if something *was* planned, is there any harm in just letting it be a surprise?"

He chuckles and presses a kiss against my neck, then he inhales, his eyes closed. I lower my hands to rest on top of his, enjoying the quiet intimacy of how it feels when he holds me like this, the way my blood begins to heat just slightly.

I've heard about the seven-year itch, but I can't begin to fathom what it must feel like. Each passing day makes me want

311

more time with my husband, and I'd bet my life he'd say he feels the same about me.

"You look beautiful," Reid says, his eyes opening and his gaze raking me up and down in the mirror. "Have I seen this dress before?"

I shake my head. "Briar picked it out when we did that trip to San Francisco."

He hums, the sound low and gravelly and sending a ripple down my spine. "Well, I like it," he tells me, his thumb caressing my hip.

We make a striking pair in our reflection, each dressed to the nines, something we so rarely have the occasion to do. It's a special celebration tonight, and that means a chance to get a little gussied up, even if we're just going to the other side of the lake.

"I especially like," Reid continues, his hand dipping lower and finding the short hem of my blue floral dress, "how soft it is."

I inhale softly when his fingers slide between my thighs and gently stroke the skin just below the edge of my underwear.

"We don't have time for this," I mumble, though my protest is half-hearted at best.

We're running a little late, and I know people are waiting for us, but I wait with bated breath to see what he'll do. Anticipation threads through me as he traces my bare skin, teasing me, his eyes still locked on mine in the mirror.

"We can *always* make time for the things that are important," he says back, his words a whisper. "Isn't that right?"

I hum in response, my mouth opening slightly when Reid drags his thumb over my clit, the material of my panties still a barrier between us. Instead of shifting them to the side, he just stays right there, stroking me through the fabric, his movements infuriatingly slow. My breathing picks up, and even though we're several feet from the mirror, I can still see the flush in my face and the frantic need growing in my eyes.

"God, I love how you still respond to me," he says, his other hand roving, his pace leisurely as he caresses my body...my hip, my stomach, my breasts...before resting gently on my neck.

Then he tilts my head to the side and presses his mouth to the skin there, his tongue stroking against my pulse.

"Reid." His name falls from my lips like an exaltation, and he groans quietly in my ear before *finally* slipping his fingers beneath the fabric and gliding them through the slick wetness between my lower lips. I close my eyes at the relief his touch brings, my head falling back against his chest.

"Is this for me?"

Nodding, I find his eyes again in the mirror. "Always."

He doesn't smile, but I can see the joy he gets from my response as he circles the nub of pleasure, over and over again. "Good." And then his fingers are pressing into me, first two and then, after a few strokes, a third that makes me whimper, my legs threatening to give out.

"God, look at you," he whispers, using his other hand to lift my dress completely above my hips so we can see his movements in the reflection. He groans again at the sight, and I can feel his cock, thick and heavy, pressing against my ass.

I lick my lips, wanting to feel him inside me. But when I try to shift against him, he shakes his head. "This is just for you. A little early Christmas gift." Then Reid smirks. "But it's just as much for me as for you, because watching you fall apart is entirely selfish."

My head falls back as he continues working me over, and when he finds that perfect rhythm of thrusting and rubbing against my swollen clit, I give in, biting my lip to keep from shouting as a wave of white heat rushes through my body.

Once I've ridden my orgasm to the end, I slump back, my heart pounding an erratic beat in my chest. Reid slips his hand from my panties and adjusts my dress, and apart from the flush in my neck and cheeks, nobody would be any the wiser.

"Mom!"

My eyes widen at the sound of Junie outside our bedroom door.

"I can't find my green shoes. Have you seen them?"

"I think they're in the garage, sweetie," I call back, clearing my throat.

"I already looked there."

"In the bag with your swimming gear, not near the doorway."

There's a pause. "Oh! Thanks!" And then I hear her running through the house, presumably back toward the garage.

"She loves those shoes," Reid says, chuckling.

I shrug, running my hands over my dress, still feeling a little mentally flustered. "Which I normally don't have an issue with, but she has such a cute dress picked out for tonight and…neon green sneakers?"

My husband laughs again and shrugs. "Funky is just her vibe. She takes after her mom."

I chuckle and press a kiss against Reid's lips. "Don't I know it."

Crossing the room, I slip on a pair of pumps before turning to look at myself in the mirror again. Then my gaze snags on the sight of Reid tugging on his jacket, and my head tilts to the side as I drink him in.

"That suit still looks great on you," I say, watching as he

walks toward me.

"You say that every time I wear it."

I grin. "Because it's true every time you wear it."

I reach out, adjusting the knot of his tie, my mind wandering back over the other times he's worn this navy blue suit.

The first time—the reason he bought it in the first place—was our wedding. It was a tiny affair, just our family at a small ceremony in my parents' back yard a few months after Reid proposed. We considered planning a full wedding, inviting half the town, blah blah blah, but when we actually thought about the logistics, it sounded like a lot of fluff that we didn't need. So instead, we kept it tiny, and we each picked one thing to splurge on. For me, it was a really good photographer to capture the important moments. For Reid, it was his suit.

Since then, he's worn it to any nice occasion we've been to, like Rusty and Bellamy's wedding a few years ago and his twenty-year high school reunion last year. He looks just as good now as he did the first time he wore it. Maybe even better, especially with that little bit of gray coming in at his temples and along the edges of his mustache.

Once we're ready, I go in search of Junie, who I find sitting next to the fireplace, her little legs dangling over the couch as she watches TV, our aging Sydney snuggled up at her side.

Our pup is a bit too old to be sneaking out of the house anymore. Reid finally figured out how she was escaping from the blue cabin all those years ago by setting up Junie's baby monitor to watch her, and we couldn't believe it when we saw the video of Sydney hopping up and shoving the sliding door open all by herself, then nudging it closed once she was outside. The little escape artist. Apparently, she could have lived another life as a trained show dog.

Junie's head snaps to the side when I walk into the living room, and she lifts one leg dramatically into the air, showing off her bright green tennies. "Found 'em!"

I grin. "Awesome. Are you ready to go?"

Junie nods and jumps off the couch, turning to pet Sydney and give her a kiss before following me to the door.

"Jacket," I say, pointing to Junie's winter coat hanging by the door as I pull on my own.

"Alright, let's get to this fancy 'Christmas dinner'," Reid says, smirking and using air quotes.

I purse my lips and Junie cackles as we follow him out to the car, a dark blue SUV we bought after his truck finally broke down a few months ago.

"He totally knows about the party," Junie whispers loudly as we round to the passenger side, her breath coming out in a fog against the cold evening air of late December.

I wrinkle my nose and she giggles, but we stop talking as we hop into the car and Reid blasts the heat, giving the windshield a chance to defog for a few minutes before we pull out on the long gravel drive that leads to our cabin in the woods.

After Reid and I got married, Junie and I moved into the blue cabin, the three of us beginning our life as a family in the same place where we fell in love. About a year in, we realized we wanted something bigger. It took a few years of saving, but eventually we found a spot in the northwest corner of the lake. A single story with three beds, two baths, and a den. Most importantly, it has a property line that touches water. That's why it took so long for us to find the right spot, because we both knew we wanted to be on the lake. After Reid got the right permitting to build a dock, we were in heaven.

It's so wild to sit on our back deck during the summer with

Sydney, watching Reid and Junie in the water. My mind almost always drifts back to years ago, to the days when he spent hours teaching her to swim. Now he's her father, the man who has shown her consistency and stability and never fails to show up for her.

After Reid and I had been married for a year—a time period during which Jay didn't visit or call once—he asked how I'd feel if he adopted Junie. I cried, because I was so overjoyed and overwhelmed in the same breath. Then Reid contacted Jay himself and handled it all. Getting his permission, the legal paperwork, the appointments with the court…all of it.

The day everything was finalized felt like a new beginning, for all of us. It's strange to think there ever *was* a Jay to begin with. He might have been Junie's father, but Reid has *always* been her daddy.

When we come to a stop outside my parents' house, there isn't anything suspicious to give away the surprise birthday party waiting inside. All our family and friends were instructed to park at neighboring houses and come in groups. I received a text right before we left the house saying everyone was ready to go, and I sent a response as we turned into their driveway.

I can't help but chuckle at the fact that Reid knows about the party, because we have kept this thing under lock and key.

He looks at me as we walk toward the door, a smirk on his handsome face.

"How did you know?" I ask, my voice a whisper.

He shrugs. "Nothing is a secret in this town."

I purse my lips and just glare at him.

"Also, the caterer called the house last week to confirm."

"Jersey called the *house*?" I roll my eyes. "Figures."

I shove through the front door. "Mom?" I call out as we take off our winter coats. "We're here!"

"Dad and I are in the living room!"

The sound of my mom's voice has Reid chuckling quietly to himself. If there was ever a giveaway of the surprise in the next room, it's my mother shouting across the house to us instead of coming to greet us at the door.

Junie bounces excitedly through the entry and over to the living room ahead of us, and when we come around the corner, a loud "Surprise!" is shouted by the crowd of people waiting.

I grin when I look at Reid, because as much as he said he 'knew' about tonight, part of me thinks he didn't know exactly what to expect. The look on his face says this was much more of a surprise than he was anticipating. It might be Christmas Eve, but my parents' living room is filled with close to thirty people: my siblings, all of Reid's friends from around town, his family—everyone we love was invited to celebrate my husband's 40th birthday.

Of course, once the cat's out of the bag, the entire room is chaos. Hellos and hugs are exchanged and drinks are poured before everyone heads into the back yard. Over the back porch, a canopy has been erected and outdoor heaters have been set up, the entire space decorated with flowers and twinkle lights and one long table to seat everyone.

It's a magical evening, and the joy on Reid's face is unmistakable. For a man who prefers a quieter life, he sure knows how to come out of his shell in situations like this one. I watch as he chats with his friends, his family, and my family, never missing a beat. He's laughing constantly and smiling nonstop.

Reid's fears about the future are still a reality. He's still in therapy, still meeting regularly with his doctors, and has even started a new injection regimen that has had some moderate success in helping men with Kennedy's disease delay onset of certain symptoms. He also finally opened up to more people in his life about what the future looks like for him, and thankfully, that settled the nagging sensation in his chest that made him feel like he was constantly hiding something.

"I think it will be easier to be myself when the people I love know the truth," he said one day after he shared his diagnosis with Nick.

And it really was. Something blew open inside Reid when he gave himself the freedom to be honest. It started with me and then trickled on to other friends and family members, and now, he isn't carrying his burden alone. He's surrounded by people who not only love and support him, but who also know what he may face in the future, and that makes such a huge difference.

We've been lucky in a lot of ways, though, and we feel constantly grateful for our very happy life. His symptoms have only progressed slightly, primarily as tremors in his left hand. It's enough that he's brought on an apprentice to work the shop, a young man named Everett who will eventually take over the primary woodworking if Reid gets to a point where he thinks it would be best to take a back seat. I was worried at first, but then I saw the smile on Reid's face when he and Everett were talking one day after work, and I knew it was all going to work out just fine.

"It's like chatting with my dad about the trade, but this time, *I'm* the one on the teaching side of things," he told me one night as we sat on our porch, looking out over the lake. Then he looked at me with a big smile. "It's going really, really well."

I haven't felt even a little bit worried about it since.

"Think he was surprised?"

I glance at Briar where she's washing dishes on the other side of the kitchen island. For the most part, everyone has gone home to snuggle in for the remainder of their Christmas Eve, only my siblings and their families staying behind to help with cleanup.

"He had an inkling of what was going on," I tell her honestly, "but he had *no* idea it would be this big."

She smirks. "Nice. I was worried for a while."

I shake my head and finish scooping the roasted potato leftovers into Tupperware. "No, it all went perfectly. He was very surprised."

"You talking about me?"

Looking over my shoulder, I smile when I see Reid and Andy walking through the sliding door to the back yard.

"Always."

"Hey, why don't you guys take off," Briar says. "I'm just about done, and Andy can finish up with the leftovers."

He nods, bumping his hip against mine as he takes my place at the counter.

"Normally, I'd protest and stay to help, but I'm exhausted," I say, giving Andy a hug. "Thank you for offering." Then I round the counter and hug Briar. "We'll be back in the morning."

My sister nods. "We're doing gifts and stuff with the kids and Andy's dad in the morning," she replies. "But we'll be here probably around lunch time. Do you know what everyone else is doing?"

I shrug. "All I know for sure is mom is adamant about a big family photo since we're all here together. Apparently, it's been more than ten years since the last one."

I hitch a thumb in the direction of our last family photo that hangs on the wall in the living room, taken on the dock out back.

"Didn't Ruby take that picture?" Briar asks, drying her

hands and crossing over to take a closer look.

We're all jumping off the dock together, fully clothed, laughing and looking completely ridiculous.

I nod, remembering the summer when Boyd met his wife. "She did, and then Boyd tugged *her* into the water as well."

It's my favorite picture of our family, probably because it was taken before life got complicated. I was barely 19 at the time. Now, at 29, I'm trying to imagine what a new family photo will look like, with my parents and all my siblings and our spouses and kids. Three generations of Mitchells.

I smile, because what an amazing new memory that will be.

We finish saying our goodbyes to everyone before grabbing Junie from where she's been hanging out upstairs with Briar's kids. Once we get home, she collapses fully clothed, face down in her bed, with barely a muffled good night. Then Reid and I head to bed, making quick work of our evening routines before we're snuggled up together.

"Tonight was perfect."

"Yeah?"

He nods, bringing me in against his chest. "Yeah."

I wrap my arms around his waist, satisfaction blooming within me. Every year, I try to do something to make my husband feel special on his birthday, and seeing the joy on his face at being celebrated always sends a thrill through my heart.

Reid lifts my face up so I'm looking into his eyes, which are twinkling in the moonlight stretching across the room.

"You have a way of making me feel...so seen, and loved, and..." He shakes his head, his gaze boring into mine. "I'm just so thankful for you. For your love, but also *how* you love me, each and every day."

My eyes grow misty, feeling the truth and depth of each

word, and also knowing the same is true in reverse. This man knows how to love me and cherish me in a way that fills a space I didn't know was empty before him.

"I love you so much," he whispers, dipping down and pressing his lips to mine.

As our tongues tangle together and we lose ourselves in each other, I can't help but think for the millionth time how lucky we are to have found each other, and to have been given this beautiful happily ever after.

For more stories from Cedar Point and the Mitchell family, including bonus content, visit my website:

www.jillianliota.com/cedar-point

jillian liota

acknowledgments
from the author

Writing this story was an incredibly emotional journey, for two reasons. Firstly, because of the storyline and all of what Busy and Reid go through to find their happily ever after. But secondly because it's such a reminder that each day is precious, and how important it is to hold those we love close.

And while I am devastated that this is the final chapter in the Cedar Point series, I still need to take a few moments to thank a few important people, without whom, this story would not have been what it is:

Danny: my best friend and soul mate - thank you for your never-ending encouragement. Your kind, gentle heart is the root of who Reid is as a character, and I could not have written him without your love.

To **Julie** for always pushing me to be better and work harder and keep my nose down.

To **Marylou, Caitlin, Cheyenne** and **Jaelynne** for demonstrating to me what exceptional motherhood looks like. I could not have written Busy as a loving (but exhausted) mom without witnessing your incredible patience and love for your children.

To **C. Marie** for always making my words and story shine in a way I couldn't do without you. And for letting me send you things last minute.

To **The Jillybeans**, because your excitement over the Cedar Point series fills my happy little author heart.

To **Jenny** and **PenPal PR** for the exceptional help in getting this story out into the world.

And last but certainly not least, to anyone who has picked up this book and given me a chance. As an indie author, it means the world.

<3 always,
Jillian

If you loved the Cedar Point series, keep reading for a the first chapter of *Bitter Truth*, a forbidden romance between a chef and his boss' younger sister set at a small town vineyard.

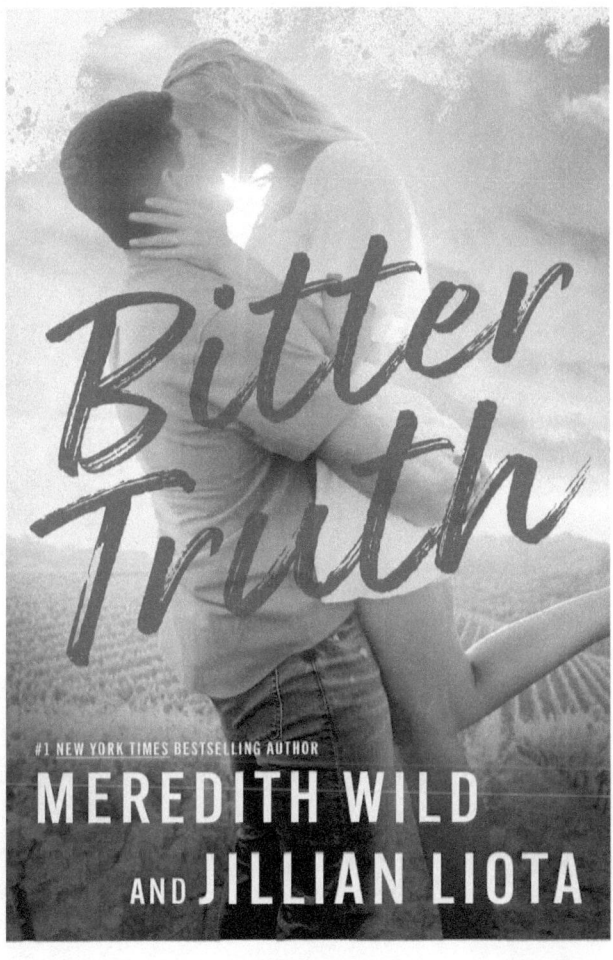

chapter one

- Murphy -

The sign for Rosewood streaks by, the lights from my car illuminating it for just a moment before it disappears behind me with the fading sunlight.

Twenty more minutes until I'm home.

I sigh, wishing not for the first time that things were different.

That this wasn't the way things in my life were falling together.

Or, I guess, falling apart.

The eight-hour drive from Venice Beach hasn't been that bad, but once I crossed the bridge taking me out of San Francisco and into Napa, it felt like time sped up. The drive I had earlier wished would pass more quickly now feels like it's coming to an end far too soon.

Because the fact I'm heading back to my hometown is finally starting to sink in, and I wish I could slow time for a little while. Just long enough to figure out . . . well, to figure out a lot of things.

What I'm going to say.

What I'm going to do.

But most importantly, how I'm going to cope with the aftermath of what happened back in LA and what it means for my life.

I take the next exit and catch myself grinding my teeth, my jaw flexing with the anxiety that overwhelms me with each passing moment.

As I leave the freeway and begin the final stretch out into the country, everything I see is a reminder of why I left. All the reasons I couldn't ever imagine a life here beyond the one forced on me as a child, when I had no choice about where to live and what to do.

The truth is that I hated Rosewood the moment we arrived. I was just four years old when my father, my brothers, and I showed up with a carload of belongings and a truckload of emotional baggage.

I take a deep breath and let it out long and slow, hoping it will help ease the anxious energy beginning to build in my chest.

It doesn't help.

And then I make the turn onto Main Street, crossing the short stretch of downtown. Rosewood has one of those quaint downtown areas that doesn't seem to exist anymore. It's a stretch of road that hosts a bar, a restaurant, a café, a coffee shop, a bakery, and of course, little shops filled to the brim with every wine-related tchotchke a tourist might desire.

In the years since I left, I've come to realize just how different Rosewood is from so many other places. Though I haven't yet decided whether that's a good or a bad thing.

It's particularly different from Venice Beach and Santa Monica, my stomping grounds when I moved to Southern California. People everywhere, beachy weather, tattoo parlors, and weed shops. The grunge and grit of the place make it feel like a town that brought out the wild, slightly unhinged parts of people. The social niceties of small-town life wouldn't be a blip in the minds of anyone who stuck around there long enough.

Rosewood is . . . the exact opposite. Clean and quaint and perfect in a way that is also absolutely infuriating.

Which is why the idea of being back sits in my belly like a stomach bug, a nauseating feeling that has me cracking my window for a little fresh air as I come to a stop at the end of the street. The familiar smells of wine country—damp earth and grapevine—flood my senses.

Memories from my childhood rush in, some bad, some good. Like the shared stresses of a bad year for the grapes, or seeing my father, covered in debris and sweat in the middle of the crush.

"Five generations have worked this land," he'd say after another day of tireless physical work. "It's our family legacy. You should be proud to be a part of something as beautiful as this."

By *you*, he meant my brothers and me. We'd share eye rolls whenever Dad launched into one of his "family legacy" sermons. I often wondered if he was trying to believe the words himself, more than he expected them to mean something to us. After all, he'd left Rosewood as soon as he was eighteen, wholly uninterested in the family business or the pride of legacy, only to return with his tail between his legs after tragedy struck, two children and a newborn in tow.

I wince a little and rap my fingers against the steering wheel. Maybe we're a lot more alike than I thought, my father and me.

Not that I'd ever tell *him* that.

I finally turn off the main drag, which takes me down the long highway out to my family's vineyard and past the Rosewood High School football field and Chantry Winery—two landmarks of my younger years.

High school in a little wine country town didn't offer much. I wasn't popular, but I wasn't unpopular either—kind of falling into that middle space that most high school students are in. I was invited to some parties, went to some school activities, had some friends.

Come to think of it, my high school experience is basically a metaphor for my life as the middle child. Not too much attention, but not enough.

Maybe that's the real reason I left.

It sucks to feel like you're just noticeable enough to be intentionally ignored.

I'd rather believe I bounced from Rosewood because I wanted more.

More fun.

More people.

More experiences.

Definitely more men.

The guys of my youth were mostly consumed with the quest for the two Ps. As my friend Quinn would repeatedly remind me—and possibly herself—as we spent countless nights on her living room couch watching reality TV, "All they're after, Murph, is popularity and pussy. And if you can't give them either, you have nothing they want."

She had a point, and it only became clearer to me when I moved away just how true it was of pretty much every guy, everywhere. I can hardly remember a first date when the guy didn't seriously think he was going to get laid at the end. Or at least get his dick sucked.

Not my style. Sex has never been a bartering chip for me.

My entire body shifts at that thought. The emotional whiplash of what happened back in LA makes my stomach turn over.

And then, as if the universe has decided to gift me one final middle finger on this emotional journey home, I hear a loud pop and my car begins to bounce and shudder, the wheel tugging to the side in deference to what I can only assume is a flat tire.

Fuck.

I know that nobody ever really *needs* a car issue, but this is seriously the last thing I need right now.

Something wells up inside my chest as I continue driving, hoping my memory is correct that there is a one-pump gas station around this bend . . .

I take a shuddered breath when I see it, and my car hobbles its way off the highway and into the dirt lot before I roll to a stop next to a beat-up old truck.

It feels like a great effort not to burst into tears as I shove my door open and then slam it closed, my irritation and frustration getting the better of me. When I round to the back and take a look, I see that the back right tire is pretty much flat on the ground. Thankfully I didn't damage my rim in that final few hundred yards.

I haven't ever changed a tire by myself before, which makes me even more upset, especially since my dad *and* my older brother offered to teach me several times when I was in high school.

Rolling my eyes at the irony, I head toward the tiny shop, hoping that somebody can help me out.

But as soon as I push inside, I know I'm out of luck. The woman behind the counter looks to be in her seventies at least, and when I ask if there's a mechanic on-site, she gives me an empathetic smile.

"I'm sorry, honey. But I've got a landline if you wanna call somebody."

I give her a thin smile and shake my head, knowing I'm eventually going to have to resort to calling my brother. The amount of shit Memphis is going to give me . . .

Sighing in disbelief at just how bad my luck has turned out, I head back to my car, staring at the flat tire as if I'll be able to will it to inflate.

If this doesn't sum up my life right now, I don't know what would. Getting so close, almost there, and then having everything fall apart.

And then, it just all becomes too much. The dam breaks. My emotions rush in—a culmination of my return home settling into my soul on top of all the other bullshit I've been dealing with. I burst into tears, overwhelmed and broken. Dropping down into a squat in the middle of the dirt parking lot, I hide my face in my hands and just let it all out. All the sadness and frustration and disappointment.

"You okay?"

My sob cuts off in the middle and I look to the side, embarrassment coursing through me as I realize someone has been watching me have a breakdown.

I stand quickly, wiping at my face and staring studiously at the man's feet, not wanting to see his likely judgment of the woman sobbing in the gas station parking lot.

"Yeah, I'm fine, I—"

But my voice cuts off. I can't even force the fake smile and customer-service voice that I've perfected over nearly ten years. Instead, I start crying again.

"I'm sorry, I'm going through a lot," I say, looking back to my car. "My tire popped and I don't know how to fix it, and it has just been . . . the *worst* day."

My observer is silent for a long moment, and when I finally glance over at him, I feel a second wave of embarrassment. Heat prickles at the little places behind my ears and at my wrists when I see the concern evident across his brow.

"I might not be able to fix your horrible day," he says after a long pause, "but I can handle the tire for you. Get everything fixed up so you can head on your way."

I blink a few times, feeling a little off-balance at his offer. I've spent the past decade in LA, where nobody slows down for a moment, and definitely not long enough to help someone in a shit situation. I almost forgot people do that kind of thing.

I nod, thankful that the emotions previously welling inside me seem to be dissipating.

"Yeah, that would be great, actually."

"Don't suppose you have a spare tire in there, do you?"

I wince, wishing I could say yes and preparing to tell him the story of when I sold it to a friend for fifty bucks during tough times. But before I can, he dips his head toward his truck.

"No worries. I have a spare in mine."

And then he strides toward his truck and drops down to the ground, sliding underneath the bed and working at something for a minute or two before he tugs out a tire and shimmies back out, his shirt and jeans now covered in dust.

"I'll have this fixed up for you in just a few minutes," he tells me, looping one strong arm through the tire and hoisting it over to my car along with a couple of tools.

I watch for a few minutes as he works, twisting a wrench for a while on the lug nuts before lifting the car with the jack.

Now that my earlier overwhelm has eased, it's hard not to

appreciate just how handsome this Good Samaritan is. I've never been one to give elevator eyes before, but I can't help it now. My gaze lingers on his broad shoulders and flexing forearm muscles as he works on removing my flat.

My mind briefly flitters over the idea of what else he's capable of with those hands, but I clear my throat and scratch idly at my cheek, trying to shove that thought aside.

"I really appreciate you taking the time to do this," I say, not wanting to hover awkwardly in silence.

He glances up at me and grins, his hazel eyes warm and kind, then looks back at the task at hand. "I'm happy to help. You feeling a little better now?"

My face flushes and I let out a laugh that surely betrays my embarrassment. "Yeah. Sorry about the tears. I was feeling overwhelmed."

"You don't have to apologize. Life is overwhelming sometimes." He looks at me again and shrugs. "I had a good cry just last week."

I purse my lips, trying to hide my smile. "Oh yeah? A good cry, huh?"

He nods. "And a nice long bubble bath."

Shaking my head, I can't help when my smile gets the best of me. "Sounds soothing."

"You should really try it out. See if it helps."

I tuck my hands into the pockets of my shorts and lean back against his truck. "I will definitely consider that. Thank you so much for the suggestion."

He chuckles and continues working for a few more minutes before hopping up and tugging the tire off and setting it to the side.

"This isn't a permanent solution," he says, his voice slightly strained as he shoves the spare into place. "You'll still need to get a regular tire put on here. But this should be good for tonight."

I nod, watching as he puts the lug nuts back on and begins tightening them, and when he finally drops my car back to the ground and gives the trunk a tap, I say the first thing on my mind.

"Can I buy you a beer or something? As a thank-you? There's a bar about a mile up the road."

He looks off to the side, in the direction of town, and seems to consider it for a moment. But ultimately, he shakes his head.

"Not really a bar kinda guy."

I lick my lips, my ego slightly bruised.

Any other night, I would have said *Okay*, thanked him again, and gotten on the road. But something makes me try again.

Maybe I'm not ready for him to go just yet.

Or maybe *I'm* not ready to go.

Either way, I want a few more minutes with my rescuer, even if it's just in this parking lot.

"Or maybe I could grab us some cheap wine coolers from inside?" I stick my thumb toward the gas station. "I don't want to ask for help again, but I'd appreciate it more than you'll ever know if you give me a reason not to go where I'm headed."

He grins at me, licks his lower lip just slightly, then nods his head. "You know, a cheap wine cooler actually sounds great."

I beam at him. "I'll be right back."

Then I race inside and hurriedly pay for two of the little bottles that I used to sneak back in high school.

"All right, I've got mojito or margarita," I say as I approach where he's seated on the dropped tailgate of his truck.

"I'll take the mojito."

"Good choice."

I hop up next to him, then pop the caps off our bottles with my car key.

"That was a neat little trick," he says, taking his drink from my hand.

I smile and clink my bottle against his. "Desperate times teach you some wild things."

He smirks and raises his drink to his lips, mumbling, "Isn't that the truth."

We both take a sip, and I wince immediately, the flavor not at all what I remember from my youth. "Oh wow."

"Yeah."

"That's terrible."

"So bad."

"I remember it being so much better when I was in high school."

"Everything against the rules tastes better when you're young."

We both laugh. I swing my legs and cast my gaze over to the sun that has dipped low on the horizon, enjoying the simplicity of the moment.

I know once I hop off this tailgate and make the short drive down the road to the house, all the stress is going to rush back in. But for now, the peace and quiet, and sitting next to this handsome man who was willing to take time out of his day to help me, is exactly what I need.

"Thanks again for the tire save . . . and for sitting here with me."

His leg, dangling next to mine, bumps me so lightly I'm not sure if it was accidental or on purpose. I'm partial to the latter.

"And sorry you're covered in dirt now. I hope you don't have somewhere important to go tonight."

Chuckling, he shakes his head. "Nah. And I figure you did me a favor. Now I have an excuse to take another bubble bath."

My lips turn up and he winks before taking another sip from his wine cooler.

I watch as he does, and I can't help the way my gaze drops to his lips for one long moment, wondering what it might be like to kiss a man like him. And when he looks back at me, I see his eyes dip as well. Just for a moment, for a quick, almost invisible glance, before he turns his head and stares off into the distance.

My hand between us is braced against the lip of the tailgate, and a shiver of anticipation slides through me when his hand does the same, the edge of his palm grazing against mine.

"So what was the deal earlier? It seems like you might have had more on your mind than just the tire."

I nibble on the inside of my cheek, trying to decide how to answer. I want to keep talking to him, but the last thing I want to do is share all my dirty laundry. Ultimately, I settle on vague truths.

"Change is hard, especially when it feels like you're not really in control of the course your life is taking." I shrug and take another sip from my bottle. "I think earlier was like . . . a dam breaking, you know? The tire was just the last straw on a very large haystack."

He bobs his head. "Yeah, I know what you mean."

Even talking about it brings the emotional magnitude up to the surface, and I bat away a tear that breaks free.

"Hey now." His gentle voice, warm like a blanket I want to crawl into, wraps its way around me. His hand reaches up and cups my cheek, his thumb stroking where another tear has fallen. "No more tears tonight, hmm?"

I give him a watery smile, my emotions calming again.

"You seem to be able to keep my tears at bay better than I can," I tell him. "Maybe I should keep you around."

His lips turn up at that. "Maybe you should."

The world fades away in that moment, when our faces are so close together, our thighs touching and the evening humidity making everything feel hazy and warm.

I feel a little drunk, and there's no way it's from the wine cooler that I've taken only a few sips of.

No, it's this man holding my face in his hands.

I'm intoxicated with everything about him, and what I do know is very little.

All I know for sure is that it's been a long time since I've been this interested in a man.

So I do the only thing that makes sense.

I lean in and press my lips to his.

He seems surprised at first, but that fades almost immediately, and the hand on my cheek slips around to the nape of my neck as his mouth opens against mine.

The taste of mint and lime explodes on my tongue, along with something else even more heady that makes me groan just slightly.

I shift my body so I'm facing him more, and my hands reach out, bracing against his strong chest. I love touching him, feeling the strength and warmth of his body beneath my palms.

The kiss doesn't last long, and he nibbles gently on my lower lip before we eventually pull back and look at each other, each of us with smiles on our faces.

"That was unexpected," I say, trying to keep the smile on my face small so he doesn't see how wildly incredible I feel. I'm sure I barely succeed.

"It was," he replies, his fingers stroking gently against the back of my head before he lets me go.

We sit there for another ten or fifteen minutes, taking little sips from our drinks and glancing at each other every so often with knowing smiles. It's the kind of magical night that I would have dreamed about back in high school, when I would have been up all night with a pen and a notebook, trying to capture the experience in lyrics.

When we finish our wine coolers, he hops down and crosses over to a trash can that butts up to the back of the gas station to chuck them.

"You think the tire will be enough to get you where you're going?" he asks as he walks back to me.

"I should be fine."

He nods. "Good." Then he takes my hand and helps me down, my feet kicking up a little bit of dust as I drop to the ground. His muscles flex as he pushes the tailgate closed, and the sound of it slamming shut feels jarring against the quiet of the evening.

The toe of my shoe skims over the dirt between us, and I wonder if I should ask for his number. Or if he'll ask for mine.

He watches me for a long moment, and my heart throbs rapidly in my chest, the anticipation of what he might say growing until it's a living thing inside of me. As friendly as he seems to be, he's also very hard to read.

"You know, in another life, I would be asking for your number right now," he says. "But things in my life are . . ."

My heart falls. "You don't have to explain," I tell him with a thin smile, not wanting to hear another rejection. "My life is messy right now too, so . . ."

I trail off, not knowing what else to say.

So . . . I wouldn't give you my number anyway?

So . . . we're better off leaving things like this?

Neither of those are really true, so it doesn't even warrant saying them.

"Thanks again." I take a step back, in the direction of my car.

His eyes skim over my face, and I can't help but imagine that he's trying to commit me to memory so he can remember me later.

Doubtful, though.

Instead, he's probably trying to figure out how to say goodbye and get on the road without having to talk to me anymore.

Oh, how quickly all my warm and fuzzy feelings have begun to fade.

"All right, well, have a safe drive."

I nod, and we both turn to get into our respective vehicles. I glance at my phone briefly, seeing a missed call and a text from my brother.

Memphis: *Let me know when you're ten minutes out. I'll come help with your stuff.*

I take a deep breath and send off a quick response, letting him know I'm just a few minutes away, then drop my phone in the cup holder and glance to my left.

My Good Samaritan is already gone, and I can see his taillights in my rearview as he pulls out onto the highway.

Part of me is glad he took off so fast. As fun as it was to give my mind a chance to create a reality where something more might have happened, I'm not in the market for that kind of distraction. I have too much on my mind as I prepare to face my family for the first time in nearly a decade.

They always disapproved of me leaving town in the first place, and I know they will have plenty to say now that I'm back.

I only have to drive a few minutes before I'm pulling off the highway and down the long dusty road to the house I grew up in, but my eyebrows scrunch in confusion when I see a familiar truck parked off to the side next to some of the other equipment.

When I come to a stop, I scan the area around the truck, trying to understand why that truck would be here.

As soon as I step out of my car, I hear a newly familiar voice.

"Did, uh . . . did you need something else?"

I squint through the dark, finally seeing the form of the guy from the gas station heading toward me.

My head tilts to the side, and I cast my eyes up to our house, trying to make sure I didn't pull into the wrong driveway.

But no, even with just the porch light, I can see the same dark-brown front door and the same silver door knocker that my younger brother, Micah, picked out from Home Depot: a circular grapevine with a stem of grapes dangling in the middle.

The man from the gas station is standing about fifteen feet away from me with his hands on his hips, looking at me like I've followed him home.

But before I can say anything—ask him what he's doing here, tell him I live here, or any other thing that would actually make sense—I hear my name.

"Murphy?"

I turn and look back to the house where the front door is open, the light from inside illuminating a tall, strong figure that I know without a doubt is my brother.

"That was fast," he says, walking toward me. "I didn't realize you really meant only a few more minutes."

"Yeah, I got a flat so I was at the pump when I texted you,"

I reply, then look back over to where the Good Samaritan is still standing near his truck.

"Hey, Wes." Memphis greets him briefly and then stops at the trunk of my car. "This is my sister, Murphy."

My eyes stay on him—on *Wes*—and I watch as his body language changes, the tense way he'd been standing relaxing just slightly.

"Nice to meet you, Murphy," he says, his voice tight.

"You, too." Then I turn to where Memphis is tugging my suitcase out of the trunk. "Just the suitcase. I only have a few other things and they can wait until tomorrow."

He shakes his head. "We can get it now. Wes, you mind carrying a box or two?"

I sigh, feeling awkward about having him help when I still haven't processed the fact he's here right now.

"So how do you two know each other?" I ask, assuming that Wes and my brother are friends or something.

Memphis pauses, eyeing us both. "Wes works here," he tells me, hoisting a box out and handing it to Wes, who is suddenly right in my space and still smelling deliciously of dust and sweat and the faint scent of mojito wine cooler.

"Doing what?" I ask, watching as Wes stands silently, looking just as shell-shocked as I feel.

"He's the chef of the new restaurant." Memphis tucks a box under his arm. "So he'll be your boss."

I blink a few times, all of his words hitting me at once. There's a restaurant? There's a chef? Both are news to me. But one thing stands out the most, and my voice grows tight as I glare at my brother.

"He'll be my *what*?"

Murphy and Wes' epic romance continues in

Bitter Truth

Available on Amazon and Kindle Unlimited

jillian liota

about the author
Jillian Liota

Jillian Liota published her first romance novel in 2016. Since then, she has become known for writing stories filled with emotion, real-world themes, and most importantly, love. She has had her writing praised for depth of character, strong female friendships, deliciously steamy scenes, and positive portrayal of mental health.

Jillian is a Southern California native currently residing in Suwanee, Georgia, where she lives with her husband and three-legged pup.

To connect with Jillian:

Join her **Reader Group**
Sign up for her **Newsletter**
Rate her on **Goodreads**
Visit her on **Facebook**

Check out her **Website**
Send her an **Email**
Stalk her on **Instagram**
Add her on **Amazon**

additional titles
from jillian

For an up-to-date list of titles, visit:
www.jillianliota.com/books

For bonus content, visit:
www.jillianliota.com/bonus

www.ingramcontent.com/pod-product-compliance
Lightning Source LLC
Chambersburg PA
CBHW020930260626
47169CB00006B/1646